MORE THAN A KISS

"Don't," he murmured, cursing himself for suggesting something that so obviously caused her distress. "Don't cry." He reached out and touched her cheek.

She reached up and covered his hand with her own. She moved such a little bit that her skirts barely rippled, but it was as if she'd crossed some invisible barrier that let a magnet inside his body draw hers closer. He didn't know if he pulled her tight or if she pressed against him, only that she was there, nestled against him, his chest bearing the sweet weight of her with each breath he took.

He wanted to pull her closer and yet dared not move at all for fear that she would step away, and also because her nearness intoxicated his senses so thoroughly that no part of his body seemed inclined to obey the demands of his brain. He wanted only to feel her, to breathe in her scent . . . to taste her.

She lifted her face toward him and he indulged in his wish.

Her mouth beneath his pulsed with her life force. It molded softly against him, warm and insistent, driving his hunger for her to a fevered pitch. . . .

BOOK YOUR PLACE ON OUR WEBSITE AND MAKE THE READING CONNECTION!

We've created a customized website just for our very special readers, where you can get the inside scoop on everything that's going on with Zebra, Pinnacle and Kensington books.

When you come online, you'll have the exciting opportunity to:

- View covers of upcoming books
- Read sample chapters
- Learn about our future publishing schedule (listed by publication month *and author*)
- Find out when your favorite authors will be visiting a city near you
- Search for and order backlist books from our online catalog
- Check out author bios and background information
- Send e-mail to your favorite authors
- Meet the Kensington staff online
- Join us in weekly chats with authors, readers and other guests
- Get writing guidelines
- AND MUCH MORE!

**Visit our website at
http://www.zebrabooks.com**

JUST THE WAY YOU ARE

DONNA JORDAN

ZEBRA BOOKS
KENSINGTON PUBLISHING CORP.

http://www.zebrabooks.com

ZEBRA BOOKS are published by

Kensington Publishing Corp.
850 Third Avenue
New York, NY 10022

All Kensington titles, imprints and distributed lines are available at special quantity discounts for bulk purchases for sales promotion, premiums, fund-raising, educational or institutional use.

Special book excerpts or customized printings can also be created to fit specific needs. For details, write or phone the office of the Kensington Special Sales Manager: Kensington Publishing Corp., 850 Third Avenue, New York, NY 10022. Attn. Special Sales Department. Phone: 1-800-221-2647.

First Printing: September 2001
10 9 8 7 6 5 4 3 2 1

Printed in the United States of America

PROLOGUE

London, 1614

John Bradford's arms hurt with the effort of holding them still at his sides as the little one crept toward him, seeking reassurance.

"I'm scared, Johnny."

Tears tunneled through the grime coating the young child's face. John's arms twitched, aching to pull the child close. His instincts, though, told him to back away, ignore the tears, deny the child the comfort of his embrace.

He was glad his mother wasn't alive anymore to see her son deliberately withhold comfort from a frightened child.

He edged back a step, irrationally wishing that his parents had died long, long ago when he was as young as the crying child. Maybe if they'd died when he was little more than a babe, he wouldn't be able to remember what it was like to curl up against another human being for the sake of love rather than the need to stay warm. Maybe if he'd grown up in Groat Alley, he'd believe that this stinking crawlspace was as good as a real home. Maybe he'd believe that God would forgive stealing and begging or sins too foul to even think about, knowing that a hungry belly drove a body to do things a body shouldn't have to do.

"Johnny."

The child murmured his name again, but this time with resignation rather than sadness. His head drooped, his whole body quivered. John remembered the moment when he, too, had realized he was truly, utterly alone in this world. The moment when despair and loneliness had made it seem life was not worth living.

It didn't seem right that little Benny should have to learn those harsh realities so young. Didn't seem right that John Bradford would be the one to steal the child's last illusion of innocence. John's own sorry heart wasn't sufficiently toughened, it seemed.

Knowing it was the worst thing he could do for himself, knowing that he'd only set himself up to assume a role he wasn't prepared to fulfill, he crouched in the fetid dirt and gathered the child into his arms.

"Johnny," the child whispered again, but now with a hint of hope.

He silently issued enough profane embellishments to ensure himself a thousand-year stint in Purgatory, and then he took a deep breath and tipped young Benny's face upwards.

"Aye. I'm here, Benny. It's not so bad when someone's with you, hmmm?"

"I wish Rob was still here," the child said. "Rob would know what to do."

John added another few years to Purgatory by cursing the dead man. Man? Hell, Rob Marton had been no more a man than he was himself, but he'd been the oldest survivor among the Groat Alley orphans, and they'd all looked to him for leadership. And now, by taking the weeping Benny into his arms, John had silently assumed the role.

"Now there, Benny, stop your crying, else you'll look like one of those zebras what came through with the circus last month."

The jest failed to rouse even the hint of a smile.

"I'm scared, Johnny. There's men outside trying to catch us like rats."

John swore again. Curse *and* damn Rob Marton for dying and leaving John in charge of all these little ones at a time like this.

Benny pressed close, his slight frame shivering as if he'd just emerged from a midwinter dip in the Thames. "They snatched Willy Tyler right in front of the Drum and Spangle, and folks laughed every time he screamed. They chased Tommy Stallworth down the middle of Connelly Lane, and he fell and split his head open like a melon. He's dead, Johnny. Maybe . . . maybe Tommy should've let them haul him off to Virginny. Maybe he'd a' liked tobacco farming."

"No, Benny. Tommy did the right thing." John crouched and scraped a scattering of dirty straw into a heap that would cushion Benny's sharp-boned hips. He patted the straw, inviting Benny to sit. The boy leaned against him with all the quivering need of a frightened pup seeking its master's reassuring caress. John groped for soothing words; instead, rage surged through him, impotent for all its ferocity, for one such as he had no means of fighting against men who would steal wretched freedom from those who possessed nothing else.

His hand curled into a fist. He stared down at it, watching his knuckles turn white. Rob had taught him the motion. He'd claimed that a Groat Alley lad who possessed nothing had to hold on to the only things that belonged to him: his thoughts, his feelings, his freedom. Closing his hand around his rage would mark it in his mind and trap it within, where it could fester and grow until a man had the ability to make things right. One day he would get his vengeance—he would have to teach the pursuit of vengeance to young Benny, just as Rob had taught it to him.

"Nobody likes Virginia, Benny, or they wouldn't have to snatch likely lads off the street. Tommy's pride made him fight them, and if he hadn't gotten killed, he would have kept on fighting them."

"Seems silly to fight if'n you can't win, Johnny. There was too many of them and only one of Willy."

"A man might be forced to do something against his will, but he is never defeated if he vows to avenge the wrong. That's winning, in a way, when you gain your vengeance."

"What do you win, then?"

"Your dignity, Benny. A man can endure anything, so long as he holds onto his dignity."

Dignity. Not many among these rag-clad, homeless orphans even knew what the word meant, let alone cared a snap for it. John supposed he'd learned about it, absorbed it into his very bones, before his parents died. Benny, an orphan almost from birth, obviously cared nothing for dignity; he seemed more concerned with the threat from the impressment crews.

"I shouldn't have run straight here, but I was

scared. What if one of them followed me, Johnny? What if they find our hideout and get us, too?"

John allowed himself a humorless laugh to cover the rush of apprehension slithering through him at Benny's words. He couldn't afford to let the fear blossom. Lice-ridden and stinking it might be, but the hideout offered some measure of safety, a place to call home, and he'd always felt an almost irrational attachment to it.

"They won't take two steps into Groat Alley before the smell drives them back, or Mistress Briscoe douses them with her slops, eh?" Encouraged by Benny's wobbly smile, he pressed on. "Besides, look at us. They went after the other lads because they had a bit of meat on their bones. Not like us, all skinny and gangly."

Benny held out his arm and frowned at it, while John felt an odd lurch at the realization that Benny looked more like a frail four-year-old than the lad of seven that he was. Constant near-starvation did that to a fellow—look at his own body, almost embarrassingly tall, and yet lacking the weight and rippling muscle his long-dead father had possessed.

His mother had always promised he'd grow into his body one day. That was before she'd died, too, and he'd nearly followed her—would've followed her if Rob Marton hadn't found him wandering the streets, looking for food. Rob had led him to the Groat Alley hideout and let him earn his place among the dozen or so starving orphans who huddled within its noisome shelter.

John had never been able to decide whether Rob had saved him or condemned him.

Now he was inclined to believe he'd been condemned. Fever had sent Rob shivering and coughing his way into hell, leaving John friendless and bereft, and sticking him with Groat Alley and all its responsibilities.

It was enough to drive a body to tears. Except that now he had to teach Benny the survival lessons that he'd learned so well. Crying blurred a man's eyes and made him vulnerable to attack. A soft heart could be broken, so it was best to harden it with indifference. A heart incapable of feeling another's pain wouldn't ache when an anguished young boy pressed against one's knee, desperate for reassurance that couldn't be offered.

Crying and caring—who needed such weaknesses? Thank God Rob had taught him that males finished with that wet, messy business early on, well before they reached John's advanced age, whatever it might be. John's parents had died before it seemed important to know exactly how old he was, but he thought he might be eighteen. Or nineteen. Or maybe he'd reached twenty, which meant he wouldn't live much longer. Those who scratched their existence from places like Groat Alley seldom did.

"You run straight for the skip hole if they come after you," John ordered. "There's no shame in running—only in giving up."

"I will, Johnny," Benny vowed. "Faster than ever I run after filching a purse."

"Faster than if you were dodging Mistress Briscoe's slops," John said, grinning.

"Aye, so fast that fat old Constable Malmford—"

The sickening screech of rotting wood being wrenched from its pegs drowned their feeble jesting. A gust of slightly less fetid air and sunlight streamed into the hideout. Man-sized shadows quickly blocked the rare illumination. John's instincts roused his blood, setting a chorus of *run, run, run* pounding in his ears even as his mind dispassionately realized he stood no chance of escape. He'd long since outgrown the child-sized skip hole. But Benny . . . Benny could get away.

He shouted the command to run and pushed young Benny toward the hole, all in the space it took for him to be surrounded by a circle of hard-breathing, mean-eyed sailors.

Fat old Constable Malmford squirmed his way into the hideout, wheezing hard to draw air through the stained cloth he held clamped over his nose. One seaman curled his lip with derision and jerked his head toward John.

"They ain't but one street rat here, Henry, and you promised us a dozen of the little pests nested in this pit."

"Aye, but he's the best of the bunch. Look at the size of him."

John held his tongue, though he yearned to shout a protest against their discussing him as if he were a fresh-roasted joint of beef. He inched back until his backside pressed against the wall, and he rested his hand, palm down, against the straw-littered dirt—the perfect position for springing toward freedom. He narrowed his eyes into slits and lowered his head as he studied his enemies. As much as he hated the filth matting his tangled hair, it concealed most of his features. Rob had taught him that virtually everybody gave away their intentions with an unwitting glance or a flicker of interest. He'd stand a better chance if the sods couldn't guess his intentions.

"Skin stretched over bones," scoffed the seaman. He studied the hideout with a sneer twisting his face and then turned toward John, snapping his fingers in the manner of one demanding a dog's attention. "A ship's hold ought to seem like Buckingham Palace to you, eh, mate?"

"Go bugger yourself and all your friends."

The sailors took offense at John's insult. They muttered obscenities and tightened the circle around him while he shifted his weight onto the balls of his feet. He'd escaped mobs before; he knew what to do. He swallowed, tilting his jaw upward defiantly, knowing any show of spirit would infuriate them. Anger might goad one of them into charging, and he could slip through the break in their ranks.

The break never came. They stepped forward with all the precision of the king's guards. Two of them went straight for his hair, winding it round their fists, their eyes glittering with malice when his long reach enabled him to land a few telling blows to their guts. His bellowed protests drew only laughter. They captured his flailing arms and legs, one man to a limb, and hauled him bucking and screaming into the alley.

It hurt. And he tired almost at once; none of the Groat Alley lads could sustain physical exertion for more than a few minutes without exhausting their meager strength. Still, he strained against their grips for what seemed like hours, shuddering into resignation only when his breath deserted him, when he ached so much it seemed he'd rent himself in two from crotch to gullet. Tears, from the pain, from humiliation, pricked his eyes and thickened his throat.

"The Virginia Company is pleased you've decided to join our colony," announced the seaman.

The jibe prompted John into another paroxysm of useless twisting.

"Let it be, boy." Unexpected sympathy softened Constable Malmford's expression. "It's bound to be better for you there than here. Those tobacco farmers will be grateful for your help. They'll give you a home and good, honest work to do. In seven years you'll be finished with your indenture and you'll be a free man. You could even have a tobacco farm of your own one day."

"Take my place for yourself, then, if you find the idea so pleasing."

"There's room enough for all of us, boy. I'm giving up my commission to become a colonist myself. Mind your tongue and study on your blessings—could be I'll buy your papers myself and you can work for me."

"I'll work for no man."

They laughed at him.

John's struggles had dried his throat, but he managed to form a respectable wad of spittle and send it flying Constable Malmford's way. It fell short, sinking into the dust at the Constable's feet. The damp spot it made would soon be trod over by one of his captors, or the waning sun would dry it into oblivion. It would disappear from Groat Alley with no trace, just like John Bradford, accomplishing nothing and leaving no mark to prove it had ever existed.

"If I . . . if I were quality, you wouldn't touch me," he gasped, trying to catch his breath. "You wouldn't dare do this to me if I had money or family."

"Aye," agreed one of the seaman. "And if ye was the queen of England, ye'd have a fine lady-in-waiting t' wash yer bum after ye take a shit." His captors chortled companionably while they hoisted him to his feet. With well-practiced movements they bound his arms tight against his sides, never once giving him the slightest control of his own body.

John felt a faint flicker of hope when the adult residents of Groat Alley slunk into view and gathered in a nervous knot to watch, huddling together just beyond the sailors' reach. His hopes that someone might make an objection quickly died. The familiar faces reflected dull acceptance, perhaps even a glimmer of satisfaction that with him gone there would be one less hungry belly willing to do whatever it took to be fed.

A seaman nudged him into motion. John stumbled, awkward with his arms tied. Constable Malmford bolstered him with his shoulder and caught him by the chin, forcing him to look at a syphilitic crone standing alongside her one-legged, blind husband.

"Take a good look, boy. That's the best you can hope for if you stay here—that God might strike you blind so's you don't have to look at the poxed hag you're diddlin' every night."

John wrenched his head free and managed for a moment to hold his ground. "Seek salve for your conscience elsewhere. One day you'll be called to account for this. All of you will pay, especially your damned Virginia Company. I'll get my revenge. I swear it."

Constable Malmford, witness to countless acts of Groat Alley desperation, paled at the threat. The seamen merely laughed, clearly unimpressed and confident of their mastery over him. Their leader, grunting with sudden recollection, slapped the purse hanging at his belt.

"I almost forgot! The Company means to prove its goodwill by giving you this to use as you please in Virginia." He fished a silver coin from the pouch and tossed it and caught it, tossed it and caught it, while his gaze skipped over the rags cloaking John's rigid form. "Hell, you ain't even got no pouch nor pockets to keep it safe."

With a deft motion that left John no time to object, the seaman hooked his finger in the corner of John's lips and slipped the coin into his mouth. It rested hard and cold between his inner cheek and teeth.

"More money than you've ever seen. Use it well, lad." Constable Malmford spoke barely above a whisper while the seamen propelled him back into motion toward the docks, toward the ship that would tear him away from the only safe haven he had known.

With him gone and Rob Marton dead, there would be no one at all left to look after the little ones. The most helpless wouldn't last out the month. What the more adaptable might be forced to do for survival didn't bear thinking upon. They were all as good as dead. The sorrow that gripped him told him he'd failed miserably in sealing off his emotions. He could almost hear Rob scolding him, telling him he would have to do a better job of it if he meant to survive.

He tightened his jaw, causing the coin to scrape against his teeth. Bitterness, flavored by metal and hatred, filled John's mouth, but he would not spit it away. 'Twas the taste for vengeance, and he vowed he would feast upon it one day.

CHAPTER 1

Virginia Colony, 1621

Lacey Cochran gripped the ship's rail and stared across the short stretch of open water toward land. She'd anticipated this first glimpse of the Virginia shore for weeks with a thumping heart, with a kind of breathlessness that she'd called excitement.

The reality of what she saw now also illuminated the truth she'd been hiding from herself: She'd pretended excitement to deny bone-deep dread.

"It's not as crowded as the London docks," said her friend Clara. Clara's usually loud voice was muted with either dismay or fright; Lacey couldn't be sure.

"It's nothing like London. Nothing at all," Lacey answered. She could be grateful for that much, for all along she had been praying that no part of Virginia would resemble London in the slightest.

She wanted no reminders of the mistakes she'd fled.

Huge trees towered within sight of water, and between the trees and water's edge lay a vast, empty stretch of sand beach so unlike London's crowded, bustling port that it did not seem possible Englishmen inhabited both places.

"So many men," Clara whispered.

Clara brushed away a strand of loose hair, and Lacey took no relief in realizing that her friend trembled just as she did. A milling mass of men clogged the shoreline. Every now and then one would leap up above the crowd like a trout aiming for a passing fly, shouting something impossible to decipher from such a distance. The whole lot of them would respond with a roar—with agreement, with disapproval; Lacey could not tell.

The hungry masculine noises rolled out over the surface of the water. The sound hit her with the impact of a wave, hard and foreign and threatening to suck her away from all that was familiar.

"Do you really think one of them will want to marry me?" Clara asked.

"The Company promised every woman on this ship would find a husband," Lacey answered as she'd done countless times throughout the journey.

"I wish I were as confident as you," said Clara.

Lacey tried to summon a smile and wondered when Clara would notice that Lacey's confidence had seeped away the moment she'd caught sight of the men waiting to claim a bride.

Not just any bride, but a pure and virtuous woman.

Lacey's purity and virtue were but distant memories.

"Maybe they won't be too choosy," Clara said,

oblivious to Lacey's turmoil. "One hundred twenty-five pounds of tobacco does not seem much to pay for a woman."

"The tobacco merely pays back the Company for our transportation costs," Lacey reminded her. "The men aren't buying *us* for tobacco—why, that would be nothing more than slavery, Clara."

"Call it what you will. The fact remains that we're something of a bargain. Why, a man would spend a great deal more on jewelry and fancy gifts if he were courting women like us back home in England."

Women like us. Lacey knew that Clara was just doing her best to cheer herself—to bolster her confidence—and could not possibly know that Lacey was nothing like her, nothing at all, in either physical or social standing.

But whereas Clara would never know the extent of the deceptions Lacey was playing, there would be no way she could hide them, at least not all of them, from the man who paid her transportation and took her to his bed. What would happen when her new husband learned he'd been cheated, that he'd paid for a tainted bride?

"I think I'm going to be sick." She pressed her hand against her belly and moaned.

"Don't be ridiculous." Clara's gentle squeeze of her hand removed any sting from her scolding. "You never had a bout of seasickness throughout the entire journey; you won't have one now that we're safely anchored. Besides, you'd ruin your best dress."

Like most of the women who'd made this journey, Lacey had saved her best dress for her arrival in Virginia. *Her* dress—ha! That frivolous, expensive, frothy silk was no more her own than was the identity she had assumed.

She stroked her fingers over the fine silk covering her midsection, and at just that moment another male roar drifted over the water. Irrational fear stabbed through her. It was almost as if the men knew that among all the pure and virtuous females aboard the *Talisman*, only Lacey Cochran was familiar with the way a man's hand felt against her belly. Almost as if they sensed that only the very flimsiest covering hid her true self from the world.

Soft giggling drifted from the foredeck. A few other women had come up from below, decked in their finest, their hair coaxed into the best styles they could manage considering the awful lack of washing water that had plagued them during the last week of the voyage. They leaned over the rail, laughing and waving, prompting even more vigorous outbursts from the men.

"Strumpets," Clara muttered. "In another minute they'll be jumping over the rail and swimming for the first pair of open arms."

Lacey swung her gaze back toward the men. She had hoped one of them might be her salvation. Their arms didn't appear to be waiting so much as seeking and grasping, eager to enfold and crush.

"Lacey, don't you think they look rather like that odd creature Cook once tried to trick us into eating for dinner? Oh, what was it called? Cook claimed people from Mediterranean areas considered it a great delicacy."

Clara's comment so closely mirrored the image in Lacey's thoughts that she had to laugh, relieving some of her tension. "An octopus," she said. Impulsively she leaned over and gave Clara an affectionate kiss on the cheek. "I'm going to miss you so much."

"Miss me? I daresay we'll be at each other's houses at every opportunity," Clara said.

Lacey smiled to cover the ache in her heart. If she were indeed the pure, virtuous woman she had professed to be, then certainly she and Clara would grow old with their friendship deepening with every passing year.

Lacey looked once again toward the waiting men. One of them would claim her. One of them would marry her and take her to his bed and discover she was not the innocent virgin he had paid to import. She'd be thrown from his house and disgraced.

Once the truth about her became known, it would be impossible to continue her friendship with Clara. Following her cohort Amanda's advice, Lacey had been no more honest with Clara than she'd been with the representative of the Virginia Company who had booked her on this ship. "Hold your head high and brazen your way through," Amanda had advised. "No one will question you're a lady if you act like a lady."

Lacey now found it hard to believe that she'd thought getting accepted as a tobacco bride would be her most difficult hurdle. She'd never anticipated how every step of the journey would reveal new challenges and raise the cost of revealing her deception.

For example, once Clara realized how thoroughly Lacey had deceived her, she would no longer want to be her friend.

"I wish I had your skill," Lacey said. "I wish I could call forth a witty comment, a humorous observation. Do you have any idea how many arguments you forestalled when we were all confined to the hold for days on end?"

"You can't pack women together like herrings without expecting some of them to turn into fishwives," Clara said, but she blushed a little and Lacey realized she was pleased by the compliment.

Funny, how making Clara happy eased a little of the distress inside herself. She wished she'd done it more often. Compliments had been so rare in her life that she supposed she didn't know how to recognize when one was called for. She'd seldom received a compliment herself; serving girls had no reason to be acknowledged for performing their duties as required. Nor did serving girls offer compliments. Doing so was as apt to draw a scornful "who're *you* trying to cozy up to?" as a smile.

Now that it was too late, she realized she ought to have emulated Clara's consummate ladylike behavior rather than that of her former mistress. Amanda Stivington had possessed an impulsively generous nature, but nobody knew better than Lacey how well buried her generosity was beneath layers of selfishness and petulance. She had understood Amanda so well because in many ways they were alike. Neither of them could resist a dare, and both tended to follow rash impulses that inevitably led to trouble. Both of them had allowed their hunger for passion to overrule their senses, but only Lacey had suffered the consequences.

More women came up from below; soon all those who had survived the rigors of the journey stood on deck, waiting to meet their futures. The excited laughter died. The feminine hum of words dwindled away into silence. It was as if all at once they'd realized this would be the last time they would be together, all unmarried, all exercising an unusual freedom in coming here. Soon they would be wed to men they'd never met, and never again would they have the right to decide the course their lives would take.

"This seemed like such a good idea when I heard about it." Clara sounded wistful, as if she'd just abandoned a long-cherished dream.

"It *is* a good idea," Lacey answered firmly; firmness often prevailed over reality, as she'd learned from Amanda. "We are doing our duty for the glory of England."

Clara arched one skimpy red eyebrow, and they both burst into laughter.

"*You* may be doing it for the glory of England," Clara gasped eventually. "I came because I heard every woman in the Company's first group of brides found herself a husband. I'm twenty-seven years old and haven't received a single proposal. Even my family's name isn't enough to overcome my looks and lack of fortune. I'd wager that every woman on this ship is here for the same reason— or because she's running away from some awful thing she's done."

Lacey managed to keep a smile pasted on her face, even though Clara's observation made her feel seasick once again. She and Clara had shared a thousand whispered confidences throughout the tedious and uncomfortable journey. They'd marveled at their own daring in accepting the Virginia Company's offer to sail across the ocean to wed a complete stranger. They'd speculated endlessly on the other women's motives. Somehow, Lacey had managed to keep her own reasons for leaving England a secret.

No. She hadn't kept a secret—she'd lied. Out-and-out lied to the woman who'd grown closer than a sister, and Lacey was too ashamed, and too frightened of losing Clara's friendship one minute sooner than she had to, ever to tell her the truth.

"Those men in England were fools," Lacey said, deliberately quelling her guilt. "If one of them had a lick of sense, you'd have been married long enough to have five children clinging to your skirts."

Clara shook her head, mingled regret and resignation marking her plain features. She blushed—a dull, brick-colored flush that could cause someone who didn't know her to wonder whether she might be suffering an apoplectic fit.

Lacey felt a surge of pity that she would never be unkind enough to reveal to Clara. The blush was like everything else about Clara: simply too much. She was too tall. Too slim. She tried to minimize both attributes with clothing that was both too bold and too youthful. Her hair was so carroty-colored that she could scarcely be called a redhead. Her nose was too big for her too-thin face, and her eyes, which protruded just a bit too far, were such a light blue that the irises almost melted into the whites. Her skin was too pale, except for areas over her cheeks and along her forearms where too many freckles dotted the skin, like a profusion of water lilies bent on choking off the surface of a pond. It even seemed as if she had too many teeth, for they stuck out too far every time she laughed.

And the whole unfortunate-looking package covered a heart too warm and open to shield Clara from the snide remarks and rude glances often directed her way.

Lacey prayed that the man who claimed Clara would be kind, and observant enough to recognize the treasure that lay within before rejecting the outer woman.

As for herself, well, if God had erred in making Clara too much, then He'd gone the opposite direction and given Lacey not nearly enough. For most of her twenty-three years, she had simply blended in and carried on unnoticed. She considered herself unfashionably small and far too ordinary, with ordinary brown hair, ordinary brown eyes, ordinary skin.

Perhaps if she had possessed a bit more color, a bit more flash, Amanda Stivington wouldn't have deemed it such a challenge to pretty up her lady's maid. Perhaps if she hadn't always wished she were a beautiful woman capable of inspiring passion in a man, Lacey wouldn't have accepted the dare to try to pass herself off as Amanda Stivington's country cousin.

Most of all, perhaps if she had been born beautiful, she wouldn't have been so grateful for Pumphrey Fallsworth's inappropriate attentions, and she would have held on to her virginity and then none of these troubles would have ensued, leaving her feeling sick to the stomach and sick at heart while she gazed at the Virginia shoreline.

"Lacey, what if no man likes the look of me enough to . . . well, I mean, if they march all of us before the men and none of them think I'm worth paying the passage . . . Oh, Lacey, this could be so humiliating!"

"Clara." Lacey sought for something to say to reassure her friend. "Let's make a pact. Neither of us will marry until we both find a husband."

"That wouldn't be fair to you. Why, the minute you step onto shore some man will scoop you up and claim you for himself!"

Lacey wrinkled her nose and pretended disbelief at the notion of a proper English gentleman doing such a wild thing, even as something inside her surged with pleasure at the thought of provoking such a passionate response in a man. She quelled the feeling, deliberately tamping it to death. She'd had her fill of passion. It wasn't nearly as satisfying as she'd dreamed it would be, and it had led to nothing but trouble.

"It has never made sense to me that we might be expected to marry within minutes of being asked. I think it makes a great deal of sense to postpone marrying for, oh, say two weeks after we receive our proposals." In fact, even as she spoke the words, Lacey felt a glimmer of hope. If she did have two weeks to decide to marry a man, then he had two weeks as well—and perhaps during that time he would find a few things about her that he might like well enough to overlook her flaws.

"If you were willing to wait—oh, it wouldn't seem quite so awful if there was another woman who didn't marry immediately."

"Swear it, Clara. No matter what, neither of us will marry for at least two weeks."

Clara's eyes glimmered with tears of gratitude. "I swear it. And I swear I will never forget your kindness."

Lacey had to look away. She could not meet her friend's eyes, witness Clara's loving appreciation, when she had made the offer more out of her own needs than for Clara's benefit.

"The only drawback to our pact is that the other women will have the first choice of the available servants," said Clara. "They'll also have the advantage of extra time to get their households ready for entertaining."

Although talk of servants made Lacey uncomfortable, she couldn't help sighing. "We've talked about this over and over," she said. "There will be no servants. And we will not likely do any grand entertaining."

"You're still determined to believe that Virginia's wild and untamed. Goodness, they've been colonizing this place for at least a dozen years! There must be a dreadful glut of servants awaiting mistresses—don't you remember that six or seven years ago the Virginia Company shipped over hundreds of orphans?"

"Six or seven years isn't such a long time." Lacey's father had worked his small plot for decades, until it killed him, and he'd never been able to provide enough food to keep his children's bellies full. Her mother, a gentle-born lady come down in the world, had taught Lacey everything she knew about manners and speech before tearfully sending her out to service with the Stivingtons. Lacey had counted herself lucky each time she ate a meal at Stivington Hall, but she never quite vanquished the hunger for her loving family, for the place that had once been her home.

Even when she'd needed a refuge, a place to run away from Pumphrey, she'd been too ashamed to return home and tell her mother what a mess she'd made of her life. Unless she was very, very lucky, she would never have a place to call home ever again.

"Look at this place, Clara. I see no manor houses rising tall. I see no liveried servants. I see exactly what I told you I'd read: this is a wild, primitive land and we can count ourselves lucky if we survive our first winter."

Clara sniffed, calling to mind all the times Lacey

had heard her mistress make the very same sound in the very same manner. Perhaps only true ladies of quality were born with the ability; she'd never managed to make the sound without looking and sounding ridiculous.

"Gossip," Clara said with another sniff. "You know you can't believe everything you hear, Lacey. It sounds like below-stairs prattle to me, no doubt inspired by the jealousy of those who long to emigrate here."

Lacey had indeed gleaned her knowledge from the servants who worked below-stairs. They'd often shaken their heads in puzzlement over some young nobleman who'd announced his intentions of striking out to the unknown to make his fortune. None of them had seemed jealous, but rather quite content to remain right where they were. She alone had looked upon the savage new land as a possible sanctuary, an opportunity to hide and recuperate from the mistakes of her past.

Its allure had mysteriously begun to disappear in the past few moments.

"I wish it were true," she said softly. "I wish it would be possible to step onto that sand and find everything is wonderful."

"Things will be wonderful. Better than wonderful, because we'll have husbands." Clara paused and then cocked her head toward Lacey. "You know, you never did tell me what sort of man you'd really like to marry."

"Oh, I never had any special sort of man in mind," Lacey lied, hoping her light tone would fool her ordinarily discerning friend.

She wondered what Clara would say if she revealed the dreams she'd nurtured, dreams of a kind, gentle man who might welcome someone like the *real* Lacey Cochran. Not a useless ornament as most of her fellow travelers were, but a strong, small, and rather competent if nondescript girl. Someone like her mother, who would give up everything for the man she loved without ever looking back, who was willing to learn from her mistakes and work hard to earn the respectability she craved. Someone willing to cook and clean and bear his children, even if she had closed her heart to passion and knew her soul was too wounded ever to love again.

During the days when she and Amanda had concocted this scheme, and during the long weeks of the voyage, she had managed to convince herself that her modest dreams could come true. But now, faced with the reality of knowing that any man who claimed her would know all her secrets, she knew she'd only been fooling herself.

The best thing to do, the right thing to do, would be to confess the truth, beginning with Clara. And then be equally honest with any man who showed an interest in marrying her.

In her heart, she knew nothing but disaster would follow. Clara would be humiliated and furious to learn she'd treated a common serving girl as an equal. No man would want a woman who possessed a very unladylike streak of lust, a streak so strong and deep that she'd given herself to a man for the sake of a few pretty words and phrases.

Nobody had any use for the real Lacey Cochran. She couldn't imagine now why she'd thought running away across the ocean would change anything.

Trapped. With the boundless sea surging behind her, and an untamed wilderness stretching before her, she found that the best she could hope for was a life of endless deceit. At worst—well, it didn't bear thinking of what would happen if she were found out. Perhaps it was a fitting punishment for all her sins.

"They're lowering the boats," Clara said.

While they'd been talking, the seamen had loaded the first of the small boats with women and lowered them to the water. The women remaining on deck cheered and waved at their departing sisters.

"Check his teeth—they do it when they buy horses!" called one woman as she leaned over the rail.

"Save a few good ones for the rest of us," called another.

"I don't mind waiting for a less-crowded boat," said Clara.

"Neither do I."

The two of them clasped hands and looked once again toward the shore, toward the cluster of men. Somewhere among them stood the man who might take Lacey to wife. It couldn't hurt to pray that he might be kind, but then it didn't seem right—that she would hurt a kind man. Better if he were . . . oh, not unkind, but just . . . not capable of being hurt.

Could such a man exist? And if he did, could she possibly be lucky enough to end up with someone who didn't care?

The air shifted, blowing from shore, charged with expectation. An almost palpable male hunger reached over the water. Something inside Lacey answered with a quivering that heightened with each wave that slapped against the side of the ship.

She dug her fingers into her palm until the fingernails bit into her flesh. She was furious with herself—and worried. She had been so certain that she'd brought her unfortunate wanton tendencies under control.

"This way, ladies." A seaman gestured toward them and motioned them into a boat. "There be some gentlemen over yonder mighty anxious to meet up with you."

Lacey moaned, and this time Clara joined in.

John Bradford leaned against his bale of tobacco and yawned with pretended boredom while Malmford, the former constable turned tobacco factor, pawed furiously through his sheaf of official papers.

"There must be some rule or regulation in these papers to stop you!" Malmford blustered. "You can't just walk in out of the woods and claim one of those brides. The Company intended those women for—"

"For any unmarried British subject who can reimburse the company one hundred and twenty-five pounds of tobacco for his woman's passage." John abandoned his casual pose, straightening into his body's natural, straight-backed posture. "I'm a British subject. I stand here before you with one hundred twenty-five pounds of tobacco. I demand a bride."

The factor's gaze swept over the fringed buckskin John wore in defiance of what passed for fashion in the colony. Garbing himself like an Indian was just one way he'd discovered to set himself apart from the British settlers he so despised. The smaller man blinked, his nose twitching intermittently, reminding John of a startled mouse held spellbound by a cat's predatory stare.

Malmford let loose with a mouselike squeak of frustration. "No! Those women are meant to be wives for the colonists who were brought here to do the Company's business."

"I was brought here by the Company. If you remember, you had a hand in my coming, *Constable* Malmford."

Malmford flinched at John's soft comment and reddened, appearing to regret mightily being part of that long-ago abduction that had torn John from his Groat Alley hideout. He gave an angry shake of his head.

"What of it? You never did a lick of Company work, did you? Ran off to the woods the minute your feet touched Virginia soil, without doing so much as one minute of work to pay back the Company's investment in you."

John laughed mirthlessly. "By my reckoning, the Company owes *me* for surviving that wretched sea journey. I warned you when you took me that I would never work for another man. Just as I'm warning you now that I mean to have one of those women, no matter what you say."

Malmford shuffled the papers again and blew an exasperated sigh toward his forehead. "There must be something in here about a man growing and curing the tobacco himself. There must be! It cannot be possible that you can pay for a bride with tobacco acquired by ill-gotten means."

"There's nothing ill-gotten about selling fresh meat for tobacco," said John. "I daresay the men who traded these leaves for a haunch of venison considered it a satisfactory trade."

"Only because there's never enough food!"

"And whose fault would that be?" John asked. "Not mine. Whose, then?"

Malmford compressed his lips into a grim line. " 'Tis your precious Virginia Company's fault,"

John said, since Malmford seemed disinclined to admit the truth. "The damned Company you're so worried about offending is the same Company that has you all breaking your backs growing tobacco instead of tending to your own needs. Each year it's more difficult to find enough game to feed you all."

"The Company has an investment in this colony," Malmford said. "The investors must be appeased."

"Ah, yes, the investors." John fingered the coin that hung from a thong around his neck, the coin that had been shoved into his mouth that day so many years ago, the coin that the faceless investors of the Virginia Company had thought sufficient to reimburse a man for his freedom. "They ought to be thanking me, then, for keeping you alive through the winters so you're fit enough to work like dogs on their behalf the rest of the year. They ought to be *giving* me a bride to appease *me*."

Malmford's face mottled. "I'll be damned if I'll let you have one of those women!"

"Damned if you do, and damned if you don't."

John tore a tobacco leaf from its bundle and shredded it. He approached the agitated factor. Giving him a lazy smile, he hooked one finger in the edge of Malmford's lips and pushed the wad of tobacco into his mouth, the way the sailor had shoved the Company's blood money into John's cheek when he'd been conscripted.

"Chew on this, Malmford, and tell me why you treasure it so dear. I never developed a taste for the stuff as a vice. Not even the hungriest belly could call it food. Come winter any man among you will trade every ounce of tobacco he has for any scrap of meat I bring to the settlement."

Malmford spat out the tobacco. "You're in league with the devil! It's not enough that you rob us of our earnings; you have to claim our rewards as well. Men who have lived without women as long as some of our settlers would value them higher than gold."

John smiled. Malmford had just as good as admitted he wouldn't stand in his way when it came to choosing a woman. It had been worth every minute of the six years, eight months, and seventeen days he'd waited to exact this small measure of revenge against the entity that had robbed him of his freedom, and against the men who had carried out the orders.

What exquisite retribution, that he should have fared so much better than those who had blindly followed the Company's dictates. He, the gutter lad who never bent to the tobacco hoe, would claim a bride years before some of the Company's staunchest subjects could hope to acquire sufficient tobacco. He'd savor his victory all the more knowing that he could demand his choice of the commodity they all valued most.

The revenge would be so sweet. The woman herself would be the blush on the peach.

"Sell the tobacco to the Company, John," Malmford urged. "They'll reward you handsomely."

John stroked the coin at his neck again. "I have all the money I need from the Virginia Company. There's nothing I can buy with it here anyway."

"Use the money to buy passage back to England since you're so unhappy here."

The suggestion caused an unexpected jolt of dismay within John. *Return to England?* Once he'd dreamed incessantly of that very thing. Eventually, though, he'd adjusted to the strangeness of this new land. Eventually, he'd been better able to spend all his hours plotting his revenge.

"I'll return to England when I'm ready," he said quickly to divert Malmford from recognizing the way his suggestion had affected him. "And I'd sooner burn my tobacco at dockside than hand it over to the Company, no matter how much it's willing to pay."

"You're willing to pay the Company with this tobacco for a woman."

"Aye, but only because I know that claiming a woman will annoy them more than anything else I can do." He fingered his coin again. "Imagine: using tobacco I never lifted a finger to harvest, tobacco I think so little of that I'm willing to burn it. I'm using something of absolutely no worth to me in order to claim something of great value from you."

Malmford worked his mouth and spat, whether from the vile lingering taste of tobacco or from disgust with John's scheme, John could not tell. Nor did he care.

"Go to hell. It's where you belong."

"Ah, but I was in a sort of hell when you found me and forced me to come here. You should have left me be."

"I wish I had."

John brushed his hair back from his forehead, not caring for once whether his demeanor betrayed his pleasure in this moment. This was as near an apology as he was apt to get from Malmford, and it lightened something within his soul. The fleeting thought struck him that if someone, anyone, had apologized to him long ago, his anger might never have festered to the point where it had threatened to consume him.

In the absence of anger, he might have stayed within the settlement rather than bolted to the wilderness to make his own way. He might have managed to remain friends with his fellow conscripted orphans rather than earned their enmity for refusing to endure the shackles of indenturehood.

The brief lightness deserted him.

None of those things merited pondering. It was too late to worry over what might have been.

The quick vanishing of his enjoyment at besting Malmford just proved that he could not be satisfied with anything less than the total revenge he had planned.

"I shall choose first from the women," he said.

Malmford appeared near to tears of frustration, but he made no objection to John's demand. "You can't have one unless she agrees to it. These maids have come with the Company's assurance that they need not marry against their will. Rest assured I shall do what I can to convince anyone you choose that you are the worst scoundrel to roam this land."

"Then I must see to it that she is not tainted by your opinion," John said. "Nor the opinion of anyone else. I leave it to you to spread word among the men that I am to be given first choice, that none of them are to approach the women until I have selected the best, and none is to dare attempt anything to stop me from taking the one I want."

"Even if you find a female dull-witted enough to accept the likes of you, she will not be content with you for long, wed to an outcast."

John couldn't resist twisting the knife just a little. "Truth to tell, I care nothing about the woman's contentment at all. Her opinion of me does not matter, nor does her happiness. When I choose the best of those available, everyone will know that John Bradford, who never did a lick of Company work, has made a bigger success of himself than any man who cast his lot with the Company. Each time I bed her, I'll relish knowing she should be spreading her legs for one of the Company's drudges, who had the foolishness to believe themselves better than Groat Alley riffraff."

He waited for the long-anticipated glow of satisfaction to wash his bitterness away. This was the first time he'd ever voiced his plans to another human being. Instead of satisfaction, he felt a shocking touch of embarrassment, an inexplicable urge to call back his crude remarks. He laughed, mirthlessly as he always did, to cover his discomfiture.

His discomfort increased when he noticed that Malmford had a true smile upon his lips.

"Mayhap this revenge will cost you dear," Malmford said. "It is apparent you know nothing of women, or of the misery an unhappy woman can cause a man."

"I know that a man has to care before he can be hurt."

He didn't care about anybody, and had no intentions of falling prey to such weakness. Which was why he would enjoy this revenge so well, John reflected.

Malmford's expression unexpectedly softened with something alarmingly akin to pity. "Just let it all go, John. I'll admit we were wrong for bringing you here against your will, but it's too late to change that now."

"Too late to change. Not too late to make you pay." John had been haunted for too long by the inner whispers that said *They did you wrong, Johnny.*

Someone has to pay. He would not give up his one chance to appease that whisper—certainly not just because someone had finally apologized.

"John." Malmford reached toward his arm, but drew back short of touching him. "Something's gone wrong in your head. You spent too many years living with that scum in Groat Alley, and too many years here off by yourself in the woods. Why don't you let loose of the past and join us, lad? Live a normal life, make some friends, help us build this settlement into a thriving community. Maybe then you won't be so eager to cause others pain."

John shook off the surge of yearning prompted by Malmford's fervent plea. "I learned years ago that there's no profit in caring about other people. I'm doing this because it makes *me* feel good."

He turned on a mocassined heel. His lengthy strides carried him from the factor's hall toward the sad cluster of buildings that marked the Virginia Company's grandest settlement. He glanced toward the docks. Every woman-hungry man from the surrounding hundreds had thronged there, eager to greet the brides, even if they could not pay the price to claim one for themselves.

He spotted Malmford scurrying toward the crowd, and knew the factor would instruct the men to hold back as John had directed. He paused, listened. Sure enough, within moments angry protests drifted through the air, and some dared turn and scowl at him.

But nobody dared confront him.

They seemed to draw closer together, drawn together by their fury but impotent to act against him. Many against one.

He'd imagined this moment for so long. He'd dreamed of his triumph when they all stood united against him and had to acknowledge that they were helpless against his will. Now that the moment was at hand, he couldn't understand why emptiness, rather than gratification, had lodged itself into his heart.

He shifted his attention to the sea. The ship sat anchored several hundred yards offshore in the deep water. A handful of rowboats had been launched from the ship and were approaching. The women. The colors of their garments were still bright, not yet having been exposed to the rigors of this new climate and the toll frequent wearing and washing would take.

By this time next year everything would be faded, including the women themselves. They'd all be wearing the same nondescript gray; they'd all have lost the luster in their hair, the hope in their eyes.

It didn't have to be that way. If only they'd let him show them . . . if only they'd look to their own needs before those of the Company . . .

Angrily, he shook away those thoughts and returned his attention to where it belonged. The woman—he hadn't yet chosen her. Perhaps that was the reason for the empty feeling; his revenge was not yet complete. He needed to claim the best of the lot. He would choose her and use her, putting an end to the emptiness and the goading inner whispers.

And then what? He had no more use for a woman than he had for a hundred and twenty-five pounds of tobacco.

He remembered how he'd taunted Malmford with the idea of burning tobacco at the docks rather than give it to the Company. Maybe he could do something similar with the woman to show his disdain. Claim her. Use her. Then banish her from his home as if she were unwanted chattel. That would be a delicious addition to his revenge. To not only take a woman the Company meant for one of its own, but to set her aside as of no value when he was done with her, knowing that she could not marry anyone else.

Choose her. Use her. Lose her. The refrain echoed in his mind like a musical childhood chant.

He understood little about highborn English women, except that he was certain they were nothing at all like the Indian women who sometimes slaked his needs. Indian women worked alongside their men. They expected no gentle treatment. An Englishwoman, accustomed to pampering and coddling, was probably much like a lapdog in her eagerness to please and her craving for affection. John knew himself well enough to realize that all his gentler impulses had been successfully battered into oblivion. He had no affection to bestow—none, not for dogs or women.

Choose her. Use her. Lose her.

He'd sometimes happened across abandoned dogs in Groat Alley, and he'd always raged at the cruelty of someone who had thoughtlessly abandoned a creature utterly dependent upon another for survival. Perhaps there had been a glimmer of truth in Malmford's observation that something had gone wrong in John's head. He ought not be completely cruel to the woman. He could afford to show her a hint of kindness. He would discard her when she served her purpose, but free her from any vows. In this female-starved wilderness, she might find happiness with some Company drone who could be content with John's leavings. That would, in a way, give him yet another layer of satisfaction: knowing that he'd had her first.

Yes, the revenge could be even sweeter.

So why did it seem that the empty feeling within him had grown inexplicably heavy? He quickened his step, but he could not move fast enough to shed the weight.

CHAPTER 2

Lacey and her thirty-six companions clung together near the shore. The incoming tide lapped against her soggy skirts; the ground beneath her feet rocked and swayed worse than the deck of the *Talisman*—or so it seemed to her after so many weeks at sea. Otherwise, she might have backed farther away from the hundred men, maybe more, who stood lined in rows across the landing area, looking for all the world like a battalion of soldiers awaiting the word to charge.

"Oh, my God!" Clara's fingers tightened like talons around Lacey's forearm as she rasped her dismay. "You were right about this place, Lacey! It's so . . . squalid. And the men—they're nothing but . . . *farmers!*"

A paralyzing silence stretched between the two groups, broken only by the water lapping the shore and the seabirds circling overhead. Their plaintive cawing echoed the confused curiosity racing through Lacey's mind.

One largish structure, built of what looked like driftwood, tree trunks, and mud, called to mind an enormous beaver dam but appeared to be some sort of fort, judging by the lone sentry standing at the corner with a musket resting against his shoulder.

A few tiny planked structures, looking every bit as squalid as Clara's appalled whisper had suggested, littered the landscape near the fort. Barrels stood stacked in front of one—a shop, perhaps? Another had a crude cross attached crookedly to its sloping roof—the colony's church?

Clara clapped her hands together and laughed with delight. "Take heart, ladies. I know what's happened. We've accidentally landed in a rural village. After all, this cannot possibly be James City. James City is known to be the crown jewel of the Virginia Colony."

"Maybe we've landed right at Malvern's Hundred!" cried one of the women. "Maybe they decided to save us the trouble of traveling from James City and set us straight down where we'll be living."

"I don't want to live here," someone sobbed.

"Where are the grand homes?" whispered one of the women.

"What are all those plants growing everywhere?"

One particularly robust weed choked every otherwise open inch of ground, save for one wide path that Lacey thought must be the settlement's only street. The weeds stood about waist-high, the leaves nearest the bottom a rich dark green while those above grew progessively spotted with yellow.

"Those must be tobacco plants," she said to Clara.

"Impossible. I am quite certain that tobacco is a civilized crop grown in fields, not planted willy-nilly in every spare corner."

"Yes, it is tobacco," confirmed one of the other women. "My brother described it well to me in one of his letters."

"These must be wild seedlings, then," said Clara. "I am sure the main crop is somewhere beyond those trees."

Lacey said nothing. She remembered how her parents had cultivated every inch of their small plot of ground in their frantic attempts to grow enough food to feed their family. She sensed a similar desperation in the placing of the tobacco plants.

Of all the women who'd just arrived, she might be the only one to recognize the irony. Land abounded, but all of it wooded, with huge trees shading the ground, with miles of tough roots making the ground difficult to cultivate.

Tobacco could not fill an empty belly. And yet these colonists appeared to tend it as carefully as an English peasant might nurture the cabbages that would see him through the winter. Lacey doubted any of them had ever dreamed they'd be cramming a cash crop into inches of ground that would at home be given over to marigolds and daisies.

Flowers. The tobacco was thriving, but there were no flowers to be seen.

Nothing of refinement broke the squalor: no mansions, no high-spired church, no blooded horses drawing fine carriages. No simple pleasures, either: no tree-shaded lanes, no flowerbeds. Not even a decent dock, if truth be told.

Lacey had imagined the Virginia Colony would afford rough conditions, a lack of comforts, but she never anticipated the desolation that hung like an invisible fog over the settlement.

"Farmers," Clara repeated.

Clean, *respectable* farmers, Lacey hoped. She took heart from the obvious care the men had taken in preparation for greeting them. Judging from the pale areas on their necks and faces, most of them had had their hair recently if inexpertly clubbed, their beards newly shaved. While most wore wide-brimmed hats designed to keep the sun from their eyes, a few incongruously wore the cocked and feathered hats of a dandy. Some sported silk cravats against shirts so much-mended and faded from hard use that it was impossible to tell the garment's original color. On them all, their garments hung far looser than fashion dictated in England, though they showed signs of recent vigorous brushing.

They might have been fancy gentlemen in England, but here in Virginia Colony they showed themselves to be just hard-working, hopeful colonists, obviously united together with the common purpose of taming this wild place.

She remembered what she had heard of the sort of man who had come to this place: younger sons with no hope of inheriting; men whose fortunes had been squandered; men who had run from debt and sought to make a fresh start in a new land.

One of these men might not mind too much if the woman he took to wife proved to be less than noble herself. A woman familiar with a hard-scrabble life, a woman willing to work hard and take pride in what they might accomplish together. A glimmer of hope sparked in Lacey's breast. She decided, just this once, that she would let it flicker.

"Where are the other women?" asked one of Lacey's traveling companions. "Where are all the first tobacco brides?"

An older man stepped forward and acknowledged the question with a gracious bow. "Factor Malmford at your service, ladies. Most of the other women are at their homes, on the hundreds, not here in James City."

"This cannot be James City," Clara insisted.

"I'm afraid it is, madam. You will be on your way to Malvern's Hundred within an hour or two," he said. "Every one of the ladies who arrived on previous ships is wed, happily so. Since many of the wives are, shall we say, expecting happy events, it was deemed best for their health and modesty if they remained—"

"They couldn't shut up all of us!" With an inelegant shriek, a woman clawed her way to the forefront of the group of men. Her garments, like the men's, hung loosely on her thin body, except for where a far-advanced pregnancy swelled her belly. "Modesty be damned! They made the others stay home because they're afraid you'll learn the truth in time to save yourselves. Get back on that ship, girls, and never look back on this hellhole!"

"Mistress Crawshaw!"

Some of the men looked embarrassed—and guilty. Several others murmured apologies. Two strong men moved quickly to grip the woman by her arms and then hustled the screeching Mistress Crawshaw away. "Run, girls!" she shrieked, tugging against their determined guidance. "Run for your lives!"

"Oh, God," Clara moaned. "Oh God, oh God, oh God."

Mistress Crawshaw continued imploring them to leave, her voice growing fainter, but the warnings no less troubling. The woman's voice was silenced abruptly, and the absence of sound disturbed the quiet in a manner that was, if anything, worse than the tense silence. One prospective tobacco bride swooned in a dead faint, and a dozen more burst into shoulder-heaving sobs. Another whirled and splashed into the sea, staggering to a halt only when the water reached above her knees.

Lacey found herself looking at the men with new awareness, noting hollowed cheeks, circles like bruises beneath their eyes, hands callused and dark with embedded dirt. Those loose-fitting garments had fit well at one time, she realized with a start; back in England those work-hardened hands had probably held nothing heavier than quill pens and silver spoons.

These were men who had run from their old lives and embraced the new—men who had turned their backs on luxury and comfort in order to work hard to conquer this wild place. Why, instead of cringing away from them, they should all be proud that such men would choose them as their wives!

"Ladies," she found herself urging. "Ladies, please. These men . . . they *need* us."

The sobs ended in little hiccups. Clara's incessant, "Oh, God" dwindled into inaudibility. The woman standing in the water peered back over her shoulder.

"They need us," Lacey repeated. "Leave off with all that sniveling. We're here to help them make this place our home."

One man's head snapped up at Lacey's comments. He made a quick motion to smooth his already neat blond hair. Then, with a smile broadening his face, he strode forward, hand extended toward Lacey, his blue eyes beaming a welcome.

Oh, he looked fine! Respectability virtually oozed from every well-brushed inch of him, and he seemed interested in meeting *her*. He embodied every dream Lacey had ever nurtured, every hope she'd scolded herself for cherishing. Maybe her doubts were for naught. Lady Amanda had been right to urge this Virginia refuge upon her after all. In running from Pumphrey, she'd thought herself to be a coward. By coming here to start anew, she might prove herself brave and smart and resourceful—the qualities she knew in her heart that she possessed.

Such a fine gentleman. He drew closer, and there was no doubt he was headed straight toward her. Dare she hope her new life could begin so easily?

"Hold up there, Peter."

The blond gentleman scowled but stopped at once in response to the quiet command issued by the older man who'd first greeted them. Malmford, the factor.

"Remember, *he* is to go first, and we are not to interfere."

Peter tightened his jaw and gave his head an angry shake, but he stepped back.

The women whispered among themselves while Lacey swallowed her disappointment. The disappointment was somewhat tempered by curiosity. What did that mean, *he* is to go first? Who was to go first? Some important personage, no doubt, to have inspired such deference in men who were obviously eager to meet them.

But not all of the men seemed inclined to wait

until the mysterious important person revealed himself. There was a small commotion at the rear of the gathering, and then someone bullied his way through the crowd and on toward where Peter stood frozen in place. None of the others called out a warning for him to halt and wait. He did not stop where Peter stood, so it was for just a fleeting second that they stood side by side, but it was long enough for Lacey to notice the dramatic contrast between them. One man, a neat blond gentleman any woman would be proud to call her husband. The other, an . . . apparition.

Lacey had never seen such a tall, black-haired, green-eyed savage of a man. He wore what looked to be animal skins embellished with claws and feathers and fringes. The garments, outlandish and primitive as they were, fitted his taut length with a flattering precision any tailor would envy, revealing that he had not endured the deprivation that had turned the others so thin. His hair looked clean enough but hung loose around his face and shoulders. He carried his head low, as if accustomed to avoiding eye contact with any other, an impression enhanced by the way in which his hair fell to shield his eyes.

One of the women whimpered; another said, "Will you look at him!" He must have heard. He cleared his line of vision with a toss of his head and faced them all with a challenging glare, and all Lacey could think of was Stivington Manor's stud horse, so fierce and unpredictable that it was stabled in isolation because it could not be controlled.

She felt a quickening within herself, something wild struggling to break free.

Oh, lord.

She'd thought she'd tamed those wayward yearnings. All those months in England, hiding in seclusion with Lady Amanda while they concocted this scheme for her escape from Pumphrey, and then the long miserable weeks on board ship—she'd spent virtually every minute reminding herself that ladies did not ache with unfulfillment, that ladies did not dream dreams that wakened them in the night wet and quivering and hungry for the feel of a strong man's arms.

She bit her lip, hoping the pain might drive her wanton sensations away. What was wrong with her, letting slip her tight control over the sensations of her body? That's what came of thinking about unruly stallions when she ought to be focused on the most important moment of her life! What had happened to her common sense?

It was *his* fault. The savage's. He looked every bit as wild and free as that nameless thing inside her yearned to be. She took a step backward, distancing herself from him. He matched her maneuver. His economical and oddly graceful movements, the way his peculiar clothing clung to that fine-honed body, all conspired to rouse such a hammering in Lacey's heart that she felt sure the others must hear.

She wished it was fear that caused her body to behave so, but fear didn't sizzle pleasurably up and down one's spine and leave one weak in the knees in quite this way. She recognized the symptoms; they'd been her downfall, leading to her disastrous affair with Pumphrey Fallsworth. But that was all they had remained—symptoms—never bursting into full life, never quenched, despite Pumphrey's attentions.

The wild man made no effort at all to rouse her

womanly urges. In fact, he no longer paid any of the women the slightest attention. He'd dropped his head again, allowing his hair to swing down and over, shielding his face from them all. He circled the women like a sheepdog intent upon keeping its charges under control. As he prowled, he seemed to be studying their skirts.

Their skirts. Now and then he would pause and lean closer to a woman, peering at the folds of her skirt as if he found nothing more fascinating than the pattern of flowers sprigged on silk. One pert miss cocked her knee and waved it suggestively beneath his nose. He ignored her antics and reached toward the hem of another, and rubbed the cloth between his fingers as the lady wearing the dress tugged and tried to pull it away from him.

His presence angered the other men, though none seemed disposed to risk his ire head-on. They spoke in low, angry tones and cast him furious glances, muttering not-quite-discernible slurs against him. He pretended to ignore their slights, but Lacey could tell by the proud tilt to his jaw and the stiffening of his broad shoulders that he absorbed every mumbled insult.

Outcast, Lacey found herself thinking, feeling a brief surge of kinship.

She shook it off and resolutely blocked the outcast from her mind. She smiled at her blond champion, who blinked in astonishment before grinning back.

"Peter Cheltenham at your service, my lady." He called the greeting without coming closer, which struck her as somehow cowardly. "I must tell you how encouraging I found your—"

"Shut up, Cheltenham."

The voice, low-pitched and husky, lodged itself somewhere in Lacey's middle and provoked another round of knee-quaking. She still refused to look at him, but it seemed her wayward body did not need to see him to be affected by his presence.

"I say, Bradford!" Peter reddened, and for a moment Lacey thought he meant to turn tail and run. But then he swallowed and clenched his fists at his side. "I'll have you know, John, that I intend to ask this lady—"

"You'll ask her nothing."

She couldn't resist looking at him now. It ought to be safe, she reasoned, since he was engaged in an argument with someone else. He would not be paying the least bit of attention to her.

At least, that's the way a sensible man would behave. This one . . . this one ignored Peter so thoroughly, he might not have existed.

The man called John Bradford swept his brooding green-eyed gaze disinterestedly past her face, and lower, and settled on her skirts. He crouched down on his heels, and without even asking her leave lifted her hem and rubbed his fingers over the silk of Amanda Stivington's fanciest day dress. He gave a quick nod of satisfaction. A slight smile, showing nothing of warmth or humor, curled his lip, and then the outcast savage jerked his head toward her.

"This one's mine."

CHAPTER 3

Mine.

He'd done it—claimed one of their women right in front of them all.

While his announcement still echoed, he caught her by the hand and pulled her away from the rest of the female gaggle. An extremely satisfying silence marked their passage through the crowd of men, who parted to let him pass towing his prize. None of them dared say him nay.

She stumbled, and he glanced back to see why she was having difficulty in keeping up with him, and what he saw brought him to a standstill.

The color had drained from her face. Her eyes were wide and stricken with dismay. She hadn't stumbled—she'd deliberately tried to get away! As soon as he paused, she tried pulling her hand free. He clamped tighter by instinct, and when she realized she lacked the strength to get loose that way, she twisted her hand in his grip until he thought her slim wrist might break.

"Don't," he said.

She went still. He started walking again, but hadn't taken two steps before she dug in her heels and nearly threw him off balance.

From behind them came nervous laughter, the sound of movement, greetings hailed with false heartiness and anxious giggling. The men moved toward the women; the women took hesitant steps toward the men. They seemed excited—eager, even—about making acquaintances that they hoped would last a lifetime. He swung his attention back to *his* woman and found her pale-faced and so rigid that it seemed she would rather die and stiffen on the spot than marry the likes of him. A roaring commenced in his ears and intensified until he could scarcely think.

Despite Malmford's warning, he had never considered that the woman might object.

He had never considered that golden-brown eyes brimming with tears and panic would drain him of every ounce of vengeance, and all but hammering him to the spot with the sudden realization that women were nothing like dogs, nothing at all.

"Don't you worry, miss. He can't claim you if you're not willing."

John jerked with surprise. He hadn't even noticed that Malmford had disengaged himself from the rest of the crowd until the tobacco factor spoke, placing an arm around John's woman's shoulders. He gave her a fatherly squeeze, and only John's inexplicable paralysis stopped him from wrenching Malmford's arm out by the roots.

Malmford, not realizing how closely he flirted with danger, gave her another, rather less fatherly squeeze. He cast John a reproachful but triumphant glance. "I told him that this was one time he wouldn't be able to do as he pleased. You women shall all have a say as to whom you'll marry."

She smiled wanly at Malmford's comments. "I had expected we might have some time to make everyone's acquaintance."

"And so you shall, if that's what you want to do." Malmford reassured her.

Another woman—a redhead who'd been standing next to John's woman before he had chosen her and pulled her away—hurried over, her face flushed, her breathing agitated.

"Oh, Lacey, I'm so relieved to find you."

Lacey. His woman's name was Lacey. She tugged again, trying to get away from him.

"Unhand her," the redhead ordered.

"Mine," John said.

Lacey tugged.

The redhead dismissed his declaration with a sniff. "Pay him no mind. You have two weeks, Lacey. Two weeks. Neither of us will marry for two weeks. Perhaps longer, since banns must be called before we can wed."

"Oh, you can wed within minutes if you choose. I'm afraid some of our more civilized customs have fallen by the wayside." Malmford nodded toward John. "Godless men such as John Bradford don't bother attending church anyway."

"Clara speaks for me," said John's woman. "I will not marry anyone for two weeks, banns or no banns."

John ignored Malmford's barbed criticism in favor of studying the sound of Lacey's voice. Smooth, melodious, ladylike, it made him want to close his eyes again and let its warmth wash over him. And yet, here and there, buried deep in her soft tones, something rang wrong, a barely audible sour note in the symphony of well-bred speech.

He glanced once again for reassurance at her skirt. It took a moment to transfer his regard from the way the soft folds clung to her gently swelling hips and concentrate instead on the fabric's weave and texture. Pure silk, no doubt about it, though not half so shiny and soft-looking as the wealth of chestnut brown hair framing her face . . .

What ailed him? He'd never had such trouble focusing on the important matters. Rob Marton had taught him to recognize cut and quality long ago, claiming that cheap flash and frills often hid an empty purse, while excellence indicated wealth and status. Her garment, coupled with the manner in which she'd rallied the other women, marked her as the leader of the lot. The best. How galling it would prove to the Company, watching John Bradford walk off with their best woman.

"This one is mine." His strength of purpose seemed to seep back with speech. "Mine."

"Well, I'll admit she's a comely lass, John, but why are you so set upon her?" Malmford sounded genuinely interested, but John mistrusted the peevish gleam in his eyes.

"Yes, why me?" She laughed, a light, politely amused sound, but once again John's ear caught an off note. This time it wasn't a matter of a misplaced accent. This time he detected a subtle yearning, a craving so long buried that it lay in danger of suffocation.

Or did he only imagine it, mistaking it for the similar nameless hunger he sheltered within himself?

"You, because . . ." His voice trailed away when

her eyes met his, and his good sense, along with all his careful assessment of her clothing and leadership qualities, melted like morning mist over Chesapeake Bay. "I have seen amber." He barely recognized his own voice, so witless did he sound. "It matches your eyes."

She blinked, and the beginning of a shy smile trembled at her lips. John risked tracing the back of her hand with one finger; he had to swallow and press his lips tight against the throaty, wordless sound that welled within him at touching something so wondrously soft and feminine.

Malmford stood openmouthed, gaping at the two of them, and finally bellowed in outrage, "Pretty words from *you*, John Bradford!" He spat his disgust. "Why don't you tell the poor unsuspecting lass what you're truly up to, eh?"

"I don't understand." She moved the barest fraction of an inch, just enough to leave John touching nothing but air. His hand curled slowly, the old childhood motion that served to capture and hold his feelings. He was not at all sure, though, that he wanted to trap the sudden sense of desolation that surged through him at her obvious eagerness to get away from him.

"He doesn't mean to do the honorable thing by you, miss. He's spent too many years nursing wrongheaded grudges to care about anyone but himself." Malmford puffed with self-righteous indignation. "Go on, tell her what you told me, John. Tell her how you mean to gouge at the Company's vitals by stealing off one of its women. Tell her your grand plan about using her only to spite the others and satisfy your sour-hearted purposes."

The woman's beautiful eyes had gone dull. She pressed her fingers against her lips and crooked her arm about her middle, as if Malmford's words prompted the urge to retch. John made a slight, involuntary motion toward her; she took a huge step back, opening a rift between them that loomed wider than the Atlantic.

"Doesn't deny a word of it, does he, miss? You'd see his cruel nature for yourself if he had the common courtesy to look you straight in the eye instead of always skulking about like a whipped cur." Malmford rose to his toes, bouncing with glee. "Get on with you, John. Go back to your hidey-hole in the woods. Spend your miserable life amongst your heathen friends and don't trouble us again. We don't need you here—never did."

"You'll all need me, come winter." John's voice had regained its familiar growling rumble; his innards had returned to their normal hatred-clenched imperviousness. And yet he backed away from Malmford's jeering, fighting an almost overwhelming urge to turn tail and run like the whipped cur Malmford had called him.

We don't need you here—never did.

He shook the hair from his eyes. There was no reason why the familiar taunt should strike his heart with such precision, save for the presence of one gloriously vibrant girl staring at him with utter loathing.

He took another step back. Nothing had gone as planned. Instead of enjoying his revenge, he'd opened himself up to further humiliation. They'd be laughing about him all winter, maybe longer, while they claimed their brides in joyful matrimony. Already the men had broken ranks as if sensing he'd lost control of the situation. In minutes they'd surround the women, perhaps even this one, and make it impossible to carry out his plan.

He could visualize Cheltenham's well-bred sneer, imagine his clipped tones, stating his vows with some woman. Maybe this very woman. For some reason, the notion tightened the crushing heaviness that encased his heart.

"No," he said, more to himself than to them. He stopped his inching retreat.

Malmford paid him no mind, being too busily engaged in a premature victory jig and waving the men closer to the women. His woman stared at the earth, looking every bit as dispirited as John had felt scant moments ago. Well, then, considering that she was already miserable, what he meant to do couldn't cause her much more pain.

He'd learned long ago the art of moving soundlessly. He'd learned that swift action left others incapable of responding until he was long gone. Neither of them noticed that it took only four long strides to bring him back to their sides.

He scooped the woman up, slapped her over his shoulder, and hauled her out of earshot well before her very delicate "oof" could alert Malmford to the abduction taking place right beneath his nose.

Lacey thought hours must have passed, that they must have covered miles, surely, before her limbs overcame their amazement and regained the ability to move. But when she pressed her hands against the outcast's back to gain a moment's leverage to lift her head, she found they were still well within sight of James City. The pompous Malmford had abandoned his ridiculous dance for a no-less-silly leaping and pointing, his arms swooping wildly. "Don't do it, John. Come back!" What was wrong with him? Why didn't he urge the other men to run after them and save her?

Some of the men turned, but instead of coming to her rescue, they shrugged and turned away. Nobody paid him the slightest bit of attention save for Clara, who stared after them with her hand shading her eyes.

The outcast forged on, so unhindered by her weight that she might have been a flea clinging to his animal-skin shirt. She knew, because she could feel the effortless movement of his muscles beneath her hands, could hear the easy rush of his breath, the steady pounding of his heart, from where her head pressed against his back.

Good God, what was she doing, meekly dangling over a man's shoulder, marveling at his strength while his hand clasped familiarly around her thigh!

"Put me down!" she ordered, with no noticeable effect.

All that wild hair, as well as her own form pressed against his ear, probably blocked his hearing.

Very well. She would pummel him to a halt. Unfortunately, from her position, the most easily pummeled portion appeared to be his smoothly shifting buttocks. She had never deliberately touched a man's buttocks, not even . . . well, she had never *deliberately* touched. She closed her eyes and grimaced, flailing her fists in a generally south-ward direction, and took heart when her blows did cause him to lose a stride.

Eager to press her advantage, she brought her feet into the act, and well-armed feet they were. Amanda Stivington's shoes boasted very sharp toes, and roused a most satisfying grunt from the outcast when her right foot connected with a spot that seemed too soft to belong to this taut-muscled abductor. She kicked the spot again, harder. He roared with pain and staggered to a halt, losing his grip on her thigh, which sent her slithering from his shoulder to land in a dusty heap near his feet.

"What do you think you're doing, John Bradford?" she demanded, just as he sank to one knee and whispered, "My God, what have I done?"

They stared at each other, both breathing hard, and then John's glance skittered away. Lacey understood perfectly John's gasping for air; judging by the way he hunched protectively, she suspected her sharp kick had all but unmanned him. But there was no earthly reason why *she* should feel breathless and out of sorts, considering that she hadn't taken a single step under her own power.

No, she had been capably, if inelegantly, toted along by the broad-shouldered man crouching in front of her. One forearm rested on his bent knee, the muscles corded even in relaxation, and she understood why he'd carried her with so little effort. His head was bowed but tilted toward the side, as if he preferred gazing around his shoulder to looking at her. His shirt gaped at the neck, fluttering with each ragged breath, revealing the strong column of his throat. He wore a leather thong around his neck, which carried a silver coin that had been pierced for the purpose. The base of the coin touched curls as black as the hair on his head—fine, swirling hairs that did little to hide the powerful planes banding his chest.

"I'm sorry, girl," he muttered in such a grating fashion that she doubted he apologized very often.

There went her breath again. She had to draw a deep inhalation to keep from swooning. What would Amanda do in such a situation? She would cloak herself in good manners and pretend naught was amiss.

"My name is Lacey. Lacey Cochran."

He shook the hair from his eyes and stared at her with astonishment, and well he might, considering that she had politely introduced herself instead of serving him with the razor side of her tongue as he deserved. Again he lowered his head to avoid looking at her straight on. 'Twas truly a vexing habit! She caught the deep drone of his voice, but she couldn't decipher the words with his head turned away like that.

"What did you say, Mr. Bradford?"

"I said, I didn't ask your name."

"Well, I'm telling it to you anyway. I don't know which I dislike worse: being called *girl* or trying to sort out your mumbling. You would sound rather . . . pleasant if you spoke up."

His head whipped back around so fast that the hair cleared his face once more. *I have seen emeralds, and they match your eyes,* she thought, staring into their fierce green depths. But she couldn't say that without calling to mind the compliment he had paid her earlier, likening her strange-colored eyes to amber. He might think she mocked him, and she just knew that mockery wouldn't sit well with him.

He might take the compliment back, and she didn't care for that notion, either.

"Wrong, all wrong, to take you against your will. And wrong again, not to ask your name," he mumbled, once again shifting his attention to the ground.

Two badly worded apologies from a man who managed to look decidedly unrepentant despite

his outwardly humble posture. His behavior merited a sturdy wallop across the face. Amanda would
have done it without a moment's pause. In fact,
Lacey ought to slap him at least once, maybe twice,
right that very minute in order to maintain the
masquerade that she was a pure and virtuous maid
highly insulted by such unseemly behavior.

Instead, the imp that had dwelt within Lacey
since birth demanded another glimpse of his amaz-
ing eyes. She touched his beard-stubbled chin with
unwarranted gentleness. From the way he jerked
in surprise, she might as well have dealt him the
blow he deserved. She shivered when his breath
passed over her skin, and shivered again when his
emerald gaze pierced her own.

"Did Mr. Malmford speak the truth?" For some
reason, she found it difficult to speak just then,
with the feel of his skin warm against her own. "Do
you really harbor such ungentlemanly intentions
toward me?"

"Aye, I do. Even worse than he said."

"I see." She couldn't think of a single reason to
explain the hurt that slammed through her chest.
She had known for a long time that nobody wanted
her just for herself. Obviously, the knowledge
hadn't protected her from harboring hope. It hurt
to have that last glimmer of hope so thoroughly
doused, to have it trampled out of existence by a
man like this one.

He wanted her, all right, but only because he
thought she was something she was not.

She dropped her hands into her lap and concentrated upon crushing several folds of Amanda's
silk between her fingers. She had no doubt John
Bradford was studying the ground with equal
intent, and this time she was grateful.

When would she ever learn? Her behavior since landing was nothing short of appalling. She'd all but melted with gratitude when Peter Cheltenham approached her. She'd *touched* this outcast savage and been breathlessly willing to forgive his unconscionable behavior, just because he had thought of amber when looking at her. And just because something about him radiated a familiarity with the sorts of wounds she hid inside herself.

Worse, the sight of him, the sound of his voice, sent all her senses leaping, reminding her that her wanton nature hadn't been tamed one little bit.

She was exactly what Lord Pumphrey Fallsworth had called her: a pathetic, affection-starved wretch who had nothing to offer beyond some mildly pleasant sexual diversions. This John Bradford person had sniffed her right out, homed in unerringly upon the one woman in the entire group who might be gullible enough to feel grateful for his attention while he carried out his cruel scheme. Even Mr. Malmford speaking up as he did had not been enough to shake some sense into her!

Pray God she would one day learn to listen to the voice of reason before she made a fool of herself with yet another man.

"I'll be going back to the settlement now," she said with as much dignity as she could muster, considering that she had to clamber to her feet. The harsh rending of ripping silk told her she'd caught her slipper in the hem; no matter, the dress was ruined from sitting in the dirt, and even if it wasn't, she doubted she would ever want to wear it again.

"Stay." It wasn't a command, nor was it a plea, and yet it echoed with both. He had the oddest manner of speaking that she'd ever heard, almost as though he seldom engaged in social discourse.

"Why on earth would I want to stay with you, Mr. Bradford? So I can become an instrument of revenge, only to be discarded at your earliest convenience?"

"It wouldn't take much of your time."

He remained hunkered down, a tribute, she hoped, to the continued effects of her kicks. He peered up at her. With his hair swept back to reveal the clean, strong lines of his face, he looked impossibly earnest . . . and handsome.

Oh, she was truly a pathetic case. She stiffened her backbone and tightened her lips.

"My time is worth something. What you are proposing is such a one-sided bargain that any woman would be a fool to consider it."

"I can teach you not to care so much," he muttered, "when people try to hurt you."

Her breath escaped in a little whoosh.

"I can teach you that it is possible to turn any situation to your advantage."

"What makes you think I am in need of such teaching?"

He didn't laugh. He didn't make light of her question. "I won't pretend to understand women. But I can recognize deception, and I sense you are hiding something important, something that could cause problems for you if discovered."

She forced herself to laugh, to pretend he was far off the mark, while arrows of fear stabbed at her. "All women strive to maintain an aura of mystery."

"Perhaps. It matters naught to me what secrets you hold."

Lacey didn't believe him. If he had some grand scheme for revenge, it would matter very much to him that the tool he'd chosen to gain that revenge was flawed in a very fundamental way.

She hated the terror that crawled through her. She'd run from one man because she'd been afraid. Not five minutes in her new land and she found herself in the clutches of another who might mean her harm.

He rose with a smooth motion, and she stepped back, almost losing her balance. With infinite gentleness, he caught her by the elbows and slid his hands to her shoulders. Supportive, not confining. Strengthening, not overpowering.

He stood sturdy and tall before her, shielding her from the ocean breeze and the sun's pitiless illumination. She watched the movement of his throat as he swallowed, and sensed a light tremor ripple through him when he tilted her chin so her eyes would meet his. She felt absurdly like a pampered lady accepting homage from her honorable knight.

She felt no fear at all.

"You are different," he said. "I cannot yet say why . . . but if I sense it, so will they, and eventually they will find your weakness and use it to exploit you."

"Unless I learn how to turn matters to my advantage."

"I will feed you, Lacey Cochran," he said. "I will give you shelter both warm and dry. I can do these things better than the others. I know all the tricks."

"You . . . you speak as though food and shelter are more important than love," she stammered. She didn't know why she would mention love to him.

He tilted his head, clearly puzzled by her statement. "A man will die without food and shelter."

Not a word as to what would happen to a man without love. Although she fully intended to live a loveless life herself, she shook her head violently at the omission and stepped away. He made no effort to hold her.

"I'll take my chances back at the settlement," she said.

He developed a sudden, intense interest in the horizon. "Well, that's it, then," he mumbled in the direction of the setting sun. "I doubt you want me to carry you back, so be off with you." With a pleasant nod, he turned on his heel and began striding toward a small boat bobbing in a nearby stream.

The ocean breeze struck chill; she hadn't noticed the cold at all before he'd removed his overly warm person from proximity to hers. She faced a long, cold walk back to the settlement, alone, while he just wandered away!

"What do you mean, 'that's it, then?' " Lacey called after him. Fury raged through her. She wasn't entirely certain whether she was angry with his abrupt desertion, or with herself for prolonging this ridiculous situation. "You insulted me, John Bradford, and if you think you can just go stomping off, why ... you ... you ... what kind of man tells a woman that a plate of boiled beef is more important than love, and then gives up without even getting his stupid revenge!"

He paused, his frame rigid, and then very slowly turned his head to peer through the tangle of his hair over his shoulder. "Oh, I'll get my revenge, Lacey, my girl. And you'll learn the value of a full plate come winter. Could be that the fine, upstanding husband you're racing off to find might well offer to trade you to me in exchange for a haunch of venison."

"You lie," she whispered.

"I never lie. Though it might sometimes profit me to do so."

She didn't know how it happened, but somehow they once again stood nose to nose, glaring at one another. "A woman would not give herself to a man lest love were involved."

No trace of mumbling marred the clarity of John's speech. "I daresay the men back at the settlement won't hesitate to swear undying love if that's what you want to hear, but all they'll be after is spending the night in the same bed with you."

"And you're after so much more."

His eyes narrowed. "Aye. If it's a warm romp I'm after, I need only visit my Indian friends. I've never scorned their women as these upstanding tobacco farmers have."

She wasn't sure why his admission made her teeth clench, but it did. She tried employing her unperfected ladylike sniff to cover her speechlessness.

"No need to snort at me. I see how it is with you women. False declarations of love make you swoon, while a good honest offer like mine earns naught but scorn."

That statement was outrageous enough to bring about a return of her voice. "Good! Honest!"

"Aye! There would be no pretense between us, Lacey Cochran. Neither of us would delude ourselves with notions of love. You need someone capable of keeping you alive until this settlement gets on its feet. I need a fancy lady to grace my arm and rub in the noses of those who consider themselves my betters."

"Fancy lady?" Lacey asked in faint tones.

"Highborn, rich, useless frippery about the house—just like your name," John offered helpfully.

A jumble of emotions surged through her. "You want a 'useless frippery.' *Useless* implies that nothing whatsoever is expected. So Mr. Malmford painted a darker picture of your intent than required. There would be no expectation of, er, sexual relations between us."

She could have bitten her tongue right off! No proper young lady would say such a thing, and judging by the color clouding John's face, even a savage understood that much.

He studied her. *Her,* this time, and not the dress she wore. His regard was so intense, she fancied she felt the brush of phantom fingers across her lips, against the pulse at her neck, over the pebbled peaks of her breasts.

A wave of lightheadedness assailed her as she waited while he considered his reply.

"Do not expect exemplary behavior of me," he said at last. "But when you come to my bed, it will be because you want to be there, not because you were forced."

When you come to my bed . . .

"*If* I come to your bed it will be because I have determined there is some advantage in my doing so," she hurled at him to cover the quickening his words aroused in her middle.

He concentrated on a leaf skipping by, propelled by the wind. "You learn quickly," he said.

"You, sir, are so disagreeable that I am quite enjoying the practice of your lessons."

"You aren't exactly an amenable companion."

"You aren't exactly the husband I had hoped to find when I got here."

She bit her tongue to keep from continuing the argument. It was true John was not the man she had hoped to find, nor was she the woman he had hoped to kidnap and use as an instrument of revenge.

"Helping you achieve your nefarious ends won't take long, will it?"

"I'm a busy man. I'm sure I would tire of this whole business in no time, and then you'd be free to go wherever you please."

She didn't know why his cool observation annoyed her. "I'll be free as a bird!" she hollered.

"Aye, and I won't feel a thing when you fly away."

"Neither will I!" She flapped her arms like wings for emphasis. "In fact, I'll whistle a happy tune when I know I've seen the last of you." She flapped wildly for added emphasis.

He looked as stunned by her actions as if he'd had a pike run through him.

She pursed her lips and succeeded in producing a thready whistle.

"Tweet, *TWEET!*" John thundered in response. And then he tucked his hands against his ribs and commenced strutting and crowing like a rooster.

No lady would have behaved in such a manner for a single minute, and yet it went on and on, until they both whirled to face each other, Lacey caught in mid-flap, John in mid-crow. Absurd positions, laughable, except for the sudden sense of desolation that seemed to grip them both at the same time.

She'd done it again. She'd responded to his sly dare with the same lack of sense that had gotten her into endless trouble in the past.

Lacey lowered her arms and folded her hands to keep them from trembling. John glared at his arms, scowling as if embarrassed to find them attached to his body, and shoved his hands into his pockets.

"So you see, then," he muttered, "how easy it is to learn not to care."

"I can't imagine why I'd ever thought it would be difficult," she whispered.

"You'll do it."

He was just what she'd prayed she might find: a man who would not care, a man who could not be hurt.

She sighed and glanced back toward the settlement. Nobody had pursued them; even Malmford had deserted his position and melted into the dockside crowd. "I don't know," she said. "I guess I belong back there, with them."

He didn't say, "So do I," but it hovered in the air, evident in his yearning stance as he stared toward the settlement. Lacey didn't know why, but all of a sudden she dreaded the prospect of making herself part of a crowd that excluded John so thoroughly. She needed some time to think; that was what she needed.

She did have time. She had two weeks. She'd made that pact with Clara.

Two weeks to gain better control over her wanton nature, to bury her secrets deeper, to polish her pretended identity. It would be much easier to accomplish all that out here in the wilderness with only this surly savage around. But her reputation couldn't possibly survive spending even one night out here alone with him, and there was no advantage to that at all, none whatsoever. . . .

Except . . .

She was not a virgin. She could not hide that fact from any man who wed her.

But she'd been abducted by a wild man. Nobody had lifted a finger to help her. She could stay out here for every minute of those two weeks, working on her disguise, and the ruin of her reputation would not be her fault. Nobody would dare accuse her of wantonness if she was later discovered to be no pure and virtuous maid.

Already, he was teaching her. Already, she was gaining value from her participation.

"All right," she said. "I'll do it. But I don't want you asking me why."

"Fair enough," he said, accepting the bargain with a nod. "Let's be off. If we hurry, we can reach my place in the woods before nightfall."

She felt a little disappointed. She wasn't sure why. This was a business arrangement between the two of them, nothing more. They would each be working it to their own advantage.

He hadn't even smiled at her. Or thanked her for her cooperation.

"You won't have to work very hard at teaching me to be hard-hearted. I won't ever care a fig for you, John Bradford."

He shrugged. "I wouldn't expect you to. There's not much about me to like."

He held out his hand. She slipped hers into his and then compressed her lips so she wouldn't blurt out that there was something about him to like, after all: she quite enjoyed the way his hand enfolded hers, all warm and strong and purposeful.

Keeping that bit of information to herself seemed a smart thing to do, considering the businesslike nature of their arrangement. Why, she could almost feel her heart hardening by the second!

Well done, Lacey, she complimented herself, though it seemed a hollow accomplishment.

She only looked back once while he led her deeper into the woods.

CHAPTER 4

It seemed to Clara that she had stood there for hours, shielding her eyes with a flattened hand, desperately trying to see into the forest where the savage had disappeared with Lacey. He would come back. Surely he would bring her back at any moment! But minute after long minute passed with no sign of a human figure emerging from the woods. Her arm grew weary and she let it fall to her side. Her hope deserted her at the same time.

Lacey was gone.

She gradually became aware of the merriment all around her. The men who had held their distance while Lacey's abductor did his foul deed had swiftly surrounded the remaining women, and now feminine laughter mingled with hearty male voices. Not one of them displayed the slightest concern that an innocent young woman had been stolen from their midst. They reminded her of those who attended the funeral of someone whose passing was not mourned. All that remained was for someone to strike up music and they'd all begin dancing a jig, she thought sourly, and she decided they required a scolding to prod them into action.

"Somebody go after them! Help her!"

She possessed the type of voice that allowed her to be heard above the din of crowds, which sometimes came in handy during social gatherings—even though she still smarted inside from once being likened to the blaring of a ship's horn. This time nobody noticed her yelling. What with the sea pounding the shore, and the raucous atmosphere of the men and women getting to know one another with laughter and loud conversation, she might have been whispering into a feed bucket for all the attention they paid her.

She realized then how alone she stood.

Her worst fear, the one she'd barely dared articulate lest saying it aloud make it true, raised its leering head. She'd made the journey for nothing. Hundreds of supposedly woman-starved men had already looked her over and dismissed her. Too tall. Too thin. Too lacking in feminine appeal. Her eyes stung. She realized that while she had told herself to expect this, she had nurtured the hope deep within that here in this new land there might be a man who wouldn't mind so much being married to a woman who did not draw appreciative glances.

All hope was gone now. She would be the one woman of all who'd survived the ocean crossing who would remain unwed. She would have been better off staying at home, where there were other spinsters aplenty, rather than this place, where she'd been told men were so anxious for wives that they sometimes consorted with savage Indian women. From the way the men and women were pairing up around her, it appeared they would all be coupled and wed within minutes while she alone remained single.

Her eyes started watering, and angrily she dashed away the tears. Lacey had ever so gently pointed out that she should do her crying alone; Clara knew better than anyone how horribly red and swollen she turned when she cried. . . .

Good God, what was wrong with her! Sniveling and worrying about her complexion while Lacey had been abducted! Lacey, the best friend she had ever had, who had intuitively understood Clara's insecurities and fears and who had sworn that she would remain unwed for at least two weeks so that Clara would not be the only woman without a mate.

That damned savage had made a mockery of Lacey's promise.

Outrage at his manhandling of her friend jolted her out of her self-pitying paralysis. She spun on her heel and marched straight into the largest group of merry-makers, noting with disgust that the tall, blond fellow who had greeted Lacey was among them. He was smiling down at another woman, looking for all the world as if he'd never tried flirting with Lacey.

"You!" She pointed a finger and stabbed him on the shoulder. "How dare you let that wild man kidnap an innocent young woman!"

He had the grace to blush and look uncomfortable, but he made no move to race off after Lacey. "John Bradford brooks no interference."

"You, sir, are a coward."

She sniffed at him and aimed for another cluster of people. The men eyed her uneasily and shifted their positions, edging away as she approached. Disbelief washed through her.

"Stop your skulking and go save my friend!"

They turned away from her.

The women who'd sailed with her, who'd pretended to be Lacey's friends, glared at Clara as if angry that she'd interfered with their courting. "Don't any of you care that Lacey has been kidnapped?" she asked, appalled.

"We can't save her, Clara."

"Nothing any of us can do, miss," muttered one of the men.

"You can send the law after him and arrest him. An Englishman has no business flinging a woman over his shoulder and carrying her off, any more than you Englishmen have any business allowing it to happen. There are laws against such behavior."

"John Bradford pays no mind to our laws. We can't make him do anything he doesn't want to do."

"Nonsense. He's only one man." A rather strong-looking man in comparison with those she was scolding, Clara had to admit. Nonetheless, he was only one against many. "Five or ten of you could overpower him and toss him into jail."

"We don't have a jail, mistress." The older gentleman called Malmford touched Clara's arm and drew her away from the crowd. "Even if we did, there'd be no way to hold him."

"You speak of this John Bradford as if he's a wild Indian. Well, sir, I saw him with my own two eyes, and he is nothing more than an Englishman just like yourself."

"No, mistress, he is nothing like me, and nothing like these other men here. He lives apart from us. He refuses to partake of Company goods. He consorts with the Indians and has learned their ways. He is more a stranger to us than you are yourself." Malmford's face drooped with misery. "I'm sorry he chose your friend. I didn't think he'd really go through with it—"

"You *knew* he would kidnap someone? And you did nothing to stop him?"

Malmford managed to look even more dejected. "We can't risk angering him. We'll need his help come winter. He keeps us supplied with meat, and—"

"Oh!" Words failed Clara and she spun away from Malmford before she could slap the excuses from his lips. "You sacrificed my friend for the sake of your bellies! Don't you know the horrible, terrible things a man can do to an innocent young maid?"

She could not articulate her fears to a man, simply could not stand there and speak aloud of the atrocities she feared this John Bradford might perform against Lacey.

"I don't think he'll hurt her, miss." Malmford toed the sand. "He has a use in mind for her."

"I imagine he does!" Clara found herself near to tears again, but this time over concern for Lacey. Malmford shrugged apologetically and bolted away from her.

She dropped to her knees in the sand, too distressed, too disappointed to stay on her feet. She didn't look up, even when a shadow blotted out the sun.

"I'll go after them, miss. Not right now, since we must be leaving for Malvern's Hundred. But soon."

At first Clara thought that the fellow who had hunkered down alongside her and made the offer was a youth—he had come upon her so quietly and had such stark fear written across his features that she knew at once he didn't have the strength of body or will to stand against a man like John Bradford.

"No, we must go after her at once. And I require someone older and stronger—" she began, but paused when her dismissal caused him to straighten with determination. Almost at once she realized that the lines creasing the skin near his eyes, and the thinning hair on his head, indicated a man of more years than she'd at first suspected.

That's what came of being overtall for a woman, and boasting an excellent posture. The man did not keep his spine as straight as Clara, but crouched down so the top of his head barely reached her nose. It was impossible to judge his height from her perspective. Perhaps he was quite normal-sized as well as mature in age.

"I'd guess John and I are of an age, but I suspect you are right in saying he's stronger," agreed the man. "Then again, he's stronger than most anyone here. Physically and mentally. We're a sorry lot, I'm afraid."

"Yes, you are." Clara cast a disparaging glance over these people for whom she'd abandoned her old life, whom she'd crossed an ocean to join. "I've yet to find a more cowardly group." But even as she agreed to the sorriness of their courage, she realized that the man had more likely been referring to the physical condition of his fellow settlers.

She had been assailed with so many strange sights, topped by the shock of Lacey's abduction, that she'd been blinded to the settlers themselves. "Goodness," she said. "You all do seem rather . . . gaunt."

"My tailor would despair if he could see the way these garments hang upon me now," said the man. "There was a time I would've cared as well. Now, the fit of our clothes doesn't seem so very important. We're all just happy to have clothes."

"Matters such as clothes tend to bother one less as one gets older," Clara said.

"How old do you think we are, miss? Most of us have yet to see our thirtieth birthdays." He smiled a little. "The Company recruited men in their prime years."

"But everyone seems so . . ." Again, her voice trailed away as she stared, dismayed, with new attention at the men who had refused to help Lacey. Many of them sported dark hollows beneath their eyes, the sure mark of illness. Their hair hung lank, dull, and lifeless. Those who were vying for the attention of the new brides showed a bit of spirit, but otherwise an air of apathy hovered over the entire settlement.

"The man who took Lacey away struck me as imposing and . . . and *confident*. There doesn't appear to be a spare shred of confidence among the lot of you."

"Not much."

"It should be the other way around! Mr. Malmford tells me John Bradford is an outcast who relies on nobody but himself. How can it be that he is fairly bursting with vitality when all of you look fit only for the grave?"

"Mr. Bradford is rather remarkable in his own way." He sounded quite impressed with the outcast savage. "Good heavens, where are my manners? Percy Bledsoe at your service, miss." He stood and executed a stiff little formal bow that ought to have looked ridiculous, considering they were both coated with sand. He extended a hand and helped her to her feet, then stepped back a bit so he could look up to meet her gaze once she was towering over him.

Well, perhaps not quite *towering*, Clara thought, since his eyes weren't more than two or three inches below the level of her own.

"Can't you press some of these men into going after her now?" she asked.

"I doubt it, miss. It's been a long, hard day for everyone—working on the tobacco and then rushing here from Malvern's Hundred when we received word of the *Talisman's* arrival. Even if there were lodgings available to us here in James City, there's stock to tend and evening chores waiting. We'll be traveling for hours to get to the hundred. Look, they're making ready now."

She saw that he spoke the truth. Men were loading the trunks of the newly arrived women onto a sort of barge. Nobody was as yet making any move to climb into the small passenger boats bobbing at the edge of the shore. Clara winced. The last thing she wanted to do was find herself back on the water, even for a brief time. The very idea made traipsing through the woods in pursuit of a savage seem like an attractive option.

"You need not go after him by yourself. I will go with you. We shall accost the scoundrel together."

"Certainly not!" Percy's diffidence transformed into conviction. "Such a thing would not be the least bit proper for a young lady such as yourself to undertake."

It had been quite some time since Clara had heard herself referred to as a young lady, and the compliment made her smile again. Strange, that despite her anxiety over Lacey, despite her despair at finding things so dismal at the settlement, despite the dousing of her hopes, she could smile twice in the space of a few heartbeats. All because of this surprising little fellow.

"To be honest, Mr. Bledsoe, at this moment I'm finding myself believing that Lacey might have been the lucky one to get carried away from here."

Percy did not object to her observation.

She studied once more her surroundings, noting the ramshackle construction of the few buildings, the lack of livestock, the absence of gaiety. She noticed that a few men were staring her way. Not at *her*, Clara Cutler, but rather at various aspects of her body. Gazes lingered most upon her breasts, traveled down her waist, lingered again at her hips. They had no interest in her as a person; they cared only for the female body she possessed.

She shivered and crossed her arms protectively over her front while she turned away from them. She met Percy's concerned gaze. Percy's attention focused upon her eyes, and concern for *her* creased his forehead. Well, of course *he* would look upon her as a person rather than a . . . a . . . bedmate. She stood taller than him and outweighed him and no doubt frightened him more than titillated his manhood.

"We'd better go secure places in the boats," Percy said. "I'll ride with you, if you like, and perhaps I can escort you to the place where you'll be staying until . . ."

Until I find a husband. Clara imagined she could feel the stares from the men behind her raking over her body. She wasn't accustomed to that sort of attention. Maybe one of them would take her after all. She should be elated. Instead, she shivered again.

"Lacey and I have vowed that we would not marry for at least two weeks," she said, taking heart from the pact they had made. "That gives me plenty of time to track down my friend and see to it that her abductor is punished."

"I'll go after them in two days. Three at the most."

Clara hated to seem ungrateful, but she couldn't understand the delay. "Why so long?"

A dull flush colored Percy's skin. "We'll have to work like demons to make up the time we lost today."

"Make up time?"

"The tobacco. It's an infernal amount of work. We can't fall behind."

"Goodness, you speak about that tobacco as if you're all slaves to it."

"We are, in a manner of speaking." Percy's flush deepened, and then he seemed deliberately to change the subject. "Come, you must be exhausted. We can sit in the boats until it's time to leave."

Clara looked once more toward the forest. Though the sun stood high overhead, the woods appeared dark, ominous, forbidding. Lacey was in there, alone with the man who had forced her to accompany him.

She choked back a sob. "Poor Lacey. Once night falls . . ."

Percy colored. "I know it is not proper to discuss such things with a lady, but John can do what he wills with your friend whether it's dark or full light."

"Yes, I suppose you're right."

Percy extended his arm for her. She took one last look at the forest and said a silent prayer for

Lacey, and then she placed her hand in the crook of Percy's elbow.

Her gown was light green and pale pink, colors John had often seen in the wild land that was his home. So there was no reason why he should find those colors so compelling that he wanted to walk backward in order to watch the way green-and-pink silk hugged her body. No reason why his fingers should itch to reach back and stroke the shining cloth, to see which was softer: the silk or her skin.

He walked ahead of her, holding back branches and clinging vines to ease her passage. He could see those things only in his mind's eye, and yet he was almost painfully aware of her following in his wake. He kept wanting to spin about to make sure she followed, to watch the movement of her skirts against her legs. She lured him to her the way a bee was drawn to the dizzying scent of a flower even when its body was so laden with pollen that it could barely fly.

He had reasons for being so distracted, he told himself. He'd planned this revenge for so long, it was only natural that he should find himself somewhat obsessed with the object that helped him achieve the revenge.

"Could we stop for a moment?" she asked.

He used the question to glance over his shoulder at her. She had paused, so he wasn't able to see her skirts swinging. He might not have been able to see it even if she'd kept walking, for she held folds of silk bunched in her hands to keep the skirts from dragging along the forest floor. She dropped the skirts when she saw him looking, and clasped her hands together in a rather demure fashion, but they seemed to be shaking a bit. He silently cursed himself for a fool. A lady such as she probably had a serving girl who followed her about to hold her garments up out of the dirt. She might've strained her hands, considering how slender were her fingers, how delicate she looked overall.

"Are you tired?"

"No, I . . ." She lowered her eyes and then tilted her head toward a thick tangle of vines. "I'd just like to go over there now."

"It's easier walking here."

She peeked up at him and he thought he saw the briefest hint of a smile, but if so it was so quickly quenched he could not be sure. "Perhaps men's personal needs are different, but I can no longer postpone a visit to that space behind the vines."

"Of course." He looked away, lest she see how his misunderstanding embarrassed him. He hadn't given a thought to her comforts. She'd been on that ship, and then on the shore, and then he'd claimed her and marched her through the woods for an hour or more without allowing her five minutes to tend to her personal needs.

Personal needs.

He heard her moving through the brush. He caught a flash of light green and pale pink amid the familiar browns and greens, and turned away so she wouldn't think he was spying on her. He'd made no special provisions for her needs at his cabin, either. Once again Malmford's warnings about how a living, breathing woman might differ from his expectations taunted him with their truth. What had he thought—that he could simply prop her up in a corner of his cabin like a doll?

She stayed behind the vines for a very long time.

He'd just about decided he would either have to go after her or give her up for gone, when he heard her moving toward him once again.

Relief surged through him.

He told himself he had good reasons for that, too. After all, his revenge would be rather minor if she'd managed to sneak back to the settlement so quickly.

When she stepped back onto the trail, it was evident that she'd had a good fight with the trailing branches and tangling vines. Half of her hair had been pulled from the loose knot at her neck. A scratch dotted with drops of blood marred the skin at her collar bone. A tear in the light green and pale pink silk marked where a thorn had torn its way through the cloth.

"Remind me again of the advantages to this plan," she said.

Once again—for the briefest space of time—he thought a smile marked her words. He couldn't understand the urge he felt to see the full version of that smile, especially to see it directed his way.

"A survivor learns to turn every situation to his advantage."

"I am a survivor," she said in little more than a whisper.

"Survivor of what? Too many cups of punch at a ball? Having your toes trod upon by a clumsy dancer?"

Her eyes blazed with sudden anger. "I survived that sea journey. I survived a fair amount of unpleasantness before setting foot on that ship. Do not mock me, sir. You know nothing about me."

"I know your kind."

"You know nothing. Nothing about *me*."

"I don't know you," he agreed. "I don't know why you came here or what you expected to find."

"I came here expecting to find a husband!"

And he'd denied her that opportunity. Remorse curled through him, and to put a stop to it he lashed out at her. "Why did you have to come clear across the sea to find a man? What's wrong with you that you couldn't find one back in England?"

She averted her eyes.

Interesting.

She was hiding something. His instincts smelled it upon her.

"Everyone will assume the worst now," she said musingly. "They will know I am no longer the pure and virtuous maid they hoped to find."

John had known that. And he'd congratulated himself on what he'd thought would be his generosity in turning her loose to return to the people who would think her damaged. Not because of something she had asked for, but because of something *he* had done.

Every time somebody looked at her, they would think of him.

Knowing this should sweeten his revenge beyond expectations. Instead, he sought to find the advantage in the situation, the advantage he had so boastingly assured her could be found in every situation.

"These people won't worry so much about that," John said. "Not the way they would back in England."

Naked hope lit her face, and his belly churned, because he knew it meant she was already looking forward to the day when she could leave him and be accepted by the others.

What of it? He didn't want her anyway.

"The entire settlement witnessed my carrying

you away," he said. "Not one of them can blame you for any stain upon your character. All the blame will fall to me."

"So a man might overlook my lack of . . . of pure and virtuous, maidenly . . . qualities."

Her comment took him aback. Lack of maidenly qualities? Her remark that he knew nothing about her suddenly took on new meaning. She was hiding something from him, and judging by this conversation it had something to do with her virtue—or lack thereof.

"Perhaps that will be the advantage you find in this situation," he said.

"A man who could overlook something that important might be likely to overlook matters of . . . lesser importance as well."

She seemed to be perking up with every word, while he felt himself staggered as if she'd dealt him a blow with a log across the head. Miss Lacey Cochran was hiding more than one thing behind her ladylike veneer. He didn't know enough about women to imagine what they might be.

Not that he cared.

She darted him a sly glance. She smiled then, and still it wasn't the sort he craved; this one had too much of a cat-falling-into-cream flavor to sit well with him, particularly when she looked away as if she meant to hide her satisfaction from him.

The strangest sensation gripped John. He found himself leaning toward her, his heart quickening just a bit, his breath bating just a bit, while everything within him demanded to *know*. It took a moment to identify the sensation: curiosity.

Curiosity? Could it be? He never experienced the slightest bit of curiosity about anybody. People were almost pathetically easy to read, their motives all the same, their actions completely predictable. He'd learned that back in the gutter, when knowing upon whom to prey meant the difference between freedom and being caught and clapped in jail.

And yet here stood this pert little miss, alone with him in the midst of the Virginia wilderness, having taken the completely bewildering step of leaving behind all she knew and loved to face the unknown—and he felt all but consumed by the need to know why.

And it was there at his lips, which even at that moment formed the question, when his common sense regained its control of him. He clenched his teeth, holding in the question.

It mattered not a whit to him why Lacey Cochran had sailed the sea. What she had escaped; what she sought. Knowing her motives would not enrich him in any way. If anything, learning too much about her might make her seem more real to him, might reveal things about her that he could actually find himself . . . liking. He gave himself a mental shake. Best to keep his distance from her in every way, particularly in that way. Best to recall his original purpose: to use her.

And lose her.

"Are you finished tending your personal needs?"

"Aye."

"Do you require rest?"

"I'm rather numb if you want to know the truth. I'd rather press on before my legs realize how tired they are."

Interesting. She had certainly embraced his scheme with her whole heart. He suspected most other women would grasp at the chance to stop and rest in the hopes that a rescue party might catch up with them.

"We have several hours yet to travel," he said. "The terrain is not easy to cover. We'll go most of the way by boat, but even so your garb will no doubt be ruined."

She nodded and never spared a glance for her fancy dress, her silly fripperies of shoes. Didn't bemoan their loss.

Her garments had meant so much to him. The quality of cloth, the cut of the dress—he'd depended on them to make his choice of a woman.

He had the feeling he'd been concentrating on the wrong things.

CHAPTER 5

They traveled for two hours, maybe more, before coming to a broad, burbling creek. Lacey swiped a hand across her forehead and licked her lips.

Though the forest was dark and cool, with just a little sun filtering through the trees, the long weeks at sea had sapped some of her strength and she found the journey hard going. The thought of splashing her face and drinking a deep measure of clear, cool water proved irresistible.

Just as she was on the verge of asking John to stop for a rest, he came to a stop.

"There's the boat," he said.

She looked along the creek bank but saw nothing out of the ordinary. Droplets of water caught the sunlight and splashed against rich soil dotted with small stones. She licked her lips again. "I don't see a boat."

"Right here."

He moved aside a branch that hung only inches

from her toes to reveal a small, narrow boat unlike any she had ever seen. It didn't appear to weigh much, judging by the ease with which John pulled it from its hiding place. The body of the boat was fashioned with something thin and brown, with thick corded seams. He dragged it to the edge of the creek and then knelt beside it, doing exactly as she longed to do by dipping his cupped hand into the water. He leaned back and let the water trickle down over his face.

He looked so *right* there alongside his boat. He with his long hair and deerskin garments, perfectly at ease in the untamed setting. He belonged in this wild place in a way Lacey had always dreamed of belonging somewhere.

She'd never managed to get it right—any child of a poor workingman knew they'd be banished from the house as soon as a place of service could be found, or as soon as a marriage could be arranged. She'd hated Stivington Manor when she first entered service, and hadn't ever felt it was her true home, even when she'd been promoted to the position of maid to the household's spoiled rich girl. Even during her brief and disastrous affair with Pumphrey Fallsworth, she'd known that there could be no possibility of marriage between them, no chance of his telling her to make his home her own.

Always, she had felt all at sea. Always, she had hungered for something more, something nameless, something that had eluded her no matter where she went or what she tried.

John scooped a double handful of water and soaked himself so thoroughly that his shirt seemed to meld to his skin.

She licked her lips again.

She swallowed, and the dryness of her throat convinced her that there was nothing more than thirst responsible for her yearning. She moved to the bank. She couldn't kneel on the rocky earth without thoroughly ruining her dress, and so she crouched, and held on to the rim of the boat for support while she dipped one hand into the water. The cool wetness felt so good that she just let the water swirl around her fingers for a bit. Remembering how the cascading water had molded John's clothes against him, she settled for daintily dabbing her wet hand against her cheeks and forehead.

The boat shifted a little from the pressure of her weight, and as she caught her balance, she realized how very small it was.

She delved her hand into the water again and pressed wet fingers against her lips. She tried to guess how many inches apart were the two roughly hewn boards that seemed to be the only places where a person could sit. Inches, mere inches. Her knees would be bumping into him throughout their journey.

"A sight different from the *Talisman*," John said, no doubt mistaking her trepidation for curiosity.

"This boat appears to be made of hides," she said.

"It is."

"I've never seen its like in England."

"I traded for it with an Indian."

"It's rather small," she said.

His eyebrow quirked. "Small? I would think that someone who just stepped off a ship would find it quite spacious. Unless you traveled in the fancy cabins. I've traveled in a ship's hold, and I remember well those close quarters packed like herrings in a fisherman's creel."

"That is true. There's some silly sailors' superstition about carrying women on a ship, and so we were seldom permitted up on the deck. We spent most of the journey confined to the hold. We scarcely had room to turn around. At first."

"More room no doubt became available as the journey progressed," John said, with the familiarity of one who had made a similar journey.

"Aye."

She let her hand trail in the water. She'd never been able to touch the water during the journey—the ship's deck sat up so high, and they'd been allowed up for air so infrequently. Some silly sailors' superstition meant that the women could not walk about as they pleased, but had to remain packed in a huddle in one small section.

Nor had she been able to talk to the other women about the way so many of her fellow tobacco brides succumbed to illness during the journey. It was as though they all had a pact of silence, as if they feared that discussing death would cause it to visit them next.

It seemed right, somehow, to talk about it to John, who would understand.

"I would have preferred to endure the crowding."

"How many died?"

"Twelve."

The tobacco brides had traveled in overcrowded conditions even after so many of her fellow travelers had died. They'd lost at least twelve of the women to illness during the long journey. Even after their deaths, the amount of space alloted to the survivors in the hold had been pitiful, and their only respite from the close crowding had been the rare trip above deck.

Compared to the vast size of the ship, John's small

boat seemed a laughable toy. And yet it offered more
room per person than Lacey had enjoyed for months.

So why did she dread sitting in it with him? She
would be perfectly safe with him in that boat—
safer than here on land where he could move freely
and do with her as he willed.

"Are you ready to continue?" he asked.

She shook away her ridiculous misgivings. Just
because she couldn't seem to keep her thoughts
under control didn't mean his intentions leaned
in the same direction. "I'm ready." She let him
help her into the boat.

He went back to the boat's hiding place and
returned with a paddle. He tucked it under one
arm, and then pushed the boat into the water. With
a graceful lunging motion he launched himself
into the space in front of her. His broad shoulders
filled her vision. He cut into the water with the
paddle, first on one side of the boat and then the
other, and with each movement his shirt drew taut
over his shoulders.

She forced herself to look away, to concentrate
on the things to be seen along the shore. "How
much longer?" she asked.

"Two hours. Maybe three."

"You don't know?"

"I've never made the journey with another
person."

"You've never taken anybody to your home
before this?" It seemed an astounding admission.
Surely she'd heard wrong.

"No."

She waited for him to elaborate. He did not. He
dipped his paddle into the water.

"This first part of the journey has taken twice as

long as usual. I don't know what to expect for the rest."

"So we will travel in this boat for two more hours. Or three." *Please God, no longer,* she prayed when her gaze was drawn again and again to the strong, fit body sitting right in front of her.

Why, with an endless wilderness to drink in, could she stare at nothing but the movement of John's broad shoulders as he plied his paddle in the swift-moving creek? One small part of her mind noted that birds unlike any she had ever seen flitted from branch to branch upon trees unlike any that grew in England. After weeks of nothing to see but gray-green, foam-capped water, she ought to be drinking her fill of the lush greens and browns and unusual sights. But there she sat, riveted in place by the way his muscles moved beneath the taut deerskin, the way his bare arms corded with strength as he pitted his determination against the current.

She might as well have just stayed in England. She hadn't learned a single lesson from her experience with Pumphrey Fallsworth. Curiosity about a man's body, and caving in to the intense yearning that gripped her middle, had led to her downfall. Making love with Percy had done nothing to slake that yearning; now it seemed she would be forced to endure it for all the days of her life, because it gripped her again, even more intensely, as she watched John Bradford carry her away from all that was safe and proper.

She brushed a stray tendril of hair away from her forehead, and then her hand hovered near his shoulder, all but itching to touch him and feel the play of muscle as he worked. She caught herself leaning forward, breathing deeply, trapped by the scent of him, wishing she could rub her cheek against his back and revel in the joy of sensation the way a horse might roll in new-mown hay. How appropriate that she should think of a mare in heat at this moment, when she found herself thrumming like a piano string for a man who was bent upon using her and destroying her reputation before casting her aside.

She had a hundred reasons for being repulsed by him, and no reasons—no *sensible* reasons—for wanting to curl up against him. She tried mentally listing all the wrongs he'd done her against the few courtesies he'd shown. It should have been the work of a moment to come to the only possible conclusion, but instead her thoughts swirled and refused to come to the proper, the necessary conclusion. Instead, she kept hearing the echo of his voice saying, *I have seen amber . . .*

"We're here," he said, jolting her out of her pondering. He positioned his paddle in the water so that the boat turned toward shore. She drew back with a start, embarrassed to find that during the intervening hours, despite all her attempts to convince herself to hold her distance from him, she'd moved so close to him that she had been able to feel the rumble of his voice stir the air.

"Your eyes are sharper than mine," she said, hoping he would not notice the breathless quality of her voice. She'd been sitting, doing nothing, and had no logical explanation for it. Sitting for hours, probably, judging by the stiffness in her back and shoulders. She twisted from the waist, hoping to ease the discomfort. "I couldn't see your boat at first, and now I cannot see your cabin."

"I did not think it wise to build a home where it would be visible from the creek," he said. With a few quick, mighty plunges of his paddle, the boat skidded up onto the shore. "I'll help you out in a moment; hang on tight."

She gripped the edges while he hoisted himself effortlessly from the boat. With a quick sweep of his hand he gripped the prow and walked forward, impeded not at all by her added weight, drawing the boat behind him as easily as one might haul a broom.

"Up with you now," he said, turning and extending his hand.

She stared at his hand, his large, well-shaped hand, while dismay held her still. She would have to touch him. She'd just spent the better part of two hours wishing she could do that very thing, and thanking God she couldn't, and now with the memory of his muscles and his scent fresh in her mind, she would have to slip her hand within his, feel those large fingers close around hers, feel his strength draw her toward him.

"I think I know how to get out of a boat," she said, rather more sharply than she'd intended.

"Your position is all wrong. It's not easy to climb out of something that's tilted uphill."

"We'll see about that," she said.

"So we shall."

He didn't seem disturbed by her refusal of his help; if anything, he appeared to find her small stand for independence amusing. He crossed his arms over his chest and stood watching her while something that was almost but not quite a smile hovered at the edges of his lips.

She wished he wouldn't do that. His stance made his shoulders appear even broader, his upper arms stronger, and the subtle gentling of his expression made him look almost ... handsome. Ha! As if one could consider a long-haired, outcast, garbed-like-a-savage woodsman attractive. She was no doubt suffering some malady, an opposite of seasickness perhaps, where her head was all awhirl from the rapid transition from the sea to the ground, to the stream, to the ground again. The thought that she might be sick and not still overly prone to the attractions of a male body cheered her enormously.

She tried inching forward to gain purchase for leaving the little boat and found at once that John had spoken true—it wasn't easy to heave oneself out of something that tilted upward. She bit her lip and scooted to the far side of the boat, angling her legs to find better leverage.

"Take my hand." He held it toward her, open, a simple offer of assistance that froze her in place with dismay yet again. He held his hand cupped, and she couldn't stop thinking that her breast was perfectly sized and shaped to fill the empty space thus created. She couldn't help noticing the way his fingertips were toughened by calluses—not the reddened, rough-edged sort that came from unaccustomed work, but the smooth, tough kind that developed over long years of hard labor until they were almost indistinguishable from softer skin. She wondered if those calluses dulled his ability to feel through them, or whether hands that were obviously so well employed possessed even greater sensitivity than most.

With an embarrassing gurgle of dismay, she heaved herself upward, desperate to avoid his hand, and nearly toppled headfirst into the mud of the stream bank. He prevented her fall. With the hand she'd refused, he caught her by the back of her dress and hoisted her out of danger the way a mother cat might lift a kitten by the scruff of its neck.

She breathed a prayer of relief as he stood there patiently, arm outstretched, supporting her weight while she found her footing. This was fine. No part of him touched her. Her position was so embarrassing that she had no room for improper sensations. She shot him a grateful smile that faded at once when she saw him flinch as if her smile caused him pain. He took a small step back, as if trying to distance himself from her even as she dangled from his grip.

Horror lit his eyes, and before she had time to bristle over her smile causing such a reaction, he fell flat on his back.

She landed right on top of him.

His arms closed around her, clamping them together like a human toboggan while he skidded feet-first toward the stream. She heard his feet splash into the water. She realized how very much taller he was than she when she noticed that her feet remained perfectly dry.

"I slipped," he said, sounding strangled.

She couldn't think of anything to say except to apologize for her stubborn refusal to accept his help. "If I had taken your hand . . ." she began.

She couldn't finish. The breathlessness that had assailed her in the boat while watching him paddle returned with renewed force.

Lying nose to nose with John Bradford was worse, much worse, than touching his hand.

Her hands rested against the shoulders she had so recently yearned to touch. Her breasts, which she had so recently imagined the right size to fill his hands, were flattened against his chest. She could feel it rise and fall beneath her, causing her garments to slide against her skin, creating the most inappropriate tingling . . . all over.

And it didn't help one bit that his breathing sounded as labored as her own. As if he, too, were as affected by their being virtually glued together. She could not let herself dwell on the thought that he might find himself attracted to her in the same inappropriate way as she was attracted to him. He had been very clear, very explicit, in telling her exactly what he intended to do with her. Exactly how he intended to use her and then send her away.

There were reasons, good ones, for him to be breathing so hard. He'd just fallen and might have had his wind knocked from him. He'd been paddling and pulling the boat, all without apparent effort, but perhaps the tasks had taken more of a toll upon him than he'd let on.

He drew a great breath. Let it out. It stirred the hair at her temples, and the warmth seemed to penetrate her skin.

He cleared his throat. Took a deep breath. She felt the whoosh of his breath against her hair and wondered what he was finding so difficult to say.

"Bunch up your skirts around your waist."

Her fingers dug into the soft deerskin shirt.

"Remove your shoes and stockings."

He wanted her to strip herself naked here on the shore of a fast-moving stream, bare herself to his sight in bright daylight, expose her tingling skin with birds and who knew what manner of woodland creatures looking on. . . .

"Otherwise you'll ruin it all in the mud, and we left the settlement without the remainder of your belongings. What you're wearing will need to last you for a while."

She lay still upon him, while the heat and the tingling cooled and settled.

She remembered the carefully protected pale complexion of Lady Stivington, the dry touch of Amanda Stivington. True noblewomen were always cool and composed, as if the blue blood flowing through their veins ran chill as river water. No wanton heat and tingling for them. She would do well to remember it, considering that she was attempting to pass herself off as one of them.

"Exactly how am I supposed to virtually disrobe without dirtying my precious clothing?" she asked.

"It will be easy if you're facing the other way. Hold your skirts close and turn over."

"On top of you?"

"Aye."

Very well. He was wider than she, if a rather unconventional perch. "Unclasp me, then." His arms moved away a few inches, and she felt the welcome coolness of the air where his skin had rested. She attempted to roll over and almost slid from him, prompting him to band his arms around her again.

She felt the surge of his pulse clear through her dress. It must be a trick of her imagination to think it had quickened.

"I'll have to shift over little by little," she said, and once more he let loose of her. Quickly. As if he couldn't wait to stop touching her.

She wriggled her pelvis. Angled one leg. Curled the other. Every slight motion she made seemed to wedge her more intimately against him. Her nose found itself buried in the vee of his shirt, and the crisp hairs curling from his chest tickled her skin.

Her traitorous body commenced tingling and heating again.

Gritting her teeth, she inched and wormed her way to a somewhat sideways position. His breath came in quick gasps.

"I'm sorry. I must be too heavy for you," she said.

"No . . . I—I can barely tell you're there."

She heartily wished she were equally oblivious to him. Well, best to get this over with, quickly. She bunched her skirts around her knees—she'd be damned if she'd bare herself to the waist for him—and with one final wriggling twist, thumped over until she was lying flat on her back on top of him.

The part of him pressed tight against her buttocks did not seem to be quite as disinterested as he'd led her to believe.

She caught herself smiling and put an immediate stop to it. If he had indeed become aroused, it didn't mean it was she, Lacey Cochran, who had prompted his desire. No doubt any woman who spent five minutes or so squirming atop him would provoke the same response.

"I'll sit up now," he said. "If you move with care, you'll be able to remove your shoes and stockings, and then you can step off onto the ground."

Perhaps he truly barely noticed her weight, for he sat up easily, folding both of them into a sitting position. She bent over the bulge of her gathered skirts and quickly peeled away her slippers and stockings, and would not allow herself to wonder whether he peeked over her shoulder for a glimpse of her bare legs.

She scrambled off him then, and even though she tried to spring away from him, the ground was wet and slippery and she had to catch at his shoulder for support. But just for an instant. She pushed against him for leverage and was safely past the muddy bank when she heard a loud splash and whirled around in surprise.

He'd jumped into the creek.

So much for her worrying that he might be trying to catch a glimpse of her naked thighs.

She let her skirts drop and watched while he cavorted in the water like an otter.

A true lady would voice a complaint at being left alone for so long.

Yes, if he knew anything about highborn ladies at all, he would expect her to object to being left standing alone, and yet she could not bring herself to do anything to stop him. He seemed to be taking an almost childlike pleasure in cleaning the mud from his clothes. He let the water trickle through his hands and cascade over his face, looking so rapturous that one would think he had suffered from a lack of water in his youth.

She found a fallen log and sat down to put on her stockings and shoes. She finished and, after sitting there for some minutes, realized he had not left the water. She stood to watch him and for some reason didn't feel quite as tired as she'd felt before.

Eventually he looked her way, and then she fancied he blushed.

"I'm sorry," he said, wading out of the creek.

His clothes clung to him like a second skin. His long hair was plastered against his skull. Sunlight glinted from water droplets clinging to his eyelashes. He looked splendid, like a mythical figure rising from the sea.

"You seemed to enjoy that," she said.

"I was plastered in mud. I promised myself I'd never be dirty again."

It seemed like an odd promise to make to oneself.

"The cabin's not far," he said. He glanced down at her. "It's hard walking, though."

"It hasn't exactly been an easy walk up to this point."

"No, but back there, I realized how small . . ." He swallowed. "You'll ruin those shoes."

Back there, she'd been plastered to his front the way the mud had been plastered to the back of him. He'd washed off the mud but apparently wasn't able to rid himself so easily of the way she'd felt against him.

Nor could she forget the way he'd felt against her.

"I don't imagine I can walk through the wilderness in my bare feet."

"I could carry you. You don't weigh much."

She glanced at the deerskin molding his muscular chest. "No, my dress would just get soaked through. I'll walk."

CHAPTER 6

They had formed a large, jolly party when the boats carrying the settlers and newly arrived women pushed off from James City toward Malvern's Hundred. Percy suspected the gaiety wouldn't last, and within less than an hour he was proven right.

Gradually, their close formation loosened until the small boats weren't close enough for easy conversation. The laughter of the newly arrived women rang out less frequently. The men rowing the skiffs answered questions with grunts rather than lengthy explanations. Perhaps they were conserving their strength for the trip. More likely, Percy thought, they realized that the women who were approaching the hundred with such optimism and excitement were destined for the worst disappointment of their lives.

By the time they neared the end of their two-hour journey, near-silence had settled over the group.

"We're almost there." Percy peered over his

shoulder toward Clara. His heart softened with sympathy when he saw how she drooped with fatigue.

She straightened with a jolt and blinked rapidly, as if she'd been dozing where she sat. She stifled a yawn. "I'm sorry. I don't know what's come over me. I'm exhausted."

"A natural reaction," Percy said. He shifted so that he could talk with her more comfortably— not an easy thing to do in such a small watercraft. The boat bobbled a little, drawing a glare from the rower, which Percy ignored. "A body tends to demand rest after so much excitement."

"Excitement—and more," said Clara. She patted at her hair and smoothed her dress. "I watched my best friend get abducted by a madman. I saw my new land for the first time, met some people, and now I am anticipating the home where I'll be staying for a while. All of this has taken more of a toll upon my nerves than I expected."

Percy nodded, remembering well how overwhelming everything had seemed when he'd first arrived in Virginia.

She yawned again. "I know I should be hurrying after Lacey the very minute we arrive on shore, but I doubt I could move more than five feet without collapsing. Right now I confess I want nothing more than to crawl into a soft feather bed and sleep for the next three days."

"Uh," said Percy.

"You're absolutely right," said Clara. "I can't wait three days before going after Lacey."

"Mmm." Percy couldn't meet her puzzled gaze.

"You did tell me you would help me go after her within a day or two of reaching Malvern's Hundred."

"Aye. I did. But . . . did the Virginia Company

officials not explain anything to you before you came?"

"Of course they did. They explained everything. We would find prosperous settlers anxious to wed, and together we will work for the glory of England."

Percy didn't know what he did to betray his dismay, but she flushed and then looked away, embarrassed. "I suppose I will have to serve England in a somewhat different manner than as wife to a prosperous settler," she muttered. "I just thank the good lord that I came with my purse well filled. If no man pays my passage in exchange for marriage, I'll be able to pay it for myself. I would not be able to endure the humiliation of submitting to bond servitude."

"No woman has yet been forced into indentured labor," said Percy.

"I have been known to start new trends."

Indentured service was just one of the things a newcomer had to worry about. He cursed the faceless, nameless Virginia Company for luring these women with false promises and half-truths. He wondered if other men were at that very moment wrestling with their consciences over the predicament, desperately wanting the company of a woman and yet loath to tell her what awaited her in Malvern's Hundred.

"Let's just say that there might not be a feather bed for you to sleep upon," he said. "Even if you didn't have your friend to worry about, you would not be permitted to sleep around the clock for three days."

"Not permitted?"

"Weren't you told you'd be expected to work in exchange for your room and board?"

"No." She didn't sound haughty so much as perplexed. She shrugged. "Well, if that's so, then I don't mind working at some small task if it's expected. I can sew a fine seam, and am quite good at planning meals for large gatherings."

Percy glanced at her hands: the hands of a lady, with long, elegant fingers and white, uncallused skin. "They'll want you to work the tobacco," he said. "When you're not cooking or cleaning or tending the children."

"I fear you've been away from England for too long." Clara gave him a tired but fond smile. "Women such as I *plan* meals, not cook them. I *direct* servants to clean. I don't mind dandling a baby now and then, but one hires a nanny to tend children. Just as one hires a laborer to farm tobacco."

"It's different here," Percy said.

"Yes, I've noticed some striking differences."

"There are more than some differences, Miss Cutler. It is different here in all ways."

She looked about to protest, but something in his expression must have convinced her that he spoke the truth. She glanced down at her hands lying open on her lap; they had begun to tremble.

He shifted nervously. She'd begin to cry at any moment. Perhaps he ought to make a joke: *Cheer up, it's not like I asked you to marry me—now that would be worth crying over!* Perhaps he ought just to jump out of the boat and swim the short distance to shore.

She looked up and met his gaze with one filled with level intelligence. "I shall hope for the best and do what I must," she said.

Within moments of landing, Percy knew that hoping for the best had failed, and that she had no clue as to what she would have to do. Malmford had positioned himself in front of the most imposing structure in the hundred: a roofed shelter that protected the harvested tobacco from sun and rain. Reading from a list, he began calling out the names of the women who'd just arrived and matching them with the settlers who'd agreed to take them in.

Minor verbal tussles raged around them as women were paired with families, raising the objections of the men who'd set their sights on that particular woman.

"Let me get through this list and then we'll marry those of you who are ready," Malmford ordered. "Next ... Miss Clara Cutler! You shall be living with the Ellicotts."

Percy groaned inwardly.

"You look to be strong and healthy." Percy could not object to the way Jacob Ellicott studied Miss Clara Cutler's figure. There was no element of lust in the settler's regard; he eyed Miss Cutler with the consideration one might bestow upon a plow horse. "My wife needs a rest. Seven children tend to run a woman ragged. You look healthy enough to stand up to them for a while."

Clara gripped one hand with the other and said nothing.

"Miss Cutler may have found other boarding arrangements," Percy astonished himself by saying.

"How so? All of us willing to take in a boarder put in our names months ago and received our assignments."

Percy ignored the man's valid objection and hoped his own uncertainty did not show. "Thank you, Mr. Ellicott; we shall let you know if the arrangement must stand."

Percy tugged Clara's arm, urging her to follow him. "I don't care for this situation at all. The Ellicotts can barely sustain themselves, let alone take in a boarder. Why, they have only three rooms, no bond servants, their acres are far-flung, and . . ."

"They'll work me to death in exchange for room and board. It might be bearable for a brief while, if I expected to marry soon, but I'm not so certain now. . . ."

Percy felt a surge of kinship for the awkward woman. She really was quite a dear: bright as a new button, impulsive, and generous. Rather like himself, with a plethora of excellent qualities hidden beneath an unfortunate exterior.

Neither of them was likely to find a spouse in this godforsaken settlement. That was only one of the reasons why he was hoarding his money in hopes of returning to England on the next supply ship.

"Mr. Bledsoe, I don't see where I have any choice in the matter. Mr. Ellicott spoke the truth about that. Thanks to you, and now this, I am finding that the Virginia Company was less than forthcoming in the information it provided to us. We were told that some generous settlers would take us in on a temporary basis. We were warned that there would be overcrowding until matters shook out. Do you think I should request to be placed with another family?"

Percy couldn't stifle a smile. "My dear Miss Cutler, nobody—including those who agreed to accept boarders—has an entire extra room. Precious few have enough space under roof for their own families, leave alone an entire private room for a boarder. Look about you."

The settlement, which looked dismal and depressing under the best of circumstances, looked positively depressing when viewed with an eye toward the worst features.

"I expected somewhat more . . . imposing structures," said Clara.

"We all expected much more than we found here." Percy hesitated to vent the full extent of his disappointment. "We freemen find it disheartening to go about the day-to-day business of living. I cannot imagine how the bondsmen endure."

"Bondsmen? I thought you said no woman had yet had to enter indentured service."

"Aye, no women. There are other sorts of bondsmen. The largest group is comprised of those who sold their freedom for seven years in order to have their passage paid to this godforsaken place. Can you imagine—signing yourself into virtual slavery, with the only freedom to look forward to the chance to starve and freeze to death?"

"I suppose the Virginia Company was less than honest with them as well," Clara said.

"The worst of it is, some of them had the bargain forced upon them. That fellow over there"—Percy inclined his head toward a young man who looked to be in his late teens—"captured from the streets of London and forced to come here, and then forced to pay for the privilege!"

"How cruel!"

"One can scarcely blame John Bradford for refusing to cooperate."

"John Bradford? The man who abducted Lacey? He is a bondsman?"

"They attempted to make him one. He wouldn't stand for it. No amount of whipping or other means of convincing him were effective. He took to the woods and made his own way."

"They just let him go?"

"To give the man credit, he did eventually pay for his fare—using tobacco he acquired through trading."

"How strange."

"Yes and no. The one tangible benefit of repaying your passage—whether you pay cash money or whether you work it out with indentured labor— is that you get to claim one hundred acres of land. A headright, they call it."

"Then Mr. Bradford farms in this community. That is good news; Lacey won't be far."

"His holdings are a half day away, I'm afraid. No doubt that's where he's taken your friend. It's his refuge."

"I rather thought he wielded some control over the others. They seem somewhat afraid of him."

"For good reason. You see, he learned certain skills from the Indians that enable him to be quite successful at hunting game."

Clara laughed. "That scarcely seems a valuable skill. Gentlemen hunt all the time back home in England. Especially the younger sons, who are spared the drudgery of managing the estates."

Percy, a younger son himself, knew she spoke the truth, but only so far as she understood it. The truth as he'd understood it before coming here and learning that so much of what he'd taken for granted simply did not exist. "Aye, back in England we hunt within game preserves, with dogs to flush the rabbits and pheasants and deer, and where ammunition is plentiful. Here the animals are truly wild. We have no dogs. Here, bullets are more valuable than gold—one dare not risk wasting a bullet."

"Is Mr. Bradford such a crack shot, then, that you all entrust him with your bullets?"

"No. He may be a crack shot for all I know, but he does his hunting the Indian way, with a bow and arrow."

"Archery is not an uncommon skill," she noted.

"You can't quite call it archery, the way the Indians use their bows and arrows." The conversation was taking an unpleasant turn. "None of us here have yet managed to acquire the ability. We're all working too hard with the tobacco. If not for the game John Bradford brings to us, we would all starve during the winter. That's why nobody stepped forward when he abducted Miss Cochran. They fear that angering him will send him deeper into the wilderness, and he might never come back when we need him."

"He must care about you to keep you all fed."

"Some say he cares only about the wealth he acquires. They resent that he doesn't give us the food, but makes us pay for it. So many pounds of tobacco for a deer. A certain amount more for a bear. While most of us work our fingers to the bone on the tobacco crops, he wanders through the woods. He hasn't lifted a finger to harvest a single tobacco leaf, and yet his stores dwarf those of anyone in the community."

"He must have used some of that tobacco to pay Lacey's transportation fee."

"Aye. You cannot know how it galls some of the men who haven't yet been able to amass the one hundred twenty-five pounds of tobacco they need to pay for their own wives."

"He seems completely driven by greed."

Percy found himself disagreeing. "No, Miss Cutler, there's something more to him. But nobody has ever managed to get close enough to him to learn anything. That bondsman I just pointed out to you claims that John Bradford was leader of the band of orphans they both belonged to. He took care of them, kept them safe as was within his abilities. I can't help feeling somehow that he's doing the same thing with these settlers, but not admitting the truth of it to himself."

"Will Lacey be safe with him?"

Percy hesitated.

"He appears stronger and more able than most of the men I've seen so far."

"Aye. And perhaps he tells those tales just to keep us frightened and close to the settlement, so he can continue to have the hunting to himself."

"What tales?"

"Not tales exactly. Warnings. About the savages. The Indians—he claims they cannot be trusted." Percy pointed out a group of men that included two Indians. "You see how they circulate among us as friends? Sometimes they bring us game and never ask to be paid. There are those who say that John's warnings against trusting them are merely to ensure that we continue to rely upon him for food. They claim he's afraid that befriending more Indians will mean they will keep us supplied and we won't be reduced to paying him for food anymore."

"Do you believe that?"

"I can't say I do, Miss Cutler. I've already mentioned that I believe him to be more caring than he reveals. He strikes me as very able, very cunning, very smart. If he says we should not trust the Indians, then I believe him."

He realized with a start that he'd led Clara straight to his own lodgings. "I live here," he said. "I'm one of the very fortunate ones; I have my own room. It's not much of a room—a storage space, really, but it affords privacy unique to the settlement."

Clara glanced back toward the tobacco shed where Jacob Ellicott could be seen gesticulating his displeasure at possibly losing his unpaid servant.

Percy couldn't let her go there. She was doomed to enough disappointment with this place. He had never before seen a woman ignored so thoroughly as Clara had been ignored. No doubt some man would grow desperate enough eventually to offer to pay for her fare and make her his wife, but by then she could be certain that it was an act of settling rather than something the man really wanted.

He and Clara were an awful lot alike. He fancied he knew she'd been settling all her life. For once, she ought to have something a little better.

"My room," Percy said, "it's yours."

She blinked at him and then reddened, something she ought never to do, for it make her look apoplectic.

And then he felt himself redden too when he realized how inappropriate his offer must have sounded.

"What I meant was, I'll ask Mr. and Mrs. Hedgings to accept you as their lodger in my place."

"Where will you go?"

They both glanced back at Ellicott.

Percy cleared his throat. "The weather is fine. I'll not mind sleeping outdoors for a bit."

To his dismay, tears sprang to Clara's eyes.

"Please, Miss Cutler, it will not be so bad. And,"

he added with a gallant little bow, "the arrangement will surely last for only the briefest time, until one of the men here recognizes your fine qualities and offers to become your husband."

She stared at him solemnly. "This is the very nicest thing anyone has ever done for me."

John wondered what she thought of it.

He hadn't expected to care whether or not the woman he brought here would like his home. But as they crossed the small clearing toward his cabin, he heard the soft rustle of Lacey's silk skirts mingling with the rush of the breeze through the trees, noticed her flowery scent vying with the perfume of the forest.

She came from luxury, had been pampered, used to servants running about at her beck and call. Through her eyes, the structure that had always roused so much pride within him must seem crude and primitive.

Like himself.

He hadn't expected to care what she thought of *him.*

"The journey was not so rough as you led me to believe," she said.

A sharp pang of disappointment that she'd made no comment about the cabin took him by surprise.

"You're a good traveler for a woman," he said with grudging praise, grudging because he resented handing her a compliment when she had none to spare for him.

"I didn't realize you were such an expert on traveling with females, Mr. Bradford." A smile curved her lips, and humor tinged her words. Perhaps she considered her observation to be some sort of joke. He didn't know how to joke. In fact, he was rapidly learning that he didn't know how to deal with her at all.

"I don't know much about women," he said.

"Oh really?" Her smile broadened.

He wished she wouldn't smile. It lit her eyes and curved her lips. Soft, bright things were such rarities. He shoved his hands into his belt to keep from reaching toward her to touch, to see if she felt as wonderful as she looked when she smiled.

"I didn't realize females were so strong. When I helped you over rough spots, I noticed . . ."

He should just hold his tongue, as he usually did. He'd noticed a lot more than just muscular strength, but he swallowed before blurting out that information. He didn't know what was wrong with him. Why this sudden compulsion to explain himself? She was the most provoking woman, somehow managing to trick him into letting down his guard. He would have to take better care around her.

"You told me you had some familiarity with Indian women. Aren't they strong?"

"Of course they are. But they work hard. They're not like you."

"They are women."

"You've been cosseted and pampered all your life, never expected to perform the simplest tasks."

Her smile faltered, vanished. She averted her eyes.

He felt guilty, as if he'd clubbed her, and damned if he understood why. He'd done nothing but express the truth, and yet he'd somehow wounded her.

Maybe it was because she was such a little bit of a thing, small-boned, delicate. She looked as if a stiff wind might carry her away, and yet she'd kept pace with him on the journey through the woods, and when he'd lent her his hand to traverse a particularly rough stretch of ground, he'd been startled at how little of his own strength she drew upon.

He missed the smile, too.

"Here we are," he said, pausing at the door of his cabin.

Once again, the inexplicable urge to explain himself all but overtook him. He wanted to tell her how hard he'd worked to clear this patch of ground from virgin forest. Wanted to tell her that possessing clear ground, and deliberately keeping it open and free of the omnipresent tobacco plants, was the surest sign of wealth in this new land. He wanted to tell her that every one of those logs forming the walls had once been a towering tree felled by his own axe, had been laboriously debarked by him, had been shaved and hewn until scarcely a gap existed where one log touched another.

He wanted her to understand that when the people in the settlement taunted him as a man who did nothing but stroll through the woods, waiting for an unwary deer or rabbit to come his way, they had no idea of how hard he worked or why these kinds of jobs were important to him. Why raising tobacco for the Virginia Company was the last thing on this earth he ever intended to do.

There was nothing to gain by telling her all that. A lady such as herself would have no appreciation for the hard work. She would probably scorn as worthless those things he treasured most.

He clamped his teeth together lest he give in to the urge to brag, to point, to lay it all in front of her as if his worldly possessions were treasures gathered solely for her.

She started to reach toward the door, but all at once twisted her hand back toward herself, pretending she'd only meant to push a lock of hair back behind her ear.

John reached over her shoulder and pushed open the door. As it swung wide, he realized that before now no human being other than himself had ever stepped inside. No longer would it be his refuge alone. Even when he had used her and returned her to the settlement, nothing could erase from his mind the image of Lacey Cochran lifting her pink-and-green skirts up to her trim ankles so she could step into the home he'd built with his own two hands.

Lacey couldn't stop a small gasp of pleasure at the homey sight greeting her inside John's cabin.

"I know it's not as luxurious as the places you're accustomed to inhabiting," John said. He stood stiff as a rail, his words clipped and emotionless.

He'd misunderstood her reaction. "It's quite—" she began, but bit off embellishing her enthusiasm when he flinched as if she'd insulted him. "Quite adequate for a temporary arrangement," she finished.

"There's only one room." He seemed determined to force her to find flaws with the cozy cabin.

"Yes. One room that is far larger than the space I was expected to share on the ship." Lacey walked to the window and lifted her face to the sun streaming through. "Fresh air and sunshine. Rare commodities when confined in the hold during rough seas."

"I have no glass for that window. When the

weather turns cold I cover it with a well-scraped deer hide."

Lacey had never known anyone so resistant to being complimented. "I have little fondness for glass." Let him make of that what he would. She would not tell him that she'd spent more hours than she could count endlessly polishing Stivington Hall's multitude of mullioned panes. She curled her hands reflexively, reminded of how the cold would settle into her knuckles, how the odor of vinegar would all but choke her despite the chill winter air gusting through the gaps around the frames.

No, she would not tell him that it was her excellence at window washing that had earned her a promotion to laundry maid, and that meant her window-washing skill had landed her here in his windowless home. As a scullery maid she might never have been noticed by Amanda Stivington, daughter of the house. But as a laundry maid responsible for delivering clean garments to Miss Stivington's room, she'd come to that spoiled, pampered darling's attention. Amanda had been supremely annoyed to see a common serving girl who bore such a remarkable resemblance to her blue-blooded self. Later, Amanda had decided it would be great fun to have a lady's maid whom people might mistake for her sister, and so Lacey's dizzying rise through the ranks had occurred.

She'd never wanted any of it.

She didn't want this situation, either. So let John carry on with his delusions about her being cosseted and pampered all her life. The delusion suited her purposes.

Let him think that she pined for a drafty, dark manor hall. He had no need to know that her soul felt oddly at home in this charming, rustic room in a way it never had in the vast, echoing corridors of Stivington Hall.

"Does this lead to the garden?" she asked, crossing the room to a door that stood directly across from the one they'd just entered. There seemed to be little need for two doors in a one-room house, but it would be rather convenient to step out quickly if the kitchen herbs were grown in the back, rather than going out through the front and circling the cabin for a handful of parsley.

"No, the cabin backs up to a hill."

She opened the door, revealing a dark, cave-like cellar. In the gloom she saw bits and pieces of wood—shelving, no doubt. "A root cellar right next to the kitchen—how convenient," she said, for some reason perversely intent upon getting him to admit this cozy abode had some nice features.

"It's an escape hole. The door leads to a tunnel that cuts through the hill."

An underground tunnel? She doubted very much that such a feature had occurred naturally. How many hours, how many days or weeks, had it taken him to fashion such a bizarre appendage to his house? "I've heard of castles with secret passageways, but nothing like this," she said.

"You must be prepared for when trouble comes calling, lest you be caught like a rat in a trap."

Lacey considered her own situation, and how fleeing to the colonies had seemed her only escape. She wondered what it was in John Bradford's past that had forged this belief within him.

"Is it so very dangerous here?"

"The least appealing refuge can become a target for the unscrupulous."

"Do you deliberately speak in riddles? Are you

trying to tell me that I need fear the settlers will storm out here and attack us while we sleep?"

While we sleep. The words seemed to hang in the air while they were both stunned into immobility by what those words implied. She had agreed to live for a while with this man and had never considered the sleeping arrangements. There didn't seem to be many options in a one-room cabin.

A one-room cabin with one bed.

"You need not worry about the settlers," he said. "If danger comes, I suspect it will be the Indians who cause us trouble."

"I suppose we are vulnerable out here alone."

"Less vulnerable in many ways than they are back in the town. They trust the Indians. I have no illusions about them."

She shivered despite the warm sun streaming through the window. She wrapped her arms about herself and moved through the room. The place was almost painfully neat, and the sweet scents perfuming the air did not come from the outside but rather from within. She recalled him saying that he had vowed never again to be dirty; it seemed he applied it to his home as well as his body.

Here and there he'd set bowls filled with dried pine needles, or herbs, or dried flowers. And next to the bowls she noticed things that might have been considered trash if not for the impeccable cleanness of the room. One perfect leaf. A large feather, iridescent green. A stone, so smooth it might have been polished, flecked with gold. All placed with care and precision, as if the person who'd positioned them considered them rare treasures. And indeed they were beautiful, uniquely exquisite, proof that the person responsible for collecting them possessed an eye for true beauty.

What manner of man valued stones and leaves and feathers? For some reason, the care he'd taken with these insignificant artifacts that other men would have trod into the earth tugged at her heart.

He recognized true beauty. She wondered what he thought of her own looks.

She shifted her attention away from the table and on toward the bed.

One bed. A bed much longer, but not much wider, than the narrow beds she'd occupied in the alternately sweltering and freezing attics of Stivington Hall. A bed designed to accommodate one tall sleeper. The man who'd built that bed hadn't intended to share it with anybody.

She felt another odd tug at her heart. Though he'd explained nothing, simply standing in John Bradford's house and looking around had told her so many things about him. Not that she understood them all. But she had glimpses into his character, had some small idea of things he liked, of what was important to him. She had the overwhelming impression of a man who lived alone and intended to return to that state.

He, on the other hand, knew nothing of her except for the fake presentation she made in her hand-me-down noblewoman's clothing.

She hadn't told him a thing about herself. He didn't yet know that everything about her was a lie. He didn't seem at all suspicious.

Her plan was working even better than she had dared hope. After leaving John she would have every excuse for no longer possessing her virginity, and he appeared willing to accept the blame for that. For once in her life, things were going her way. She had never imagined how guilty it would make her feel.

* * *

"There's mud on the floor from my skirts," Lacey said. "I'll clean it up."

She reached for the cleaning rag, and John quickly caught her wrist, stopping her. "No. I don't expect you to handle chores."

Without thinking about it, he tightened his fingers around her wrist—not to hurt, but to gauge the size. So small. His fingers easily met.

Well, he'd accomplished something by touching her; he'd confirmed that she was too little, too frail, to be of much use around the cabin. Just as he'd suspected any true lady might be. So there was no reason to continue holding on to her, except that his fingers simply did not want to disengage. He ordered them to let her go, silently, but apparently the instruction from his brain failed to reach the offending fingers, for not only did they hold tight, but to his horror his thumb began tracing a light circle on the underside of her wrist, where he could feel the faint beat of her pulse. The soft thrumming seemed to echo in his head— no wonder his brain could not be heard!

He opened his mouth to offer some explanation for hanging on to her, but found himself speechless. Standing so close meant inhaling her scent, meant feeling her warmth. Looking at her only worsened matters. Her eyes were wide and wary, filled with confusion, and something more. He had not enough experience with women to know for sure, but he would swear she looked guilty over something, though apparently she'd done nothing to feel guilty about. Only he had done the unforgivable—stealing her away, destroying her reputation, all for the sake of his revenge. The gentlemen whose company she was more accustomed to certainly would never have taken such liberties.

And yet, holding on to her wrist was the least of what he meant to do to her. And she'd agreed to it.

"I assure you I am quite capable of handling . . . some small tasks," she said.

He shook his head. What he meant to do to her was bad enough; he would not humiliate her further by forcing her to act like a scullery maid.

"Well, exactly what do you expect me to do while I'm here?"

The question took him by surprise. He dropped her wrist. He could think of plenty of things he would like her to do, none of which he expected her to *want* to do. Not with the likes of him.

He remembered his mistaken notion that claiming a Company woman would not inconvenience him any more than taking in a stray dog. Ha! He could order a stray dog to sit, or stay, or sleep outdoors. A dog would no doubt at once grow protective of him, of the cabin, and be a valued partner in his vigilance against Indian attack. A dog would alert him to the presence of danger, would fight alongside him if he were attacked.

But Lacey . . . she increased his risk rather than lessened it. If Indians attacked, he knew with gut certainty that concern for his own safety would come second to worry for hers. His hand throbbed, remembering her delicacy. She was so small, so fragile. She required protection while she served as the instrument of his revenge.

He was no stranger to protecting the weak. But

always before, the threat had come from the outside—never from within himself, never from his own desires. He had to protect Lacey from the dangers of Virginia Colony. More importantly, he had to protect himself from losing sight of what was important.

CHAPTER 7

Lacey swayed when John let her wrist drop.

"You're exhausted," he observed.

Funny, how nobody had ever worried about her degree of tiredness before. "I'm quite accustomed to spending many hours on my feet."

"Sipping champagne and dancing at parties— a far cry from trekking through a wilderness," he said.

She bit back a retort. Instead of wanting to defend her stamina, she ought to be grateful that he continued to be fooled by her deception. Even so, she disliked being thought weak. "You must not be familiar with manor halls. I assure you that merely navigating the hallways requires a great deal of strength."

How well she remembered the endless hallways of Stivington. Nightmares sometimes plagued her of being lost in those long, echoing corridors, running and running, desperately seeking a way to escape but never finding an exit.

The nightmares had begun when she'd first gone into service, and had been, she supposed, merely a reflection of the reality of her life. She'd been expected to work a full fourteen hours each day— a child was thought to have endless stamina. Her promotion to laundress had meant working just as many hours, with the added burden of intense heat and odors. Stivington Manor had indeed seemed to be a prison of sorts.

Her elevation to lady's maid had been the fulfillment of her mother's dreams for her, and while the physical effort required of her had been greatly reduced, she had always been at her young lady's beck and call, regardless of the hour.

Amanda Stivington never apologized for rousing Lacey from bed, never thought twice about staying out half the night dancing. Unless she wanted Lacey at her side to help carry out one of her pranks, Amanda never cared whether Lacey catnapped with the other servants in the kitchen, or whether she waited at home to undress her and prepare her for bed.

It was during those late nights, when Amanda had been bubbling with champagne and mischief and Lacey had been exhausted beyond sensibility, that they'd conjured their plans to dupe Pumphrey Fallsworth into believing Lacey was Amanda's country cousin.

Lacey had been wide awake when she'd carried out those plans, though. Fully awake and aware— more so than she wanted to be—when lying in Pumphrey's bed. She couldn't blame Amanda for that.

She'd been wide awake when she'd consented

to be part of John's plan for revenge, too, and fully alert to the possibilities it offered to her. Perhaps his comment about her exhaustion was meant to convey disappointment, considering what he meant to do with her.

Tired she might be, but a little ripple of excitement surged through her nonetheless.

"I'll feed the fire, and then I must attend to chores outside," said John.

Before you tend to the chores inside? she wanted to ask.

He prodded the banked ash with a long pole.

The servants in the kitchens had always been quick with jokes about men and prods and poles. Always some snide comment about the gentry treating a rousing bout of sex as if it were business that needed attending.

She wondered if that was how John looked upon bedding her: as a chore waiting to be completed. That was how she ought to be considering it.

She darted a sideways glance toward the bed.

It was not dread or resignation that had her heart skipping beats.

Nor was it excitement, she told herself firmly. It was merely the strangeness of the situation— anybody would find herself in a bit of a dither. Best to get it over with. Best to keep him here and do it *now* rather than prolong the inevitable.

"I didn't see your livestock," said Lacey.

"I have none."

"Then . . . what is it you must do?"

He was silent for so long that Lacey began to think that he'd been alluding to tending his personal needs. Perhaps there were things men needed to do before . . . before . . .

"I must make a pass through the woods," he said. "Seeking sign of Indians."

Her heart skipped again, but this time from pure fear. She was aware suddenly of how utterly alone they were, how cut off from the rest of the settlers.

"We're not safe out here in the woods, are we?"

"Safe enough." He inclined his head toward the bed. "Get some rest."

"Will you be gone long?"

"A quarter hour."

Fifteen minutes wasn't much time. It had sometimes taken her hours to prepare Amanda to meet a paramour. But Amanda had never been travel-stained from a sea voyage and traipsing endless miles through a wilderness.

"I'll . . . I'll be ready."

"Ready?" He tilted his head, clearly puzzled.

She let one hand hover at her neckline; with the other she tucked a curl behind her ear, wishing he would allow her the time to wash her hair before . . .

Understanding dawned upon him. "Go to sleep, Lacey. We can tend to that business another time."

That business. Something within her plunged. Her suspicion had been correct: He didn't expect to take pleasure in making love to her.

She was suddenly very, very happy that she hadn't told him the truth about herself. If he thought making love with a pure, virtuous woman of quality was nothing better than business to be completed, then what would he think of engaging in sexual relations with someone like herself?

Well, he would be making love to her; he just couldn't know who she really was.

And she'd better do all she could to reinforce his opinion of who and what she was. She would start by behaving as Amanda would do. "I'll require hot water," she said.

"I anticipated you would." He nodded toward the fireplace, where several buckets were lined up close to the fire. "I set those out before I left. The fire has been banked ever since, so the water won't be hot, but at least it won't be ice cold."

The thought of sluicing fresh water of any temperature through her hair and over her skin made her shiver with anticipation. She tried to quell the reaction lest he misinterpret it, but a soft thud told her she need not have bothered. John Bradford had already left the cabin and closed the door behind him.

John touched the broken twig. The slender shoot had been twisted until the white inner pulp oozed through the shredded bark where it dangled from the branch. Whoever had passed this way had meant to break the wood. More important, whoever had done this had meant for him to see it.

He set his musket down, close enough to grab, but far enough to prove he was open to approach.

He squatted, balancing himself on the balls of his feet, and waited.

Waited for an Indian. If it had been a white man who'd left that sign, the woods would have been silent around him. John had never met a white man other than himself who could move through the forest without frightening the wild things into silence. All around him the forest sounded the same as usual, familiar, birds warning that the day was about to end, insects celebrating the nearing of night.

The din made it difficult to sort out subtle noises

that might indicate the arrival of John's visitor, but he welcomed the distraction. Otherwise, he knew he'd be straining to hear a hint of sound from the cabin, even though it lay well out of earshot.

His mind had no trouble tormenting him with what he could not hear: the soft swish of silk as she dropped her dress to the floor; the splash of water sluicing through her hair and trickling down her skin; the creak of the bed ropes as she settled herself onto the mattress; her sigh of pleasure as herb-scented pillows cradled her head.

I'll be ready, she had said. While part of him had thrilled to hearing her willingness, another part of him had taken offense that she would think him so callous that he would demand sex from a woman who could barely keep her eyes open.

"John Bradford."

John forced himself to remain perfectly still when his instinct was to whirl around. He cursed his carelessness; that was what came of daydreaming about a woman when he should have been watching for an enemy. He might have taken a hatchet in the back, leaving her alone and helpless.

He feigned a yawn. He rose slowly and pretended to stretch a kink out of his back, and only then did he turn to face the other man.

"Opechancanough."

The Indian grunted an acknowledgment.

Again John waited. Opechancanough had arranged this meeting for a purpose, and it was up to him to mention it.

Opechancanough hunkered down as John had been doing. John followed suit. They crouched there for a long time, listening to each other breathe, listening to the sounds of the forest as night approached.

"You bring someone to your home, John Bradford."

"Aye." John kept his breathing steady, his expression calm.

"You never bring someone before."

"This is different."

Opechancanough waited.

John sighed. "I brought a woman."

Opechancanough grunted, indicating he'd noticed as much.

"We have watched the sea. Many women have come to the place of the others."

"Not enough."

"Too many." Opechancanough made a cutting motion in the air. "Enough! Women mean children. More white men."

The hair at John's nape stood on end. This was the first time one of the Indians had articulated the anger John had sensed.

"There's room here for everyone."

"We once thought so. We no longer believe your kind can live among us."

"We keep to ourselves."

"*You* keep to yourself, John Bradford. Those others destroy our forests for the sake of tobacco. They are not content with what they have, not content to live among each other, but always increasing in number, always spreading into lands where you do not belong."

John knew it was a measure of Opechancanough's anger that the Indian spoke in his native tongue. The Indians considered it a mark of respect to have learned enough English to communicate with the settlers, but the settlers had not returned the courtesy. With astounding arrogance, the settlers simply refused to consider learning anything about the Indians—not their language, not their customs, not their beliefs.

The Indians were not so foolish. They had learned enough of the white men's language to spy out their intentions while moving among them and pretending to not understand.

But sometimes it wasn't mere pretense. Sometimes the Indians truly did not understand.

John had tried to explain to Opechancanough and to others of his tribe that the white men did not recognize the Indians' claim to Virginia. He'd tried to explain that James City had only been the starting point, that men well favored by the Virginia Company had been granted vast tracts of land known as "hundreds" and were given the task of settling and taming those hundreds for the benefit of the Company.

Just as the white man did not recognize the Indians' rights, the Indians refused to believe the land they had lived upon since the dawn of time could be owned by anybody.

"They will not plant corn or beans. Too much game is required to feed them."

"You supply them with game yourselves. At no cost. They do not value what is given to them for free. I have asked you before why you do this and you would not tell me. Will you tell me now?"

Opechancanough's lips compressed into a thin line. "They do not plant corn or beans," he repeated. "The signs say this winter will be a hard one. We fear your kind will raid our own stores to feed their bellies."

John wished he could deny Opechancanough's fears, but he couldn't. The English settlers had come to expect the Indians' generosity in matters of game, and he had heard them openly state that the Indians would no doubt be equally generous with their crops if need should arise.

Some had stated that generosity was not required—with their superior weaponry, they could take what they wanted from the Indians. John wondered if any had been so incautious as to make those comments within earshot of an Indian who understood perfectly well what they were saying.

"Summer's almost at an end," John said. "They won't be planting corn and beans now."

"The trees will soon shed their nuts. Animals grow fat in preparation for winter. Tell your kind to gather what they can, to dry and salt and make preparations for a rough winter."

"I'll tell them," John said.

"We will be watching."

"They don't often pay heed to what I tell them."

"For their sakes, I hope they listen this time."

"And if they don't?"

Opechancanough did not answer. He stood and glanced back in the direction of John's cabin. "Your woman will believe what you say."

Lacey would believe him. She had believed him when he'd told her she would find some advantage in carrying out his plan. She had believed him when he'd told her he meant to use her and then discard her.

"She's not my woman. That is, she won't be staying with me. She'll be going back to the others soon."

"If you care about this woman, maybe you should keep her with you." Opechancanough fixed him with an enigmatic look.

It was a warning. Opechancanough uttered no fighting words and issued no threats, but John knew in his gut that Opechancanough had just told him the settlers would be eliminated if the Indians perceived them as a threat to their winter food supply.

And if Lacey was with them, she would die.

He remained outwardly impassive, as if Opechan-canough's implication had not sent arrows of dread shooting into his soul. There was no logical reason why thinking that Lacey might die should affect him any more than knowing the rest of the settlers were at risk.

Yet he could think of Malmford's scalp dangling from an Indian's belt and not feel the awful churning he felt at imagining Lacey being run to the ground by a screaming Indian, and a hatchet plunging into her flesh.

He couldn't bear, somehow, to think of that soft, bright smile stilled for all time. Couldn't stand it if he never learned the secrets behind her shifting gaze, her evasive answers.

That was what came of allowing himself to get too close to another person. Less than a day in her company and he was already worried about her survival, already sick at heart to think she could be wiped from the earth, leaving him alone as ever. If he was so affected already, imagine how bad it would be if he let her worm her way into his heart.

He'd been right, in planning his revenge, to plan on sending her away.

Choose her. Use her. Lose her.

He'd figured on sending her back. Knowing she faced massacre shouldn't matter; he'd figured on losing her.

He'd just never envisioned that losing her might be so . . . permanent.

Besides, they need not die. Maybe he could make one more trip into the hundred. Try one more time to convince the settlers to change their ways. Make them listen this time. Then she could return to the settlement, find a husband, and raise a family.

She wouldn't be dead, at least not right off. But would ejecting her from his home, practically pushing her into the arms of another man, make losing her any less permanent?

He couldn't decide which alternative was worse, which meant he had to put an end to these ridiculous feelings of his at once.

"She means nothing to me."

"You have never told me a lie, so I owe you the courtesy of believing you this time as well," said Opechancanough. But the very phrasing of the Indian's comment told John that he hadn't fooled him for a minute.

That Opechancanough believed John was only fooling himself.

Well, he would show Opechancanough that John Bradford's word could always be trusted. He'd use Lacey and set her aside just as he'd planned, and he'd advise the settlers yet again to abandon their devotion to tobacco and pay more attention to the threat posed by the Indians. Then, when the settlers ignored him and ended up dead—all of them, including Lacey—he could laugh at their dead bodies and say he'd told them so all along. His revenge would taste truly, truly sweet.

So why did he feel he wanted to vomit?

With one final, unreadable stare, Opechancanough vanished into the trees.

Night birds sang now, along with locusts and crickets, uncaring of the Indian passing through the trees toward his people, or the white man sick and shivering as he blindly forged toward his cabin.

He knew the creatures would be singing and crying on the night the Indians massacred the settlers, not stopping even when Lacey died, not caring that if John managed to survive he wouldn't be any more alone than he'd always been, no more alone than he was at this moment.

She tried to move and reflexively touched her head when a tug at her scalp reminded her that she hadn't bound her hair before going to bed. Her hair had been wet, almost dripping then, and now it felt barely damp beneath her fingers. She must have been asleep for hours.

Hours, and John was just now coming back to the cabin.

He'd said he would be gone no more than a quarter hour.

She couldn't see him because the fire had burned so low it was mere embers. She could hear him walk across the floor, though, and was surprised to realize she felt so certain that it was him, that despite all his warnings about Indians—about himself, truth be told—she felt no fear. Somehow she recognized his breathing, his step, as if her senses had memorized everything about him. Somehow her nerves settled, with a silent "it's all right, he's home," and let her almost drift back into sleep again.

Almost.

He'd gone straight to the hearth and was stirring the embers with a poker. The fire flared back to life, small but bright enough to illuminate him. She watched through half-closed eyes as he collected small pieces of wood from the pile with exaggerated care, obviously trying not to make too much noise. One clattered to the floor, and he retrieved it with a muttered curse and then edged the fresh wood into the fire inch by inch, silently. He glanced back toward the bed, perhaps to see if he'd wakened her, and then he returned to tending the fire.

Warmth surged through her, more warmth than could be accounted for by a fire that had yet to respond to its new fuel.

She should call out and tell him she was awake. Feigning sleep was rather like lying, in a way. But it was obvious that he'd expected her to sleep through his return, and in thinking about it, it made more sense to let him think he'd succeeded. Amanda had certainly possessed the ability to sleep through any distraction, whereas Lacey had had to learn to sleep lightly, to jolt awake at the faint tinkling of a bell or the cross calling of her name, for it would never do to keep the gentry waiting when they wanted something done by a servant.

John Bradford had wanted a noble lady in his bed, a lady capable of sleeping straight through until noon—not a serving girl ready to spring into action at the slightest sound from her betters.

She would never be able to fall back asleep while he was making so much noise. That gave her a perfect excuse, she decided, to continue watching as he pulled a blanket from a shelf and spread it near the fireplace. She kept watching when he bent at the waist and pulled his shirt over his head. Kept watching when he passed once more in front of the fire and the golden light danced over a torso that rippled with muscle.

Lacey had never seen anything so alluring.

She caught herself before making a sound of pleasure.

Pumphrey hadn't let her see him in the nude. She'd touched him, though, and borne his weight, and had found little appealing about him——nothing that had tempted her to *ask* to see him naked. She and Amanda had giggled, in fact, that men were much more attractive when fully clothed.

She'd been wrong.

John stretched, clasped both hands behind his head, arched first one way and then the other. The firelight illuminated muscles bunching from the exertion, framed the triangular shape of his broad shoulders tapering to his narrow waist.

She'd been so very wrong. She wished for nothing more than that he would peel his breeches away from his legs and let her see him. All of him.

She closed her eyes.

When she opened them again, he'd taken to his makeshift bed, and she could see nothing but a dark huddle on the floor. A huddle that turned first one way and then the other. No doubt the floor was hard and uncomfortable.

Or maybe he was distracted, unable to sleep because of her presence in his bed.

She smiled into the dark.

She stopped smiling when she realized what she was doing.

Foolish, foolish Lacey, she chided herself, to take pleasure in thinking she was responsible for his restlessness. If she was, well, then he had reasons apart from being overwhelmed by her desirability. He was a methodical man, deliberate in thought and deed, stingy with emotion. If he was troubled by her presence, it was probably only because he was fretting over not taking another step toward completing his stupid revenge.

And yet . . . he could have taken her in this very

bed within minutes of walking in the door. But he hadn't.

But she'd been exhausted, filthy from their journey, and no doubt rank with the scent of the ship still upon her.

That hadn't prevented him from getting hard, from showing he wanted her as a man wants a woman, when she'd landed on top of him near the creek.

He twisted again. Muttered an oath. He sat bolt upright and glanced toward the bed for a long moment. Did he fear he'd wakened her . . . or was it something else?

He lay back down, and at once his breathing turned so rhythmic, so even, that she knew he was deliberately trying to calm himself. It caused an odd little feeling inside her, for she somehow knew that John Bradford seldom allowed anything to affect him that much.

She let her eyes drift closed. Somehow, his care with the fire, his concern just now, left her feeling touched and pampered.

A smile curved her lips.

Foolish, foolish Lacey, she thought as she drifted into sleep.

CHAPTER 8

The small square of outdoors framed by the window lightened from velvet black to pewter and then to silver. John waited until traces of gold yellowed the light, and then he gladly took leave of his pallet.

He'd not enjoyed a minute of rest during that long night.

The pallet could not be blamed—he'd slept on bare floors so often that the scantiest layer between himself and a floor cushioned him as well as any feather bed. No, it had been the presence of the woman. *Lacey*. The soft sounds she made as she moved on his bed; the scent of his soap lingering in the air to torment him with the image of her washing herself with water he'd drawn for her.

He turned his head, just a little, letting his hair fall down over his cheek to hide where he was looking, just in case she happened to be glancing his way.

She slept, heedless of the dawn.

He shook the hair back and studied her.

In the newborn daylight he could drink his fill of her and slake the curiosity he had not dared indulge the night before. At first he did not think there would be much to see. He'd done so much tossing and turning that he'd felt overheated, with no need of covering during the night, but she lay huddled with his best blanket pulled all the way up to her chin. She made a small, curving mound in his bed.

Her hair tumbled across the pillow, curling over the blanket—more hair than he'd ever imagined growing from one woman's head. The pale light struck against it, raising golden glints, hinting at how silky it might feel if a man were to wrap those freshly washed strands around his fingers.

He looked away, and wished he hadn't when he spotted a frothy flounce of petticoats heaped on his table. Mud stains darkened the hems, but he could tell she'd tried to wash them. She'd arranged her dress carefully over the back of his chair. Light green and rosy pink silk shimmered in the dawn, reminding him of how the folds had clung to her legs as she walked, how the bodice had fit close to her narrow waist and full breasts.

Petticoats on the table. Dress on the chair.

She had no other clothes with her.

She was lying on his bed, under his blanket, with only the scantiest of undergarments covering her skin. Or possibly, wearing nothing at all.

He forgot to breathe for a moment. When he remembered, the sound rasped harsh in the quiet. Loud enough to wake her.

The bed ropes creaked, and she sat up. She clutched the blanket close with one hand, revealing nothing, as she rubbed the sleep from her eyes.

She seemed to shrink back against the wall when she noticed him. He could not blame her. A lady such as she was not accustomed to waking to find a Groat Alley orphan staring down at her.

She wouldn't have to endure it much longer. Another day. Maybe two.

"It's late," she said, her voice husky from a night of silence.

"Not for the likes of you."

She blinked and looked ready to protest. He was in no mood to hear false niceties from her.

"I know your kind usually stays abed until noon."

She seemed to flinch away at his observation. "Not always."

He shrugged. "It suits me if you want to continue sleeping half the day while you're here. Once you return to the settlement, though, you'll find that most are up and about early in the day."

She frowned. He wondered if she thought he was trying to impress her with the luxuries to be enjoyed here, with him, over the harsh conditions in the colony.

He wondered if that was what he'd been trying to do.

She covered a yawn with the hand that wasn't holding her blanket. "It won't be difficult for me to become accustomed to rising with the sun."

Perhaps she had not understood. Or perhaps she did and had just handed him a rejection of all he had to offer.

Maybe he should have told her about his conversation with Opechancanough.

No. Just thinking about what Opechancanough had told him filled him with sick dread.

Besides, if she decided to stay, he wanted it to

be because she wanted to stay with him, not because she feared being scalped.

"I have chores to tend," he said.

"I'll help. Just let me get dressed—"

"No. Stay in bed."

She stared at him, uncomprehending.

"You might feel fine at the moment, but you still need rest. I know the toll that a sea journey takes upon a person."

"I've heard that the best thing one can do to overcome malaise is to plunge right into work."

He let a smile curl his lip at her ridiculous comment. "Women such as you don't know what it means to work."

She glanced away. Strange, but as she looked away he thought he saw tears glittering, unshed.

"What am I to do while I'm here, then?" She gave a choked-sounding little laugh. "Oh, never mind, I remember: we have a little bit of *business* to attend to once I'm rested."

No sense in denying the truth, but the words threatened to stick in his throat. "There's no need for you to do anything else."

"You didn't think this through at all, did you?"

He bristled at her criticism. "I did. I could think of nothing more suitable for the woman I chose than to offer her an interlude of complete idleness. I assure you, no man in the settlement can afford a woman who lies abed and does nothing all day."

Damn! He had not meant to brag.

She glowered back at him, and he welcomed the return of her spirit even as she heaped insults upon him. "Even the most indolent woman requires something to do. Books, or fancy needlework, *something*."

"If you were a woman of my kind, you would

know I put no value on books and fancy needle-work."

"Then you should have chosen a woman who appreciates the same things you do."

"Ah, but that would not have served my purpose. I wanted exactly what I chose: a pampered little darling born and bred to decorate the arm of a man who thinks he's better than everyone else. So go back to sleep now."

She didn't answer him. She sank back down upon the bed, then closed her eyes and curled away toward the wall.

She'd done exactly as he'd suggested. He felt no gratification.

Clara woke to full sunlight.

Mindful of the warnings Percy had issued about what would be expected of her, she scrambled clear of the pallet that served as her bed and hurriedly dressed. There was no mirror in this tiny cubbyhole that Percy had called home for many months, which might have been a hardship for him but was a mixed blessing to someone like herself.

She patted her head and found a few loose strands. She'd washed her hair and pinned it up the night before, and judging by how well it had stayed in place, she must've slept still as a stone, as exhausted as she'd been. She spotted some loose pins in the bedclothes and worked them into her hair quickly.

She must have slept so long that she'd missed breakfast, for there was a distinct lack of appetizing aromas. She didn't fancy tackling a day of back-breaking labor on an empty stomach; perhaps she could cajole a bit of bread and cheese from the cook.

Cook? Her hand wavered in the act of stabbing the last pin in place. The kindhearted Hedgingses had agreed to let her take temporary residence in Percy's lodgings, but they'd been honest and apologetic about the lack of comforts she would find in their home. The room she occupied had been built in a fever of optimism, when Mr. Hedgings had believed he might harvest enough tobacco from their 100 acres to fulfill his obligations to the Virginia Company and store a little extra for themselves.

Instead, like virtually all of the other settlers on Malvern's Hundred, he'd found himself continually trading away the little tobacco he managed to harvest for the necessities of survival. Most of the extra went for flour and tea from the Company store.

There was not enough tobacco in the land to buy milk and butter and cheese. There were no dairy cows on Malvern's Hundred. Some had arrived with the first settlers, Percy said, but they had either died or been killed for food. One team of oxen remained, shared out among the settlers, and coddled more lovingly than most children. The Company continually promised to send livestock, but the ships that arrived instead came loaded to the brim with new settlers rather than the supplies so desperately needed. Each new shipload meant the settlers' scant resources had to be stretched even further.

Like all of them, Mr. Hedgings traded a few ounces of tobacco for meat, sometimes, from John Bradford.

John Bradford, the man who'd stolen Lacey.

Clara's hand shook. How could she have slept so long? How could she have been standing here thinking of breakfast and wishing she'd had a mirror when her friend required rescuing?

In the kitchen, Mrs. Hedgings greeted her with a tired smile. She hoisted herself from her chair with more difficulty than her slight size warranted. Usually, Clara thought, only women weighed down with fat or crippled with gout moved as if each joint ached. "I kept some breakfast warm for you," Mrs. Hedgings said.

The kitchen table lay littered with used dishes and cutlery. Clara took heart from the sight. "The men have eaten and gone—to rescue my friend?"

Mrs. Hedgings shook her head. "To the tobacco."

"Percy—I mean, Mr. Bledsoe—told me it might be a day or two before a rescue party was formed. I didn't want to believe him."

"Oh, dear." Mrs. Hedgings hobbled to the hearth and from an iron pot dished out a portion of an unappetizing-looking gruel. "He ought not have promised a rescue party."

"Someone must go after her! She's been in that man's clutches for a full day now!"

"Aye. And whatever he's meant to do with her, he's no doubt done by now."

Though they were speaking woman to woman, the implications made Clara blush. Mrs. Hedgings handed her the plate of gruel and Clara sniffed at it warily. Other than the faint odor of iron from the cooking pot, the grayish, somewhat slimy substance had no scent.

"Eat your porridge," Mrs. Hedgings said. "You'll need to keep up your strength." She indicated a chair for Clara to sit.

"Milk?" she asked before remembering there were no cows. "Sugar?"

Mrs. Hedgings chuckled without humor.

Clara dug in her spoon, raised a heaping portion, and swallowed it. Food without a smell seldom had an objectionable taste, and this so-called porridge proved to be tasteless fodder indeed.

"Your friend might be enjoying fresh meat right this minute," Mrs. Hedgings said. Her stomach growled. She rested her hand against her belly and sighed but made no apology for the unladylike sound.

"Lacey can eat fresh meat until she bursts, but it is no compensation for what has been done to her," said Clara.

"There are those who would not agree."

Mrs. Hedgings's stomach growled again.

Clara lost her appetite altogether. She let the spoon clatter to the table. "Then I will visit every house in the hundred until I find those who will agree."

"You set yourself a difficult task," said Mrs. Hedgings. "You seem to be a good friend; I hope you won't take it too much to heart if nobody wants to confront John Bradford over the matter of your friend."

"I simply refuse to believe that, Mrs. Hedgings."

"Please, call me Ellie." The woman's expression softened with sympathy. "Don't judge us too harshly, Clara."

"I'm not judging anyone. I just can't believe that nobody cares!"

"We're too tired to care about much of anything, my dear. In another few months you'll feel the same."

"Never!"

"You'll see. Something happens to you here. It's a gradual thing—too many weeks of going hungry, too many hours spent working at tasks that never get done. Next thing you know, you lose all hope, and one day you wake up and realize, well, you just don't care about anything anymore."

"It's not supposed to be like this," Clara whispered.

But it was. She had felt it in the air of defeat that permeated both James City and the tiny settlement of Malvern's Hundred. She saw it in the almost-emaciated body of Ellie Hedgings, in the swollen joints and ruined teeth that spoke of starvation and overwork.

"Everybody cannot feel this way," she said.

"You're right; there are some who cling to optimism." Ellie used the table to support herself as she took a few steps. "Your Mr. Bledsoe, for instance."

Clara felt a quickening of her heart at hearing Percy called "her Mr. Bledsoe."

"He's proven himself to be a good friend," she said.

"To us as well," said Ellie. "He's out there working with my husband right now, and God knows I can use your help here in the house."

Clara decided to wait until she could speak with Percy again before agitating about Lacey's rescue. "What would you like me to do?"

"Oh Clara, there's no end to what needs doing." Ellie's shoulders slumped. "Laundry. Grinding corn. There's wild fruit and weeds to gather and dry."

Ellie continued with a list of chores that left Clara feeling more distraught with each addition. "Ellie, I don't know how to do any of those things."

"Nor did I when I came here. I know more now,

but lack the strength to do it right." She glanced around her home as if surprised to find herself sitting there. "No wonder I've grown so thin and my very bones ache."

"Why did the Company recruit the likes of me?" Clara wondered.

"Why did the Company promise men like my husband that they'd find a fine easy life here, and certain riches?" A faint glimmer of anger darkened Ellie's expression, but only for an instant. It seemed she lacked the energy to sustain much of anything at all, not even an emotion.

Clara vowed she would never permit that awful numbness to take over her spirit.

She would start by learning from Ellie everything she could teach her about how to survive.

After she saved Lacey, of course.

Lacey opened her eyes with some difficulty.

She must have fallen asleep while crying, for it seemed tears had dried and glued her eyelids together. She sat up and knew from the lethargy in her bones, from the fogginess in her head, that she'd slept many, many hours. The sunlight shafting through the window confirmed her suspicion. When last she'd seen light, it had been the pale, weak stuff of dawn, not this rich golden red that harkened the approaching sunset.

She'd slept for an entire day!

She'd never done such a thing. But *he* had goaded her into it.

With a cry of disgust she flung away the blanket and swung her legs over the edge of the bed. She'd validated his poor opinion of women.

And she'd also more firmly entrenched her lie.

He'd given her the perfect opportunity to admit the truth about herself. She could have agreed with him that wellborn ladies did indeed often sleep until noon—but that ordinary girls like herself didn't have that luxury. Except when they were pretending to be wellborn ladies.

She could have said that.

She could have wiped the satisfaction from his face, too, when he'd said he wanted a pampered little darling. Shocked him with his bad choice, and destroyed his satisfaction in his revenge.

Thinking that he could be hurt in that way—by destroying the one thing that meant so much to him—made something twist with pain inside her. Not so much at the idea of hurting him, but because it seemed inexpressibly sad to hold vengeance as a precious dream.

She resolved to tell him the truth, soon, but in a way that would let him retain some of his pride . . . let him retain some good will toward her.

She stood and fought off another wave of tiredness. This fatigue was ridiculous. She would get dressed and find something to do, no matter what he'd said about lying about. She shivered in the cool cabin and realized that this might have been the first time in her life that she'd ever been so nearly naked with no one else there to see. She got on the petticoats easily enough. The dress was another matter.

How many times had she dressed Amanda? Helped dress other ladies? Her own garments had always been easy to don and chuck off. She'd had the help of the other women on the ship while masquerading in these kinds of clothes, and she'd never suspected she might have difficulty handling the tiny buttons that Clara had helped her with.

Had it been just two days ago? It seemed like a lifetime.

She managed to fasten one button, then another, but the rest eluded her. She made a small sound of frustration.

"I'll play lady's maid for you," John said from the doorway.

She froze with her arms arched behind her. He must have walked in, quiet as a thief, while she strugged with the dress. "I can do it—" she began.

"I'd hoped the Company would've prevailed upon you women to bring more sensible clothes with you. It never fails. You arrive here with ball-gowns and fancy tea dresses that won't last through the winter."

He came up behind her and began fastening her buttons.

This was the perfect time to set him straight. To tell him that she, Lacey Cochran, typically wore sensible skirts and shirtwaists. That she, Lacey Cochran, knew well how to button a dress—from a maid's position.

"For all I know they do try to tell you what you'll need," he continued, oblivious to her inner struggle with her conscience. "Perhaps a representative gave you a list of what to bring and you tossed it in the fire and ordered your maid to pack naught but the most useless and most difficult to maintain."

He stood so close that she could feel his breath stir her hair. His hands worked the buttons at her back. His knuckles pressed lightly against her spine, moving upward with each successive button. How many buttons were there anyway? She'd been able to make short work of them when dressing Amanda, but he took infinitely longer, whether because his

big man's fingers were more awkward or because
he enjoyed lingering, she could not tell.

Nor could she understand why he was spending
so long buttoning her up when she knew he
intended to undo all those buttons soon.

"I'm not tickling you, am I?"

"I'm not laughing, am I?"

"No, but you seem somewhat short of breath."

Mortification flooded through her, and she was
very happy that she was facing away from him. "I
am merely anxious that you finish, for how would
it look if a rescue party bursts through the door
and finds us with your hands on my buttons?"

He laughed.

"It's not funny. My reputation is destroyed."

"That's not why I'm laughing."

"Then why?"

"Because you think someone will come after
you."

"Of course they will. You kidnapped me."

"There. Finished." He ignored her sensible
observation and gave her shoulder a quick pat, as
if dismissing her.

"Someone will come," she said, turning to face
him.

"It must be nice," he said, "to be so assured of
your importance in this world that you're convinced everybody else has nothing better to do than
come chasing after you."

"I'm not—" She stopped herself.

I'm not important, she'd almost said. So why had
she stopped? It was once again an excellent opportunity to tell him the truth about herself: that she,
Lacey Cochran, held no place of esteem in this or
any other society.

At the same time, his assurance that nobody

would come after her came as a very sobering reve-
lation. If he was right—and he seemed supremely
self-assured about it—then that meant she had no
value as Lacey Cochran, commoner, *or* as Lacey
Cochran, country cousin to the illustrious Stivington clan.

She wasn't sure what it meant—that women in
general had no value, or that she in particular had
no value.

But . . . she did have some value to John Bradford. So long as he continued believing her to be
the blue-blooded lady of quality that his revenge
demanded, he would treat her well.

For the moment, it seemed like a good enough
reason to hold her tongue and continue to conceal
the truth about herself. Her pride stung, too,
enough to make her consider how Amanda would
have responded in a similar situation. Amanda
would never let him believe she had no value.

"I'm not worried," she said. "Someone will
come."

"I hope they do," he said. "If they value you so
highly, it will mean that I chose well."

He reminded her at every turn that it was her
false identity that was important to him, nothing
more. With each moment spent in his company,
with each word he said to her, he proved that he
had no use for an ordinary, hard-working girl who
wanted nothing more than to find the right man
to spend her life with.

CHAPTER 9

She had spirit, did Lacey Cochran, John admitted grudgingly.

Although she definitely showed signs of being affected by his bitter remarks about her privileged life, she made no apologies for what she was; she took what he dealt without regressing into helplessness or resorting to a woman's tricks of tears.

And yet ... there was something that set his instincts on alert. She responded to his jibes with a defiance that dared him to prove what he said, rather than passing his insults off as of no consequence. She seemed just a little too determined to prove herself useful when a woman in her position ought to reveal dismay at thinking she might have to mar her pale white skin with menial tasks.

Everything about her screamed contradiction. The only matter that rang true was her desire to leave him. Whenever he mentioned her returning to the settlement, she agreed in the most amenable of manners.

Was that why he kept taunting her? Because he wanted to goad her into turning so contrary that she'd reverse her position about leaving?

He needed to get away from her for a time, to let his senses clear. He felt full to bursting from being so near. His hands tingled from buttoning her dress, the scent of her perfumed the air he breathed. The need to escape turned him clumsy; he spun and his hip banged into the table, sending his one and only plate skidding toward the edge.

She caught it deftly, with a skill that he wouldn't have expected a lady of leisure to possess.

"It wouldn't have broken," he said. "It's naught but pewter, but serviceable."

"Saves bending over to pick it up."

The observation was sensible enough, but jarring. "Your sort orders servants to clear the floor."

"My *sort* knows that keeping a house clean to begin with saves labor in the end."

"Well, maybe you're right to worry about those kinds of things. Once you leave here, you won't find many who are willing to bend toward the floor at your beck and call."

She flushed angrily. "I know how to care for a home. I'm merely defending my hard-won skills. . . ." She blushed and bit her tongue. "What I mean is, we *are* taught to manage a household, you know."

He berated himself for yet again taunting her about leaving. Not that she'd bothered to deny it—she'd merely gone and refuted his opinion of her abilities. Again.

"Careful now, Mistress Cochran, or you'll have me thinking you'd enjoy ruining your hands with lye soap and hot water. You'd have to forever wear gloves to maintain your ladylike image."

"What does someone like you know about maintaining an image? Maybe ladies of quality really do want to be more useful; maybe they'd like to exercise their intelligence, and yet must continually bite their tongues and diminish themselves in order to fit into the mold society has cast for them. Maybe that's why so many ladies of quality suffer from the vapors or take to their beds for days on end—they have nothing better to do!"

What a remarkable speech. And what a tempting picture she made uttering it. Her breasts heaved with passion; her cheeks flushed with emotion; her eyes glittered with anger.

Her senses were as heightened as his own, but for all the wrong reasons.

"I would think that you of all people might understand," she said.

With effort he dragged his thoughts to conversation rather than her physical presence. "Understand what?"

"What it's like to believe you must behave in a way that's contrary to the truth."

He tensed. He'd been so intent upon sniffing out the contradictions in her that he'd somehow let down his guard enough for her to divine something about him. "I behave exactly as I want to behave."

"Ha! You play the part of the vengeful outcast, and yet you harbor an abiding responsibility for the settlers you claim to despise."

"I do despise them."

"You feed them."

"I make them pay."

"You gave back the tobacco when you paid for me."

"You are the means to my revenge. The tobacco was part of it."

"The ultimate revenge would be for you to let them starve in misery."

The truth of her words rocked him to his core.

She wasn't done with tormenting him, either. She advanced a step closer until they stood almost nose to nose. "You take their tobacco, but I'd wager you know you could charge more and they would pay it. But you don't because you want to leave them with something. You could live anywhere in this vast land, but you've built a cabin within a half day's journey so you can be close to them. You take care of them and watch out for them and slink about with your hair hiding your face, with your eyes not meeting theirs, so they won't know the truth."

"You're wrong."

"Your actions speak for themselves."

"Then what does it say that I am here arguing with you right now when I ought to be there warning them that the Indians mean to massacre them all?"

His words seemed to echo from the walls.

"The Indians will massacre the settlers?"

"Yes."

He waited for her to react like the others—to deny the truth of what he said just because *he* had said it. He waited for her to accuse him of trying to cast the Indians in a bad light just so he might continue to profit.

She did neither. She grew solemn and still, and with a dawning sense of disbelief, he knew that for once somebody had taken him at his word.

He'd imagined he might feel satisfaction, or even

a sense of gloating, when people started believing him. He hadn't imagined . . . gratitude.

Lacey said, "Then it's all pointless."

He could not follow her logic. "I don't know what you mean."

"You will return me to the settlement."

"That is the bargain we struck." He waited, holding his breath, hoping she would ask for a revision to the terms.

"We'll all be massacred there."

"Unless changes are made, then yes, they'll . . . you'll . . . all be massacred."

"But staying here seems just as dangerous. All alone and vulnerable to attack."

She wouldn't be alone if she stayed here. She would be with him.

But all he said was, "I understand the Indians. The Indians understand me. There is a certain respect between us. They would not harm me or mine."

Me or mine . . .

She gave an exasperated sigh. "Well I am glad the Indians understand you, because I certainly cannot! You claim mutual respect, confidence that you won't be hurt—and yet you keep insisting the Indians cannot be trusted."

"They cannot."

"You just said—"

"Come. Let me show you how little I trust them."

He held out his hand. After a slight hesitation, she took it. He led her to his skip hole, flung open the door. Morning light flooded the cabin and brightened this newly revealed space as well, revealing to her everything that he knew had been little more than darkened shadows when she'd glanced in there the evening before.

The "room" he'd hacked from the hillside was tall enough for him to stand in, and wide enough to sit or sleep, but the bulk of it was occupied by something else.

"What is that?" Lacey asked.

He could not blame her for not guessing.

His odd contraption jutted from the wall—a jumble of metal with a long handle, followed by a series of shallow troughs hewn from wood leading to a basin.

"That's the water," he said, and he could feel his shoulders straightening with pride. "Watch."

He worked the lever. The squealing and squeaking had never seemed so loud to him, or the results taken so long, but all at once a gush of clear water splashed from the metal. He pumped harder; water surged, splashing over the sides of the troughs.

"We don't need to haul from the stream; the stream is coming here to us. If we get trapped inside by the Indians, we can't be forced out by thirst. Unless they find my intake."

"Intake? You can explain that to me later." She moved closer, fascination lighting her face. "We had nothing like this at Stivington."

She moved closer for a better look, and unfortunately at the same time his energetic pumping caused such a cascade that it jarred loose one of the troughs. Her cry of dismay escalated into a gasp when cold water gushed along the loosened trough, soaking her from the waist down. Water plumed up, soaking her bodice, and then another section of trough followed the first and clattered to the floor.

That's what came of being so eager to show off. He bent down to retrieve the troughs, embarrassed to realize how desperately he'd wanted to impress her.

"Not your fault," he said, and the humiliation sweeping through him made him fumble for an explanation. "I don't know why I was pumping so hard. I use a tree gum to hold the sections together, but the gum dries out. One long unseamed trough would've been much better, of course, but it wasn't possible because of the awkward angle required to pipe the water from the side rather than the ground. You'll need to know how to put this back together, because it happens . . ."

He stood there with his hands full of troughs, and his voice trailed away as he realized exactly what happened to a gown of pink and green silk when it got drenched in cold water.

It disappeared.

Oh, it was still there, no doubt, but it had molded itself to her skin so that it was no longer possible to tell whether it was pale pink silk or pale pink flesh treating his eyes.

His muscles tensed; his breathing turned harsh. *Run.*

"This can wait until later," he said.

"No, show me now."

She had no other gown to change into. Or anywhere to go. He desperately wanted to stop looking at her. Desperately wanted to keep looking at her. His skin tingled, as if wanting to cool itself against her wet flesh.

He'd been affected by lust before, but this was different.

"Show me," she said again.

"Like this," he said. He tucked the troughs under his arm and reached for a clay jar he kept on top of the contraption. A stick protruded from the jar. He pulled it free and held it out so that she could see the pine pitch he kept in it, which he used to coat the bottom edges of the troughs. He applied a liberal portion to the loosened trough and set it carefully in place atop one that had remained in place. He pressed the edges together, using his weight. "You do the next," he said.

He stepped back, giving her plenty of room. She picked up the remaining trough from him and nearly dropped it. She'd probably never lifted anything that heavy, he thought. His hand shot out to offer support, and he paused when remembering how enfolding her hand within his had affected him. Instead, he angled his arm so that hers rested atop his. His assistance should have made the job easier; instead, she seemed paralyzed.

He wished she would move, because he couldn't.

His desire coursed like a live thing through him, pounding from his pulse into hers.

The trough dropped from her hands and clattered to the floor.

"I'm sorry."

"No harm done." His voice sounded ragged.

"It broke—look."

The long trough had indeed split in two upon impact with the floor. Lacey stooped to retrieve it, and John thought how much he was feeling like that ruined trough—split asunder by confusion. Part of him wanted to pull her into his arms. Part of him knew that making love to her now, while he was so affected by her, might pierce the walls he'd so carefully built around his heart.

She gathered the broken sections of trough and held them to her breast. Distress clouded her eyes.

"It's not a tragedy," John said.

"You worked hard to make this. I can see the

marks from your tools; you must have spent hours cutting it and whittling away the excess wood."

"Time is one thing I have in abundance," he said.

He shouldn't have mentioned time, because at once his mind plagued him with the memory of endless hours spent alone, when whittling the heart from a section of tree proved a welcome diversion from the aching, endless solitude that sometimes seemed likely to kill him.

"I have extras," he said. And he did. Dozens of them, each one a silent witness to his loneliness.

But not one of them seemed more valuable at the moment than the broken, ruined thing that Lacey clutched against her breasts. Nobody had ever cared that he'd worked hard, that he'd used ingenuity and skill to accomplish something unique and different—before her.

Nobody had ever mourned the loss of anything he owned, not even when his freedom had been stolen from him.

When she was gone—when he sent her away— nobody would ever care again.

The loneliness that he'd worked so hard to deny suddenly reared up, wrenching and agonizing, and mocked him with the knowledge that this was but a hint of the devastation to come.

She had unleashed this.

She could quench it.

And she was his, for a time.

Need swelled within him once more, pounded through his veins, made it difficult to breathe. An urge so primal ought to feel familiar, but there was something different about this urgency that gripped him, this desire to pull her toward him and let her ease the ache she had roused.

He knew the way of his desires, knew that no matter how they raged, there were times when a few moments with a woman could release him to the point where he would push away the female whose company he had so recently sought, push her away and never look back at her. Maybe this was one of those times.

Choose her, use her, lose her.

Do this with Lacey, regain control over his inner demons, turn his back on her once he was whole again.

"Set down the trough, Lacey." His voice sounded rougher than the splintered wood.

She did not obey; if anything, she clutched the ruined trough more tightly, her slender fingers adjusting to curve around the wood the way they would curve around a man's arm. He wanted to rip the trough away and bend her beneath him.

He had promised he would not force her.

He closed his eyes and deliberately slowed his breathing, sickened to think that he hovered right on the verge of taking what she did not offer, simply because he was bigger, stronger . . . needier.

With his next breath he inhaled the scent of flowers, the scent of woman. The air stirred, and even before he opened his eyes he knew she had moved closer to him.

She lowered her arms. The broken pieces of trough dropped to the dirt floor with dull thuds. Her eyes met his without flinching, still wide, but the trepidation had been replaced with what seemed a mirror image of his own need.

His arms moved away from his sides, curved a little, and with a start he realized that for the first time since his parents had died and he'd been forced onto the streets, he was willingly offering his embrace to another person.

She trembled. And so did he, but not with the effort of holding his arms out for her. Rather, it was from the certainty that if she did not move forward into his embrace, he might never again manage to reach out to another.

She took a step closer. His heart skipped. She took another. He closed his arms around her, one curving around her shoulders, the other encircling her waist. She was soaked through from the water spilled from the troughs, and he did not know if it was the chill water or him that caused her to shiver, that caused her breasts to peak into hard pebbles that he could feel clear through his shirt to his skin.

He desperately wanted it to be him.

How could he know? Could he ask? His throat seemed unusually tight, his breathing too labored to fashion words even if he managed to say them aloud. He brushed his cheek against her hair, questing toward her ear with his lips, thinking he might dare to whisper the question.

She shifted and his lips brushed against her cheek, skin so exquisitely soft that he thought nothing, not even the finest silk, could compare . . . until their lips met.

Lacey had been kissed before. Quick, stolen things—not always welcome—when she was a saucy housemaid exuding too much curiosity, and a footman or steward recognized it and hoped to satisfy it. Pumphrey Fallsworth had kissed her, frequently while seducing her, less often once she'd capitulated, but always with the air of bestowing great favor upon her. She'd been so dazzled by his position, so disbelieving that she'd fooled him into wanting her, that she'd never considered that a kiss could be something more than a wet, cold, perfunctory thing.

She had never known that a kiss could surge through her whole body like a jolt of lightning, leaving every inch of her crackling with expectation that this time, maybe this time, she would find what she had been craving for so long.

John's lips . . . Always when she looked at him, they'd been pressed into a tight, grim line, unsmiling and rigid. Impossible to believe that those were the same lips that now plied against her own with . . . with . . . with invitation. Invitation to join with him in a very special banquet where the two of them might slake needs that had gone unsatisfied for far too long. Those lips betrayed an unmistakable hunger for something only she could provide.

She knew it in her soul, as John Bradford held her close and murmured unintelligible words against her lips, her cheeks, her hair, as his trembling matched her own, that he had never wanted a woman with the intensity that he now wanted her. Only her.

Within herself, something bloomed into life, free and joyous. This, this was what she had been seeking—a physical joining with a man who found her as necessary as air.

And so she ignored the inner warnings that tried to remind her that this man had promised to use her and discard her. She squelched the scolding of her conscience that screamed she had vowed to forgo passion. She turned away from the pride that suggested only someone of easy virtue would let herself be seduced by a rogue outcast in less than a single day, with scarcely a civil word exchanged between them. She ignored it all.

What difference did time make? She had known Pumphrey Fallsworth for weeks before succumbing to his seduction. And she had never felt, ever, that she was essential to him.

Pumphrey's touch had grown familiar, but had never sparked the shivering delight that John's first touches raised.

She would think of Pumphrey no more.

John brushed long fingers against her neck and then worked free the buttons of her gown. Her gown was soaked and clung to her skin, but he peeled it from her with exquisite care, greeting each inch of newly bared skin with a kiss.

He bent her back over his arm and plundered her mouth with his while his hand roamed where it would, and then a soft rattle of pebbles made him go still.

"Not here," he whispered. "Not here."

Her opened bodice fell to her waist as he swooped her into his arms and carried her to his bed.

He had said she would be willing when she came to his bed. And oh, dear God, she was willing.

She let him strip off her clothes, and then his. Something glinted in the scant light—moonlight, reflecting from the pierced coin he wore on the thong around his neck. He moved and the light changed so she couldn't see it anymore; she wondered if he'd taken it off. Her curiosity lasted only a heartbeat, for then he lay her down and joined her on the bed. His hands moved over her, tormenting her with exquisite touches, rousing yearnings she didn't even know she possessed.

She whimpered and he covered her mouth with

his and swallowed her sounds. With sure, bold touches he roused frighteningly strong sensations from her.

No timid lovemaking for John Bradford; no lady-like murmurs of protest from Lacey Cochran. If the vengeful side of him preferred to think her a weak, useless frippery by day, this passionate side of him recognized her strength and resilience and demanded everything she had to offer, all of it.

She writhed beneath him, glorying in the thrust of her hips against his, astonished at the tension of her belly pressed so tightly against his. The coin he wore lay hard against the valley between her breasts. She didn't know why such a small thing should seem such a troubling barrier between them, but then he moved a little, and its press was gone.

He parted her thighs. He thrust up against her but did not penetrate, as if to present her with the evidence of what she had done to him and what he meant to do to her. Her breath escaped her. Her insides clenched in anticipation. He moved away, just a little, and returned, probing, finding, entering, with slow and exquisite precision, allowing her to accommodate and adjust and marvel at the way her body so perfectly fitted his.

A spasm shook her. She cried out.

He made a sound too, of wonder and awe.

She felt as though her whole being were melding into his.

This was what she had been seeking.

All the years of feeling that she didn't belong. Of seeking an answer to the indefinable yearnings within. Of reaching for something that always eluded her. Here was her answer. She found it in this moment, halfway around the world from all that was familiar, with the arms of this outcast wrapped around her, with his strong body claiming hers.

He moved with a rhythm that her body matched easily, the two of them in perfect accord. "You are not alone," she whispered to him, her lone woodsman. She knew in her heart that no one but she could match him thrust for thrust, sigh for sigh. "You are not alone now."

He trembled.

His rhythm changed, as if he were trying to hold something back from her, and this she would not allow. Once again she matched him. She showed him without words that there was no place he could withdraw inside himself where she could not find him. No place he could hide away from the way she could affect him.

He said her name in a whisper, in a moan. She wanted to see him say her name; she opened her eyes and found his open, too, wide and dark and fixed intently upon her. With no averted head, no trailing hair to hide the stark need within— something that her heart told her only she could slake.

As if in confirmation, his arms tightened around her. His movements grew more possessive, more demanding, urging more from her, more and more until something seemed to explode inside her, sending tremors of ecstasy through her limbs, through her very veins.

She arched back and cried his name. Her whole body shook with the exquisite sensations. She hadn't known her body was capable of feeling such intense pleasure; she hadn't known the pleasure could escalate to even greater heights when John found a release that matched her own.

He collapsed against her. His face was buried in the valley of her neck and shoulder. She cupped his head with her hands, holding him close.

The damned coin dug into her flesh, and she wanted nothing more than to rip it from his neck.

Not yet. If it was so important to him that he would wear it against his heart always, then she would not interfere.

Not yet.

But soon, maybe.

She cradled him in her arms, knowing she had found what she had been seeking for so long.

CHAPTER 10

Their breathing gradually slowed, gradually quieted. Lacey began to notice the night sounds again, sweetened with the wild thump of his heart against her ear. For that brief, timeless space, John held her close to him, his body tense and trembling as if he meant to love her again.

In the delicious languor that cradled her, she dared to dream that their lovemaking had startled him as much as it had her with the rightness of it.

Maybe at that very moment he was seeking the words to say, that their interlude would transform into permanence, that he would never let her go. He must know now that passion for her had driven him, not his thirst for revenge.

She could not have imagined what she'd seen in his eyes, what she'd felt in his embrace. He needed her for more than the pursuit of his vengeance.

Then she felt the first brush of cool air against her cheek, and then a chill across her shoulders as she sensed the slow withdrawal of his arm from around her.

Still her foolish heart resisted accepting the inevitable. There were lots of reasons for a man to adjust his position when sharing a bed with a woman. He might only be moving to soothe an ache in his arm, or to find a more comfortable position. Moving away from her need not mean that now that he'd accomplished what he'd set out to do, he wanted nothing more to do with her. His withdrawal need not mean that at all.

She continued to fabricate reasons for his withdrawal until he'd shifted completely away from her, until a careful two-inch gap separated them as thoroughly as she had once hoped the Atlantic Ocean might separate her old life from her new.

Reality slapped her with such a cold chill that it might have been a bucket of water from that same Atlantic Ocean. While she'd been dreaming that his rigid tension meant he wanted her again, it most likely indicated that he was overcome by something else altogether.

Something like anger.

Anger, over discovering she was not the woman she had professed herself to be.

While under the dizzying spell of his lovemaking, she'd allowed herself to forget for a moment that her hour of reckoning was at hand. The last of her soft inner glow dissipated, leaving her tense with anticipation.

She'd spent endless hours dreading the moment when the man who chose her discovered her lack of innocence. But always she'd imagined herself standing chastened, with head bowed, while some faceless man she cared nothing about heaped insults upon her.

She'd thought nothing could be worse than the humiliation of discovery; now she knew it was infinitely more terrible to think of John's lips, John's tongue, hurling those accusations her way, transforming from instruments of pleasure into cold tools of punishment.

Nothing could be worse than hearing him articulate his disappointment in her.

She would rather do it herself.

"You must be sorry now that you chose me," she whispered into the dark.

He made a sound—she supposed it might be amusement; she could not tell without seeing his face. She dared not touch his lips to see if they curved upward in a smile, or if they had thinned into a sneer of disgust.

"Sorry?" he asked.

"You had the first pick of us all. You chose me. You must regret it now." She closed her eyes, but that did nothing to minimize her humiliation.

He was silent for so long that she thought he might have fallen asleep, as had been Pumphrey's habit after taking her to bed. But John made the sound again, and this time there was no doubt he found her amusing.

"If you're fishing for compliments, you've come to the wrong man," said John.

"You think I'm fishing for compliments?" She couldn't imagine how he might have misread her apology.

"I've never learned the niceties of using pretty words." He swallowed so hard she could hear it in the night. "I've never known a woman who . . ."

She shuddered, her courage shredded by the comment he'd not bothered to finish.

"You enjoyed lying with me," he said.

He said it so strangely. Almost a declaration. Almost a demand for her to agree with him. Almost daring her to deny it. She'd heard such tones before, most recently from Amanda Stivington, who'd said to her: "You enjoyed playing the game with me."

John was a man of few words, but the words he chose were diabolically clever in getting her to admit her failings.

He could not know that she had more than making love to him to atone for.

"I should not have been so . . . exuberant. Not so . . . uninhibited."

She should not have made love to him at all. He would not have forced her to submit to him. She had been the one to make the first move toward him.

She tried to summon an apology, and her voice refused to cooperate. Maybe because while her head knew that remaining chaste with him would have been the sensible way to behave, her heart told her she had done nothing to regret.

And her body—her traitorous, troublesome body—ebbed and throbbed for him and quickened at the idea of doing it with him again.

She had learned nothing at all! She made a soft sound of dismay.

He tensed. "I did not hurt you?"

"Not yet," she said, but softly so she was certain he could not hear.

"You are not in pain?"

"No. I am merely stupid."

He drew in a sharp breath and then went silent again. She waited, her heart pounding. For what? For him to say, "No, Lacey, you were not stupid;

we have found something magical in each other's arms. . . ."?

But those words would occur only in a dream.

When he spoke again, it was with the precision of a man who wanted to pin down the precise meaning of what he'd heard. "You are stupid because of what we have just done."

"Aye."

He shifted in the bed, a quick motion that made it seem as if he'd flinched, as if her acknowledging her mistake might have hurt him. Absurd. Perhaps an ordinary man would feel hurt if a woman said she'd made a mistake in making love with him, but not John Bradford. He'd made it abundantly clear that he had no tender feelings.

Amanda Stivington would never let anyone know she'd been bested.

Lacey called upon all she had ever learned from watching Amanda. She pretended to laugh. "I knew exactly what to expect from you. You didn't try to seduce me with extravagant promises or beautiful words of love."

"I did not lie to you."

"No."

"Would the pretty words make you feel . . . less stupid?"

She hadn't expected that from him. She mulled over her experiences, thought about Amanda's, before answering him. "Pretty words only leave you feeling more foolish once you learn the promises were false."

"I never made false promises to you."

"No."

She waited, hoping against hope that he might make some promises now.

"I did not trick you into this bed with lies."

"No. You told me exactly what to expect."

She was feeling more foolish by the second, remembering exactly what John Bradford had promised her: that he meant to use her and discard her.

Even though she'd known that nothing could come of her affair with Pumphrey Fallsworth, she knew she would not have gone as far as she had if Pumphrey had informed her at the beginning that he wanted her only as an instrument of revenge. He'd wooed her with flattering words and showered her with useless trinkets that reflected the shallowness of his promises. She knew he was deceiving her about his intent, even as she was deceiving him about her true identity. It had been enough to justify her behavior to herself at the time.

John hadn't done a thing to woo her. Yet here she lay, naked save for a rough blanket, speaking shockingly intimate thoughts to a man who'd made not even the slightest pretense of caring about her.

She didn't even have to ask herself why she'd tumbled into bed with him, because she could still feel it inside her. The mysterious, unquenchable longing that had tormented her for so long had responded to the way John had burned with hunger for her. Something inside her had sensed something inside him that promised that, with the joining of their spirits, each might find what they needed in the other.

She'd deluded herself into thinking she might have found it, too. For a brief space of time, she had lain naked in his arms, only a woman, and had felt treasured and cherished for herself, for Lacey Cochran, and not for what he thought she might be.

Need quickened inside her again, grew into hunger. For the recapturing of that glorious sensation of completion. For John, only a man and nothing more. For him to fill her once more, to cover her, to press her deep into the rough bed. To tell him that no matter what he might think of her, in some ways he would be right and in some ways he would be wrong—until this day, she had known something about the ways of sex, but nothing about the ways of love.

Her battered pride demanded that she try to salvage a little dignity. "You told me what to expect, and as you said I would, I have found an advantage in the situation."

His breath rasped harsh in the night. "I am glad there are no misunderstandings between us."

She wasn't. She blinked back the tears that sprang unbidden. She wished he had been hurt by her comment and had flinched away from it. She wished that he was even at that moment regretting the way they'd met and the plans he'd revealed, and that lacking that skill with words, he simply could not summon the right ones to make things right between them.

The hope that always lay within her heart leaped to life at the notion. What if they *were* both so trapped by their pride and the stands they'd taken that they could not speak the truth?

What they could not accomplish with words, they might manage by touching.

Her hand brushed along his arm. He stiffened and pulled away, and she knew she'd made yet another mistake. An enormous mistake.

"Stupid," she said through gritted teeth, and bounced her head back against the mattress. She didn't care if he heard her; he'd proven just now that she had no power to hurt him.

He rose from the waist and swiveled so that he sat at the edge of the bed, his broad back a deeper shadow in the darkened room.

"I took care that you would not be left with child," he said.

She was glad of the dark when her face burned with embarrassment. "Thank you," she said, as politely as if he'd helped her step over a puddle in the road.

He stood, and she could tell from the sounds that he walked away from the bed. She was gripped by a sudden spell of shivering, and she pulled the blanket up to her chin. She wanted to pull it right up over her face and leave it there, which was silly, because he couldn't see her in the dark. If he could, she wondered what her expression would reveal. Could he read upon her features that she had abandoned her life, risked death, assumed a new identity, all in order to start life afresh? And look where she'd found herself! Indulging her wanton tendencies had gotten her into trouble in the past, and she had vowed never again to let passion overrule her sense.

Months at sea firming her resolve, with hours spent each day praying for the strength to tamp down her unfortunately wanton nature—so much for her strength of will. Less than two days in this man's company and she'd let him toss her skirts up past her waist with no compunction whatsoever. She hadn't even given a thought to getting pregnant.

She'd lost herself in feeling, more thoroughly than had ever happened to her before. Four times she'd made love with Pumphrey Fallsworth and never once experienced the quaking in her lower reaches, the utter, mindless delight that had racked her body with exquisite sensation when John Bradford possessed her.

"You need not worry," he said.

"Yes, I know. You just explained."

"Not that. I meant, we have each taken what we needed from the other. We have each discovered the advantage we sought. Nobody need know the full truth, providing we hold our tongues about what happened between us just now."

The hot blush of shame shot through her; somehow he had sensed she was a woman who had let herself be ruled by passion, and he assumed she'd tumbled into his bed because of that. And then in the next instant she remembered him telling her that every situation could be worked to a person's advantage, and she realized that for a man of few words, he knew how to pack them full of meaning.

He was no bumpkin ignorant of what went on between men and women. There had been no innocence in his kisses, no amazement, no surprise. *Skill*. Heat coursed through her again, and not from embarrassment but from remembering exactly how skilled was his touch.

And so he knew that she was no maid when he took her.

And so he knew that she now had the advantage he'd told her to expect—she had an excuse for her lack of virginity.

But he also knew that the revenge he had planned for so long had fallen a little short of perfection.

He was a savage, an outcast, and she had spoiled his plan. If word got out that from among all the truly pure and virtuous women who had sailed on

the *Talisman* he'd chosen the only one not pure
and not virtuous, he'd be a laughingstock.

Her heart ought to be pounding in fear for what
he might do to her, out here alone in the wilderness
where no one could witness the deed, instead of
yearning for a repeat of what he had done to her.

He wouldn't hurt her. Her instincts screamed a
denial. And yet her instincts hadn't exactly been
reliable. It was bad enough that she'd forgotten to
worry about getting pregnant. Any woman with an
ounce of common sense should try to determine
if she was in great danger.

"Now you know . . . about me," she said. She
closed her eyes, as if eliminating the shadows and
darkness would make it easier to bear should she
learn he meant to kill her.

"You were no maiden."

"No."

Four heartbeats. Five.

"I thought the quality kept closer watch over
their womenfolk."

She had always assumed that once a man knew
she was no virgin, he would also immediately know
that everything else about her was pure fabrication.
But from John's comment, it seemed he still
believed she was a lady born and bred. He had not
yet figured out all of her deceptions.

Once again, she'd been given the chance to tell
him the truth about herself. Now, while the darkness and this odd intimacy made speaking such
things possible, she should tell him. He would hate
her for it, of course. Her lips parted, but the words
would not come, and she knew it was because she
still clung to some vague hope that he might not
totally despise her.

"There are moments of every day when a person

can go about as she pleases. Especially someone like me, who is not especially remarkable."

At once a feeling of foreboding overtook her; she'd made another mistake in not telling him, and now it was too late. She could only pray it would not haunt her in the future.

She felt a feather-light touch against her lips. She opened her eyes.

He'd moved silently in the dark and now loomed over her on the bed. His head was bent, but a faint shaft of moonlight illuminated his face just enough to let her see that he had all his attention focused upon her lips. He stroked her lips once again with a gentle finger, a finger that trembled when it touched her.

"A man would not find it so difficult to watch you all day," he said.

Her heart lurched. Pumphrey had been full of extravagant phrases, but she'd always known they were false, practiced, used with any number of women.

The words came so hard from John Bradford, sounding almost embarrassed. She knew with deep certainty that he'd never spoken such thoughts aloud to anyone ever before.

And then she was suddenly very, very afraid. Not that he might hurt her, but that her continued lies and deceptions had made it impossible for him ever to love her.

He had to get out of there.

John pulled himself away from Lacey before he could act as his loins demanded and claim her again. And again. Despite possessing her completely, he ached with the need for more, for deeper, for hotter, for wetter.

He hungered for her with an appetite he'd never known existed within him.

"Where are you going?" she called, her voice unsteady, as he jerked his breeches back in place and yanked his shirt over his head.

"Out."

"It's full dark."

He clenched his teeth together and tried to marshal his thoughts into order, for just then he would swear he heard a pleading in her voice, as if she wanted him to stay with her. In the dark. On that bed.

"I don't want to chase you from your home. You belong here. I am only a . . . a visitor."

Nothing could have chilled his ardor more.

She could do that. She could rise from his bed and walk from his house without a backward glance. They'd just had a calm and rational discussion about how each of them had received what they needed from the situation. Now there was no point in remaining together, and her offer to leave proved it.

He glanced over his shoulder at her. A tiny pool of moonlight brightened the bed just enough for him to see that she had sat up and clutched the rough woolen blanket to her naked breasts. He knew how rough that blanket was; he knew how soft was her skin. The ardor quickened again, driving away the doubts, and he wanted nothing more at the moment than to remove that blanket and replace it with something softer and kinder to her flesh, such as his lips.

He had to get out of there.

"I mean," she said, "after all, your purpose in

bringing me here has been accomplished. You can take me back to the settlement now.''

Use her. Lose her.

He didn't know which hurt worse, remembering the soul-sick scheme that had led him to bring her here, or realizing that she had had her own reasons for making love with him.

Now that his brain seemed to be working again, another thought occurred—one that increased his self-loathing.

''Did you think I meant to hold you prisoner here until we ... unless you ... accommodated me?''

She stared at him, her eyes wide in the moonlight.

''Is there reason for me to think otherwise?''

Tell her yes, whispered a voice inside him.

Disappear into the night, urged another.

He silently cursed his lack of skill with words and wished desperately for light. All those years of learning to read a person's true motives by watching the subtle play of the muscles in their faces, of the telltale shifting of their eyes ... He'd survived thanks to that ability, and now it meant less than nothing. He could not see Lacey well enough to judge what she meant, could not tell whether the note of uncertainty he thought he heard was real or feigned.

He dared not light a candle lest she see the state he was in.

No, that was not quite the truth of it. With light he might see that she meant exactly what she said and nothing more. That she'd come to his bed merely to get it over with, to put an end to an unpleasant business and get on with her life. Simply imagining the rejection he might see was almost impossible to bear. He could not endure it if it happened in truth.

It struck him then exactly how impossible it would be for them ever to be together. Lacey was a creature of light and air, free with soft touches and gentle sighs. He was a creature of darkness: secretive, unable to reach out with words, shying away from gestures.

He wanted nothing more than to look at her, drink his fill of the sight of her, but all the lessons he'd learned in the past conspired to make it difficult to face her straight on.

She made a small sound, and he knew that he'd waited too long to answer her question—that no matter what he said now, she would not believe him.

"I did not realize a man could not tell whether or not a woman was willing."

What did that mean? That she had or had not been willing?

"Some Indian women will love a man for food or tobacco," he said. "They are willing in different degrees."

"How so?"

She sounded genuinely curious. He edged a step closer to the door.

"Please don't go! Please stay and . . . tell me." Her plea stopped him. "Women do not speak of such things to one another. I . . . I need to know."

It seemed a strange favor to ask, a favor he had little enthusiasm for granting, but she'd asked him for nothing up until now, and might never ask him for anything again. It would provide cold comfort in the years to come, to know that he had explained to her the ways of sex, and yet it would be better than forever berating himself for not complying with such a simple request.

"A woman can be willing but disinterested. A woman can be willing and somewhat interested, and yet not spring to moist life for a man. Best of all for a man is to lie with a woman who quakes from her center, beyond her ability to control."

This last described Lacey—and yet did not even come close to describing her. She had gone wet for him. She'd shuddered for him. She'd moaned his name, shared his breath, tasted his flesh. He'd never known anything like the ecstasy he'd found in her arms.

Would never know it again.

Run . . .

"I'll take you back if you want to go."

"Now, you mean?"

"Unless you would prefer to stay."

"Until morning."

No. He'd meant would she like to *stay*. Not just until morning, but forever. With him, here in the house he'd built with his own two hands.

But he could not say those things without seeming the world's biggest fool, not after all the blathering he'd done about using her to exact revenge against the colonists. Especially he could not say it after they'd confirmed there were no misunderstandings between them. He'd given her every opportunity to say she preferred remaining with him to returning to the settlement and facing a possible massacre. She'd deflected every offer.

Groat Alley lads learned that if a toff was inclined to toss them a crumb, they'd do so after one or two requests for generosity. Continual begging usually resulted in a slap or a kick. There was no reason to believe making Lacey one more offer would make any difference.

"The trip would be more difficult in the dark. But we could leave now if you're eager."

She shrank back against the wall, moving away from the faint moonlight so that he could only guess at what she might be thinking. Would she be happy to stay . . . at least for a while longer? Or did joy light her eyes at the thought of leaving right that moment and putting him behind her?

"I'm . . . I'm a little tired. If it's all right with you, I'd just as soon wait until morning."

"Fine."

"You're still going outside?"

"Aye." While he had restrained his urge to run, he knew he had to get away from there, had to subdue the lustful urge plaguing his loins, had to wrestle with the conscience that taunted him now, reminding him that he had indeed intended to hand her straight back to them like a piece of shoddy goods. The plan reeked now with a stench that made his stomach churn.

"Why?"

"Why?" He'd explained it all to her the night before.

"Why must you go outside?"

"I have to prepare for the night." Well, at least that wasn't a complete lie. He did have to perform his usual chores, even as every ounce of his being yearned to dive back into the bed with her.

"I . . . I have some needs to attend as well."

He still couldn't see her, but he imagined she was blushing, and he berated himself for not thinking of this sooner. "You know there's a pot beneath the bed."

"It's not safe to go outside, is it?"

"Safer here than it will be back at the settlement." Shit. There he went again, sneaking in subtle little reasons for her to remain with him.

"You're safe here with me," he said, though it was a lie. He'd already proven she wasn't the least bit safe with him. "And it's only until morning. We'll go back to town as soon as you feel well rested."

"Fine," she said.

"Fine," he answered, though he'd never felt less fine in his life.

CHAPTER 11

Clara shivered and drew her cloak more tightly about her shoulders and wedged herself deeper into the crevice between two bales of tobacco where she hid. This shelter provided only a roof, no walls. Mist hung in the chill morning air. Swirling fingers of fog reached toward the ground, obscuring almost everything above eye level and distorting everything else.

Dampness always made her feel the cold more acutely, but on this morning she knew her trembling, her chattering teeth, could be blamed on more than the weather.

Nobody back in England would believe that Miss Clara Cutler stood cowering in the shadows cast by piled bales of tobacco, awaiting an assignation with an Indian.

"Hiring him as a guide seemed like a good idea yesterday," she said out loud. Her breath formed a frosted cloud in the air, temporarily making it even more difficult to see whether the bronze-skinned man who had promised to lead her to John Bradford's cabin in the woods might be approaching.

He had promised to meet her before dawn, though, and the sun was already edging above the horizon. Unless he came soon, the sun would burn off the sheltering fog. She would certainly be spotted by one of the early-rising settlers and asked to give an accounting for herself.

Let them ask! She would very happily launch into an explanation detailing why she'd been driven to such lengths. She would enjoy nothing more than telling the men of this community that they ought to be ashamed of themselves. The women as well—they all ought to be clamoring their outrage. No doubt about it: everyone in this settlement required a good scolding over their apathy and cowardice.

What was this world coming to when supposedly God-fearing Englishmen couldn't find the time to organize a rescue party for Lacey? They ought to be mortified that a helpless female like Clara had no choice but to hire a savage to help her rescue another helpless female.

The mists eddied, and coupled with her own shakiness, she wasn't sure at first that she'd spotted movement outside this roofed building that sheltered the hulking bales of tobacco that surrounded her.

She squinted and then drew back. Yes, someone walked out there—a man, a man with long, dark hair. Her pulse quickened with trepidation. He had shown up after all. While part of her rejoiced to think that at long last she might reassure herself about Lacey, another part of her wondered at the wisdom of going off into the wilderness with someone she didn't know—someone of an alien race.

Now was not the time for second thoughts. If she backed out, she'd be no better than the settlers who had turned their backs on Lacey's plight. She gathered her courage.

"Psst! This way," she hissed.

The man halted and swung his head toward her. He did not approach.

Stifling a sigh, Clara moved away from her hiding place. "Over here! You're late. We should have been on the trail a good hour ago."

"You should be inside where it's a little bit safer," he countered.

She froze. That voice—it was nothing like the awkward, guttural speech of the Indian she'd paid to meet her here.

She'd heard that voice before, though. Half-remembered echoes sent equal measures of fear and disbelief quivering through her. The swirls of fog parted, revealing a tall man, clad in native costume, his thick, black hair framing a face she would never forget as long as she lived.

John Bradford. The man who'd stolen Lacey.

"You!" A gamut of emotions surged through her. Outrage, to find herself at last face to face with this man who had kidnapped her friend. Joy, to think that he wouldn't dare show himself here if he'd harmed Lacey. Relief, that she wouldn't have to wander off with an Indian after all. "Where is she? I want to see her this very minute."

He remained unmoving as Clara stormed up to him. Once she reached him, though, she found herself stepping back a pace, startled by what seemed a profound difference in him.

Oh, physically he was as imposing as she'd remembered, and the fierce glower he directed her way would be enough to send strong men running for their lives—but something was different. The keen wariness she'd noted about him before was missing, replaced by an air of perplexity.

He blinked and cocked his head at her, quizzically, as if completely baffled by her presence.

From the first, John Bradford's confidence and determination had set him apart from the other men in the village. This new demeanor was different, too, but different in a way that left her feeling unsettled. . . . And so frightened for her friend that she swallowed her own fears and confronted him.

"Lacey," she prompted. "The woman you carried away from here. What have you done with her?"

John turned his head away from her. His hair swept down like a curtain hiding his face, but not before she noted a shifting of his eyes, a darkening of his expression.

"You hurt her!"

"I did not."

"Where is she? I want to determine her health and safety for myself!"

"She is back at my cabin. Where she belongs."

The statement must have sounded as outrageous to him as it did to her, for he scowled and looked embarrassed.

"She doesn't belong there. I mean . . . not unless she says she wants to be there. Did she? Did she stay behind willingly, or did you tie her up or confine her in some manner?"

She moved one step toward him with each accusation, and he backed away and flinched with each one.

"Well? How is she?"

"She was resting when I left her."

"So she is all alone in your godforsaken house in the woods."

"She is safe."

"Ha! Then what they say about you is right."

"What is it they say about me?"

"Surely you must know."

"I don't. I seldom venture near this place."

"Except to demand extortionate payment for the meat animals you find for free in the woods." Clara sniffed disparagingly as she reiterated what she'd heard from so many in the settlement. "And if you've left Lacey behind with no fear for her safety, then the other things they say are true as well—that you continually warn about danger from the Indians when you are only worried that they will provide us free the food for which you charge so dear."

"They are wrong." He tightened his jaw. "The Indians cannot be trusted."

Her innate honesty would not let that pass. "I suppose you're right about that, to an extent. That Indian took my money and never showed up as promised."

He tensed. "What Indian?"

"Opey something. I can't pronounce his name. Just yesterday he presented us with some fowl he called turkeys. He seemed an extremely generous and likable fellow."

"Opechancanough was here?"

"Yes, that sounds like the fellow's name. He attended church services, too, which I hear is something you never deign to do. So tell me who is the dangerous savage, hmmm, Mr. Bradford?"

He ignored her jibe. "Don't eat the turkey."

"Why? Do you fear the meat was tainted?"

"No. But accepting gifts is a step toward trusting them when you should hold them far away from you."

True enough. She'd been relaxed and trusting enough to contemplate traveling alone with the Indian. She gave a shaky laugh.

"Too late. We had it for supper last night. A trifle dry, but tasty."

He made an impatient motion with his head. "Tell me what you meant about paying him."

"He said he could guide me to your cabin."

"You can't mean you intended to go off with him alone."

Clara nodded.

John shook his head. "You're all fools."

"If you're so confounded certain the Indians mean white people harm, then why on earth are you here now, with Lacey back there all alone?"

"She will be safe. I have an understanding with the Indians."

"Oh, so *you* can trust them, but no one else should."

He shook his head. "I don't trust them. They have asked me to do something for them, and given me their word to let us live in peace for a little while longer until this matter is presented to the authorities. So long as Indians believe there is a chance the settlers will change, we are safe."

"We? You are lumping yourself in with the rest of the community, I see."

"No."

"You said *we.*" Clara didn't know why she harped on that word like a terrier worrying a rat. Except that John Bradford grew extremely agitated at being linked with the others, and she thought it a good idea to keep him off balance in this way.

"A slip of the tongue."

"Perhaps you mean *we* as in you and Lacey," she surmised. "Have the two of you decided to become a couple?"

"No." The denial fell harsh and clipped, and his lips settled into a grim line.

"So then yes, it is *we,* as it concerns you being part of this community."

"I am no part of this community."

"I know they don't think so, but apparently you do."

"I do not."

"Well then explain to me, Mr. Bradford, why the Indians have named you as their spokesman. And more important, why you have instinctively turned to your fellow Englishmen at a time when you appear to be somewhat distressed?"

She thought she'd struck her mark. A flicker of acknowledgment flashed through his eyes, as if he found himself embarrassed to reveal that he might actually need the support of his countrymen. But it happened so quickly and was so soon replaced by a mask of indifference that she thought she must have imagined it.

He stared at her for a long time. "I can't decide whether you're the bravest woman or the stupidest woman who ever lived."

"Well, I can't decide whether that's a compliment or an insult, and it doesn't matter. I want to see Lacey. And I want to know why you're here and have left her there."

"Her belongings," he said after a pause that was too long to account for such a simple reason. "Yes, that is why I have come. She needs her belongings."

It was a perfectly logical explanation for his presence, but Clara could not shake the sensation that he'd lied, that coming here to pick up Lacey's trunk was a convenient excuse that popped into his mind before he blurted out the truth.

Clara wished that those who had avoided taking a stand against this . . . this savage could see him as she saw him this moment. They wouldn't fear him nearly as much. He appeared vulnerable, confused, uncertain.

But then, perhaps men would not notice these subtle weaknesses in another man. Outwardly John Bradford appeared strong and as potentially violent as ever. Perhaps it took a woman to look beyond sheer physical strength and spot the small chinks in his armor.

Perhaps a woman had put those chinks there.

Clara unaccountably found herself smiling at the thought that her friend Lacey might have, in such a brief amount of time, rocked this stoic woodsman to his core.

John tried valiantly, but he could not summon a denial of the redheaded scold's accusation. He had come here, to this place. Now, when his heart was troubled, he had instinctively sought comfort from those against whom he had sworn to gain revenge.

He felt physically sick at the realization.

Thank God it was this bossy woman, this brash redhead, Lacey's friend, who had spotted him before he'd made an utter fool of himself.

He had never, since being forced to come to Virginia, spent one minute within the confines of the settlement without good purpose. He knew none of the settlers well, not even the few surviving men who had been boys with him in London. They had not fought the bonds of servitude so strongly as he, but had toiled as indentured servants as the

Company had decreed, and over the years they had developed a resentment against *him* for their position rather than aiming their anger at the faceless entity responsible for robbing them of their freedom.

So why, when his heart was heavy, had he come here, as if he had been seeking comfort or advice?

Because he wished he had a friend. Unprovoked, that idea flickered through his mind and stunned him to his core with the truth it held. He had been lonely for so long, but he had endured. He did not understand why, but taking Lacey had made him feel this loneliness on a level he'd never suspected. It was awful, confronting the truth of his solitude.

The female yammering away at him about Indians and turkeys was Lacey's friend. Her complexion had gone the color of bricks; her hair sprang out in wiry curls between the agitated fingers she kept raking through it. There was no doubt of her sincerity. She worried for her friend.

At the moment John could think of no more priceless treasure than a true friend. Someone to share confidences with, to seek advice from. He thought of Lacey alone there in his cabin. He'd not once bothered to go in and tell her he wouldn't be there in the morning. He'd justified his failure to do so by reassuring himself that he knew she would be safe. If he were honest with himself, he would have to admit that he'd known walking back into the cabin would mean he likely wouldn't be able to walk back out—not until he'd lain with her and taken her again and again.

He'd left her and patrolled the area surrounding the cabin to make sure no Indians lurked there watching, and then, without even thinking where he would go or why he had to go, he'd found himself here.

If he was feeling this confused, this uncertain, then Lacey might be feeling the same. She might be aching at that very moment for the comforts only a true friend could provide.

"Come back with me," he said to Clara.

She stopped talking in mid-tirade and gaped at him in surprise. "What did you say?"

"Come back with me."

"Why? So you can have two women at your mercy?"

"No, that's not it at all."

"Then what is it?"

Maybe she'll find something to like about me if I bring her friend to her, John thought. But he could not say that aloud; indeed, he didn't like admitting it even to himself.

"She needs help; she's completely inept."

"So you're looking for a housemaid."

"No, I . . ." He snapped shut his jaw before he could embarrass himself more. "If you're so worried about her, you'll come back with me. If not, then return to your lodgings and cease bothering me with your accusations."

She scowled. He had her there!

Long moments passed.

"You've certainly had a change of heart."

"I've always cautioned against trusting the Indians."

"Not about that. About Lacey. Mr. Malmford told me you meant to use her and discard her. A man doesn't haul heavy trunks and arrange for domestic help for a woman he means to rid himself of."

He reeled inwardly once more. With almost her

last words, Lacey had declared her intentions to leave him. He'd agreed to guide her back to the settlement this very morning. She was probably pacing the cabin, itching to be on her way. The last thing she would expect was for him to show up with her belongings and her friend.

But maybe bringing those things to her would say all the things he couldn't find the words for.

She would know, when she saw how he'd worked to bring those things to her, that he wanted her to stay.

Then, even though he'd not managed to say the words to make her understand, she would understand. If she still wanted to go, he would know she did so with no misunderstandings between them.

"Her things—were they left behind in James City?"

"No. I made sure they were brought here so I could keep an eye on them. And I am glad I did. These louts might just have declared her dead and gone and confiscated all her belongings."

John wished they had. Then he'd have a perfect excuse to keep Lacey just the way she'd been as he last saw her, naked and rosy from his loving, and with nothing to wear but those things he would happily provide for her.

"Let's get her things," he said.

"Mine, too. I'm not moving in without my belongings."

"I have to speak to the settlers anyway."

Percy never enjoyed the long walk home after a day tending the tobacco plants. By then his back was aching from bending all day, his legs quivering from squatting, and walking through the forest from his acres to the Hedgingses' was one layer of tiredness added to the rest of it. Now, though, he found his step quickening a little as he approached the house. Clara was there. Clara's lively conversation, her laughter, her quick wit, provided a spark that had been missing when it was just him and the Hedgingses choking down an unpalatable dinner after a long day's work.

Yesterday Clara had been watching for him. His tiredness had lifted; his spirits had soared, just because a friendly face beamed a smile his way. Now he found himself squinting through the trees for the first glimpse of her bright-red hair, and he strained to hear the first far-off sounds of her laughter. His senses failed him this day, though, because he made it all the way to the cabin without seeing or hearing anything interesting. Not that he was interested in Clara Cutler—it was just that she provided a nice change from the faces and voices and conversation that had grown tedious and familiar over the long months. That was all it was.

He trudged the final few yards, wondering why she didn't poke her head out the door. Maybe she'd popped into the necessary. Gentlemen didn't think along those lines, and especially they didn't think of tall, willowy ladies like Clara lifting their skirts to reveal long, long legs. . . .

The tricks exhaustion played on a man's mind! He shook those improper thoughts away and stopped to scrape his shoes before going into the cabin.

And still he didn't hear her.

Yesterday, she'd kept up a constant chatter while working with Mrs. Hedgings. He could hear metal clattering and Mrs. Hedgings's heavy stomp as she crossed from hearth to table. But no Clara.

"Good evening, ladies," he called as he stepped into the kitchen.

"Evening, Mr. Bledsoe."

"Evening, Percy."

Only the Hedgingses greeted him. Mr. Hedgings sat already at the table, and Mrs. Hedgings joined him in an instant. "Wash water's warm in the bucket," she said. "Rub off the dust and we're set to eat."

Percy cleaned his hands and joined them at the table. To his astonishment, Mr. Hedgings dug immediately into the bowl of stewed meat and vegetables that made up their dinner. Percy cleared his throat. Mr. Hedgings took no notice as he continued spooning food onto his plate.

"I say, shouldn't we wait for Miss Cutler?" he asked.

Mr. Hedgings let the load plop from the spoon and then harrumphed with annoyance. "We've seen the last of that one," he said.

"I don't understand."

"She up and left," said Mrs. Hedgings. "After we bent over backward to take her in, she picked up her belongings and took off."

"Took off?" Dismay shot through Percy, stunning in its intensity. A thought occurred that made his heart lurch. "Did somebody ask for her hand?"

"I fully intend to write to the Virginia Company to complain of the morals exhibited by the young women they sent on this last ship," said Mr. Hedgings. "It's bad enough that Cochran woman let him take her off, but for Miss Cutler to go as well, there's just no accounting for it."

"Please, will one of you explain to me what happened."

"Miss Cutler ran off with John Bradford."

"What?"

"They came here and she packed her belongings while Bradford regaled me with the same old cockamamie story about not trusting the Indians. He had the nerve to say we ought to yank out some of the tobacco and plant some cabbages and suchlike and hope we could harvest them before winter."

"The man has no shame," sniffed Mrs. Hedgings. "Claiming that we settlers are upsetting the Indians by not preparing for winter. As if *he* spends one hour a day doing honest work."

"Some nerve indeed," added Mr. Hedgings. "Spouting all that nonsense about Indians, and even suggesting we pick up and leave Malvern's Hundred before winter—I say he babbled that nonsense just to keep us from getting in a word edgewise about that woman he stole."

"John . . . babbled?" The notion was so strange that Percy couldn't believe it.

"Wouldn't stop talking about it, and when I told him to keep his opinions to himself, didn't he march himself off to Ellicott's and start yammering away about the same things? Malmford finally ran him off."

"And Miss Cutler went with him."

"And you just let her go?"

"What were we to do? She wanted to go."

He remembered Clara's abiding concern for Lacey. "She went to see if her friend is all right."

"As far as this hundred is concerned, the two of them can stay with that wild man. Decent folks in this settlement have no use for the likes of them."

"You're being completely unfair. Lacey Cochran

had no choice in the matter. Miss Cutler should be admired, not denigrated, for doing what she can to see to Miss Cochran's well-being."

The Hedgingses had the grace to look embarrassed.

Percy slumped back in his seat as exhaustion overwhelmed him. He had no appetite for the unappealing food congealing in the dish in front of him.

Clara was gone.

He had promised her that he would help her find Lacey . . . eventually. He'd put his own work and needs ahead of hers.

But why had John Bradford come to the hundred? Without returning Miss Cochran? Why had he tried so hard to convince the settlers to change their ways? What he knew of the man told Percy that John's advice should be heeded, not dismissed.

"Something's not right," he said.

"Eat your supper, Mr. Bledsoe. You'll feel better about things once you have a full belly."

With sickening clarity, Percy realized that what she said was true. How many times had he trudged home from the tobacco work dispirited beyond belief, aching with all his being to get back to England. A dinner, a night of sleep, and the next morning it would seem logical to drag himself out to the tobacco and start all over again.

There ought to be more to life than drudgery. Ought to be a purpose to the hard work other than satisfying the demands of a corporation. Ought to be someone whose very presence could cheer him, make him laugh, share his satisfactions and disappointments.

For the few short hours Clara had been there, his life had been a bit brighter. He'd let his apathy,

his ingrained habits, take precedence over the
promises he'd made to her.

The food before him suddenly seemed like a
symbol of all that had gone wrong. He moved to
push it away, but his hand hovered just short of
the plate. He could eat it as his hungry belly
demanded and then sleep as his aching muscles
demanded, and let apathy claim him once more.

Or he could eat and let the barely palatable food
serve as the fuel to propel his life in a new direction.

He pulled the plate closer.

CHAPTER 12

The sun had set, and a darkness unique to the forest setting began filling the cabin with gloom. Lacey sat, with no purpose, on the bed. There seemed nothing to do. She'd made bargains with herself over and over throughout the day: *If I get dressed, he'll come back through the door. If I boil some water for tea, he'll come back. If I find something to eat, he'll come back.* On and on it had gone, until there seemed but one thing left to try: sit and wait, and hope that when the sun set he would come back.

Surely he would come back.

He could not mean to leave her there alone to face the night.

Again.

"He's capable of it," she said aloud. Maybe saying it aloud and hearing the truth ring from the walls would quiet the denial her heart yearned to cry: *He left me alone right after.*

Yes, he'd left her—and he'd stayed away. One

expected a man of quality like Pumphrey Fallsworth to leave a woman's bed for the comforts of his own opulent lodgings. She knew that Amanda Stivington's parents did not sleep together despite occasionally sharing a bed, and from conversations with her fellow servants, she knew it was the same in other households.

But in grand manors, the men had their own comfortable rooms to withdraw to. Where did John Bradford have to go? What did he find more interesting than the warm and far-too-willing woman lying in the bed beside him?

She'd lain awake for an hour or more after he'd left the bed, wanting him to come back, gradually admitting that he wouldn't, until disappointment and exhaustion swept her into sleep. She'd wakened to sun streaming through the window. She'd wakened to not knowing whether he'd been back at all during the night, or whether he'd been so disappointed in what he'd learned about her that he'd left her to her own devices.

She'd wakened alone.

She ought to be accustomed to solitude. Although she seldom spent any time physically alone, women like herself learned to withdraw into themselves for the privacy they needed. A young girl sent away from home at the age of five learned quickly that cooks and maids and the quality had children of their own and no love to spare for a homesick and confused young stranger. A teenaged girl learned that the companionship offered by young men usually endured for no longer than an hour or two.

A young woman learned that while her mistress might reveal all her secrets and confidences while bathing and having herself dressed, that same mistress would look right through the maid as if she didn't exist when female companionship of her own status came calling.

Lacey knew how to perform her duties, eat her meals, and tend her personal chores with just a small part of her mind focused on the task at hand while the biggest part of her roamed wild and free. Many times in her daydreams, she had imagined all the wonderful things she would do if she ever found herself with an hour or two to call her very own, with not another person within sight or hearing.

She had found it impossible to imagine.

Until now, she had never been physically alone for more than a few moments. The only thing she wanted was for it to end. John wasn't coming back, which meant she would have to find her way back to the settlement.

They would all speculate on what might have happened to her out here in the woods. They would wonder why she'd had to find her way back to them on her own.

She could tell them she'd escaped from John.

She could tell them he'd grown bored with her and left her to her own devices.

The first choice would merely lay another layer of lies on top of the ones she'd already told. The second choice would mean she would finally tell the truth and face the consequences. Neither prospect promised to be pleasant.

As much as she dreaded facing the colonists, she feared even more the thought of making her way back there through the woods and the water.

Well, she had come halfway around the world, and she knew the settlement lay less than a half day's journey away. She would simply take herself back there. In the morning. It would be difficult enough to find her way through the forest without attempting it in the dark.

Oh, God. The mere thought of trying to find the settlement filled her with sick dread. She would have to fight like a tigress to find her way back to people who would look at her as if she were a whore. She had no sense of direction. The woods had looked all alike to her on the way here. John had seemed able to recognize clues from things like a twisted tree, an oddly shaped rock, but she had no idea of how she would ever find her way back.

Perhaps she would meet her end here in these woods, endlessly lost. Not so different from the way her soul had felt for a long, long time.

Something moved outside.

She grew even more still. She had been sitting there all day, listening, absorbing the sounds of the place. The sheer beauty of birdsong, the rich rustle of wind through the leaves, were sounds that a woman could spend a lifetime learning and loving. One seldom had the opportunity to hear nature when one's domain was her lady's chambers. She had tried to memorize all that she heard, and this sound was new.

John? Her heart leaped at the notion, and she tamed it down, telling herself that any joy at seeing him again would stem only from relief. But almost at once she wished she had allowed herself to indulge in the joy, because next she remembered his warnings about Indians.

Maybe she need not fear being lost in the woods and dying of thirst or starvation. Maybe she'd be murdered right here.

John had promised to teach her to find the

advantage in every situation. He'd told her a person had to be brave and strong enough to reach out and demand what she wanted.

She did not know what she wanted. She did know what she did not want. She did not want to die.

She especially did not want to meet her death sitting still as a stone atop a bed that had revealed her for a liar. She rose and hurried to John's skip hole. She could survive in there and escape if need be. But when she closed the door behind her, when the absolute darkness and stillness of the room closed around her like a grave, she knew she couldn't stay there either.

She opened the door to peek out into the cabin in search of a weapon. She laughed silently to realize she'd inadvertently reinforced John's idea that she was incapable of doing housework, for she'd done nothing but dither all day. She hadn't done a lick of work. She didn't know where he kept things. Specifically, things capable of causing damage to another person's head.

She would have to stay in the cellar. With the water contraption. The troughs! The water troughs that had been the start of her trouble the night before . . . Perhaps it would be fitting to meet her death while wielding one of those. She went to the water contraption and tried to wrench one free. Despite John's assurance that the pitch he used to hold them together wasn't particularly strong, it took her several good tugs and twists before she freed one of the heavy troughs.

She tried brandishing it over her head; the weight taxed her strength, and within seconds her arms quivered from the strain of holding it.

But it would have to do.

She edged out of the cellar and toward the front

door. Cracked it open. Peeked outside. And was so delighted by what she found that she flung open the door and ran outside shrieking.

"Clara! Oh, Clara, I am so happy to see you!"

John was there too, standing dark and silent alongside Clara, watching the reunion between her and her friend with absolutely no expression. Something inside her quickened at the sight of him.

He made no sound of greeting, no movement toward her. To her consternation she realized that every step she took had been aimed directly at him, toward the arms that had opened wide for her the night before. Those arms now rested stiffly at his sides.

She would not fling herself against him like a forgiving puppy welcoming home its returning master. She slowed. She had to do something to cover up the way she'd been drawn toward him. "Here." She shoved the trough at him so she could embrace Clara. "Oh, Clara, why are you here? I don't care why you're here. I'm just so happy to see you."

She was babbling. Clara laughed. They hugged. They jumped like schoolgirls, round and about, giggling.

"I explained the situation," said John. "She thought it best if she came."

Lacey faltered in mid-jump.

"He told you?" Oh, God, how it hurt to know that this man had told her very best friend about her wanton capitulation!

"I must say I'm not surprised," Clara said. "A woman of your status has no need to know how to handle housekeeping chores for a savage."

"She'll take care of the house for us," said John.

For us. Us. Lacey's heart skipped a beat while delight coursed through her. He'd changed his mind! He wanted her to stay with him after all!

Lacey didn't know whether to feel thrilled or humiliated. It was obvious John considered her completely incompetent, despite her protestations to the contrary. He had wanted her that way, and he would stubbornly continue to fit her into the mold he'd devised. But he wanted her! Given enough time, she could convince him of her abilities.

And then a second, more chilling thought froze her in place.

Clara Cutler, lady, had no more knowledge of how to handle household chores than Lacey's former mistress had.

"What makes you think Clara is any more adept at housekeeping skills than I am?" she asked him.

"She said she was."

"I see." She thought she might faint from the pain of hearing him say this. How easily he accepted Clara at her word. He'd *asked* Clara, obviously. He had never asked her, Lacey, anything of importance, and when she'd tried to stand up for herself, he'd ignored her as if she hadn't spoken.

"Why did you bring my things when you know I don't intend to remain here?"

"She thought you would want them."

Again, deferring to Clara rather than considering her own wishes.

A hot spear of jealousy stabbed her to her core, quickly replaced by something worse.

He'd gotten what he wanted from her, and it hadn't been enough. He could have returned her to the settlement, but instead he'd left her here and had gone on his own to the place he professed to hate.

He'd used her as bait to lure Clara to this place.

Sweet Clara, virginal Clara, so trusting and innocent that she had probably believed John when he'd said Lacey needed some help with the house.

He hadn't brought Clara to the cabin out of concern for Lacey's loneliness or confusion. There was no reason for him to believe that Clara would be any more likely than she to know how to perform household chores in a rough wilderness cabin.

Bringing another woman to the cabin gave him double the leverage for his revenge. And it told Lacey without words that he did not value at all the one thing she had to offer him: her body. With another person in the tiny cabin, they would have no privacy at all. There would be no more repeats of their lovemaking.

His aloofness, his refusal to look at her, took on new meaning. While she'd been carried away the night before by passion, he'd been coldly calculating ways to sweeten his revenge. He'd found it. He'd used her own lies and deceits to lure yet another woman here. Clara would no doubt be as ruined as she was, and it was all Lacey's fault for allowing him to persist in his belief that she was a helpless blue blood.

The way they looked at each other. The way Lacey leaned almost imperceptibly toward him, as if she were drawn to him by a magnetic force. The way his hand kept reaching toward her and falling back, as if he ached to touch her but could not let himself do it . . . Clara shivered at the romance of it all.

She had been an observer all her life of the

attraction between men and women. Men and other women. She had stood witness while meaningful glances seduced without words. She had felt the change in the air when a woman's smile turned from one of humor to one of surrender.

But never before had she sensed an attraction so powerful that it was almost palpable. Here in these woods, while birds screeched and trees rustled and unseen creatures scuffled through the undergrowth, she fancied she could hear the quickening of Lacey and John's heartbeats just from standing near each other.

And yet they would not look at each other. Or speak to each other. No doubt the unfortunate circumstances surrounding their meeting contributed to their agitation. How ironic if, in kidnapping Lacey, John had somehow latched on to the one woman in this world who was meant for him, but by his very actions had made it impossible for her to love him. And if Lacey had been snatched away by the one man who could complete her heart—but could not see beyond the pain and humiliation of being carried away against her will.

Why, the two of them required a matchmaker!

And she, Clara Cutler, had been matchmaking all her life.

"All right, Mr. Bradford, take our things into the cabin."

He blinked at her and stood still as a statue.

"Now!" She shooed him into action with a wave of her hands. "I swear, Lacey, I can't imagine why the good Lord gave this man lips, he exercises them so seldom."

To her immense satisfaction, Lacey blushed deeply, a sign if Clara ever saw one that Lacey was

intimately aware of the uses to which John Bradford
put his lips.

He, in turn, stared at Lacey's lips. Oh, yes, this
was going very well indeed.

Without another word, he hoisted the sticks over
his shoulders and dragged the conveyance he'd
rigged to carry their belongings on toward the
cabin. Lacey turned to follow, but Clara stopped
her with a touch.

"Let him go on ahead," she said. "We have so
much to talk about."

"Oh, Clara, I wish you weren't here, and yet at
the same time I am so grateful that you are. I am
so confused."

"I imagine you must be. I am, too. I don't have
the faintest notion of how to do chores around a
cabin."

"Of . . . of course you don't."

Clara gazed shrewdly at her friend. "That's not
what you meant, is it?"

Lacey hesitated. She appeared to be doing battle
with an inner voice. "Have you ever been face to
face with a man who portrays himself as one thing,
completely wrong for you, and yet in your soul you
feel there is something drawing you toward him?"

"Much to my surprise, I have indeed recently
made the acquaintance of a man who presents that
very conundrum."

"Who would that be?"

"You didn't have a chance to meet him. Your
John hauled you away before Mr. Bledsoe introduced himself to me."

Clara felt herself blushing.

"Clara? Did you find a match?"

"Oh, no, nothing like that. I was drawn to Mr.
Bledsoe purely on a friendship basis. He was so

kind, such a gentleman. He gave up his own comfortable lodgings just to save me the drudgery of
lodging with a family who was looking for unpaid
labor.''

"He sounds like a remarkable man."

"He is."

"Well, perhaps you and he—"

Clara interrupted Lacey before she could say anything embarrassing. "Mr. Bledsoe plans to return
to England as soon as he accumulates enough
tobacco to pay his passage."

"The love of a good woman might change his
mind."

"It might." Clara refused to let Lacey draw her
into admitting any romantic feelings for Percy,
especially since she had none. "He believes he
won't marry here, because he believes he is not
attractive enough to draw the interest of a woman.
A tragic loss to the community, I must say, and it
seems to me very shortsighted of the women who
are the right size for him to have overlooked him."

"The right size for him?"

"Someone who is not so tall as I am. Someone
not so . . . robustly healthy."

"Perhaps he wants a tall and robust woman."

Clara's face warmed. "I can understand completely how demoralizing it was to be always skipped
over in favor of someone more attractive. Why, I'd
spent no more than five minutes in Mr. Bledsoe's
company before I recognized him as pure sterling.
Pure sterling."

Too bad she was too tall, too thin, too old for
him. If they were not so physically incompatible,
they might make a good match.

But she wasn't here in the wilderness to sigh over
her own lack of prospects—she was here to help

Lacey. A very agitated Lacey. A Lacey who appeared to be on the verge of falling in love. Clara felt a pang of what might be jealousy tempered by caring. She loved Lacey like a sister, and yet she couldn't help wishing she would herself one day know what it might feel like inside to be so affected by a man.

"Tell me all about it, Lacey," she urged. "Everything. Maybe between the two of us we can figure out a way to make things right."

Lacey stared at her, her eyes welling with tears. She dashed them away and tilted her head, assuming a stance of bravery that Clara found highly commendable.

"Oh, Clara, I just pray you will find it in your heart to forgive me after I tell you the truth."

Clara squeezed Lacey's hand reassuringly.

"I never meant to deceive you," Lacey said. "Well, I mean, I certainly meant to deceive people, but I expected to deceive only a man, and never expected to find a friend as dear as you, and you cannot know how it has torn me apart to know I have not been truthful with you."

"I've just gotten here, Lacey, and so far all we've done is talk about Percy Bledsoe, a man you've never met. What is all this talk about *you* deceiving *me*? Start from the beginning. I'm afraid you're making no sense."

Part of Lacey wanted to simply blurt out the truth and be done with it. But she'd spent a lifetime keeping her thoughts to herself, lowering her head, and holding her tongue when criticized or questioned.

She was like John in that way, she realized. Hiding her features to avoid revealing her vulnerabilities. Of all the people in this new land, she might be the only one capable of understanding what lay behind his outward aloofness.

John would understand that one such as she had no business making friends with a woman of Clara's position. It had been essential to her deception that she socialize with women who were her betters. She'd always felt such a fraud, even when the possibility she would be discovered was remote.

Would the caring and concern she read in Clara's expression shift to loathing? She didn't think she could stand it just now if she lost Clara's friendship as well as John. *Keep your secrets,* whispered a little voice inside her.

But if she was right and John had figured out the truth about her, he might tell Clara, and that would be worse.

Oh, God, she'd woven such a web of deceit, and no matter which way she turned, she bound herself more tightly within it.

"Lacey, it cannot be so bad." Clara squeezed her hand.

"It is." Lacey's voice shook. "You will hate me for it."

"I cannot imagine ever hating you."

Lacey recognized the ring of truth in Clara's voice. Recognized that she had gravitated toward Clara's friendship for a reason: the two of them did enjoy a special closeness that made the difference between acquaintances and friends.

Lacey did not want to lose that along with everything else.

John had told her that someone who was strong and brave, someone who reached out to demand what they wanted, could succeed.

She could cower now, assume her lady's-maid stance, and refuse to explain herself. Or she could meet her friend's eyes and clearly admit the truth and trust to the instincts that had made her friends with this woman in the first place.

"I'm not what you think I am, Clara. I am not Amanda Stivington's distant cousin."

"Well, then, who are you?" Clara didn't sound frightened or annoyed—merely curious.

"I'm a fraud." Lacey swallowed. "An imposter. I don't have one drop of Stivington blood in my veins."

"You mean you're not related to the Stivingtons at all?"

"That's one way of putting it."

Before Lacey begin her explanation, Clara chuckled. "I'm quite glad to hear that. I never wanted to tell you because you seemed so nice and so unlike the rest of them, but I could never abide the Stivingtons."

"You . . . you know Amanda?"

"Only casually. We met once or twice at dinner parties. You weren't there, of course."

"I—I might've been."

Clara cocked her head quizzically.

"I was most likely in attendance, awaiting Amanda's summonses along with the other servants."

Clara tipped her head the other way.

"I'm a lady's maid, Clara."

"You? You were Amanda Stivington's lady's maid?" Clara clapped a hand over her mouth after squealing the words.

Lacey nodded her head miserably.

Clara burst into laughter.

Lacey's head snapped up. "What's so funny?"

"My own lady's maid was a doddering old dear who could barely bend her arthritic fingers around the handle of a brush. She was delighted to retire when I decided to go on this adventure. My parents once told me that they would never allow me to have a maid close to my own age because there was no end to the mischief two young females could concoct together.''

"Your parents told you that?"

"Aye, and judging from my friends' exploits, they knew what they were doing.''

"You mean . . . friends of yours and their maids . . .''

"One escapade after another! How I envied them!"

"You didn't think less of them for consorting with someone below them in status?"

"Oh, Lacey, status means nothing when a person is lonely. Status means nothing when the only source of love and comfort is the lap of a cook, or the warm embrace of your governess. My maid was my closest confidante. I could not have loved her more if I had been the child of her loins.''

Lacey couldn't think of a thing to say.

"So what trouble did Amanda Stivington devise, and why are you the one who is paying for it?''

Lacey had never considered her problem in quite that way, but she realized with a shock that it was indeed true. None of this would have happened if Amanda Stivington had not been bored, restless . . . and in need of a friend.

"We are rather alike physically—rather small in size, an overabundance of hair, large eyes. It amused her to let me wear her clothes and pass myself off as her cousin when we were away from the house.''

Clara nodded. "Go on.''

"We were walking through Lyndley Park one day when a man . . . a gentleman . . . by the name of

Pumphrey Fallsworth strolled toward us along with someone known to Amanda. We were introduced.''

"And?"

."And . . ." Lacey swallowed. "Amanda found him fascinating, but Mr. Fallsworth took a fancy to me."

"I see."

Lacey didn't think Clara could see at all. Clara had not been there when Amanda returned home from a tea in a vicious rage because she'd attempted to flirt with Pumphrey and he'd asked instead where her pretty little cousin might be.

"Amanda wanted to humiliate Mr. Fallsworth and so urged me to continue the ruse with him. We met secretly a number of times."

"He fell in love with you."

"He thought he did. It was not love, but more like an obsession. He frightened me, Clara. I wanted to tell him the truth and end it, but by then I'd come to recognize his true nature and I feared . . . I feared what might happen if he realized how he'd been duped."

Her voice caught as the old dread twisted through her. She could never adequately convey to Clara how afraid she'd been of Pumphrey. At first she'd assumed that her prickles of worry stemmed from the deception she was playing on him. But all too soon she'd come to realize that he meant it when he'd threatened her. Meant it when he'd said, "There is no place in this world where you can escape me, my pretty one. . . ."

"I think you're shouldering more of the blame for this situation than warranted. I'd guess Amanda played a greater role than you're telling me."

Lacey nodded, but she would not refuse to accept the blame for what she'd done. "I knew from the first that I shouldn't have done what I did. I could have put a stop to it before it went on so long. But I . . . I wanted to do it."

"Did you care for him so much?"

"No, although in my defense, I always thought my affection would grow. It did not, and I knew he would never be able to fill the need. . . ."

She let her explanation trail away. It was so hard to explain the aching emptiness inside her, the near-constant yearning that had plagued her for years. Those wayward feelings were what had led her to fall in with Amanda's crazy schemes, and what had propelled her into Pumphrey Fallsworth's arms, searching, hoping.

Never finding. Until here in this wild place, in the arms of John Bradford, who did not want her.

"I had to get away from him," Lacey said. "Amanda wanted rid of me, too, lest Pumphrey find out her role in all of this. She arranged everything. Obtained the church references, procured my passage, provided clothes and a bit of money. And now here I am."

"And what if your Mr. Fallsworth demands to know what's become of you?"

"Amanda swore she would not tell."

Clara studied her, her expression grave. "You said you were afraid of Mr. Fallsworth. He sounds like a frightening fellow. Do you believe Amanda Stivington will stand up to him if he attempts to . . . persuade her?"

Amanda never did anything that caused her distress or inconvenience, but she had been as frightened of Pumphrey as Lacey had been. Even so, they had agreed that putting an ocean between them was the best option.

No matter how obsessed he claimed to be with

her, Pumphrey Fallsworth would never turn his back on his luxurious life in England to go chasing after Lacey. Never.

"I pray she has never been tested in that manner," Lacey said.

"I must say I am astounded—and I greatly admire your daring. How I wish I possessed even a fraction of your courage!"

"I'm not daring. At this moment I'm depressed and confused and I don't know what to do."

"That's why I'm here. We'll soon sort it out."

CHAPTER 13

Lacey tugged at her neckline and took a deep breath, wondering why she felt so stifled, so *cramped*.

She and Clara stood in the middle of the cabin's one room with plenty of empty space surrounding them. Sparse furnishings and golden-bright late afternoon light streaming through the window and door ought to make the room seem huge. Certainly during those long, lonely hours when she'd sat all but paralyzed with inaction on the bed, waiting for John to come home, the cabin had seemed like an enormous, echoing ballroom.

Clara was tall but not large. She took up no more floor space than a chair. It didn't seem possible that it was her presence that made the walls seem closer, the ceiling lower, the air stale.

One additional person didn't make that much difference in the space, Lacey knew. If she were honest with herself, she had to admit the truth.

Much as she loved Clara and welcomed her company, Lacey wished Clara weren't there.

She wished John had come back alone.

She wished that partly because she harbored the fear that John had brought Clara back solely to involve her in his revenge. But she wished so even more because she wanted to be alone with him. Gloriously, wantonly alone.

Something that would be impossible now.

John walked through the door, balancing Clara's trunk on his shoulder. He lowered it and stacked it atop Lacey's, which already sat along a wall. The room seemed to shrink in on itself even more. Lacey tugged once more at her collar.

"That won't do," said Clara. "We shall both need access to those trunks to make our preparations for the night."

He hesitated for a moment, and then he lifted the top trunk away and set it on the floor alongside the other. He stood looking at the two trunks, and Lacey found herself doing the same. She remembered her first look at this cabin, how its impeccable cleanliness and touches of beauty had marked it thoroughly as John's. The trunks seemed an intrusion: overly large, shrieking of strangeness in this home he had built and furnished with his own hands.

"It's only temporary," she blurted out.

He said nothing for a long moment, and then he nudged Clara's trunk with his foot. "Aye."

She felt a plunging of her spirit at hearing him acknowledge how briefly she would be present in his life. What had she expected, that he would whirl about, grab her into his arms, and declare he wanted her to stay with him always?

He'd never given the slightest indication that his desires led in that direction.

Clara headed for her trunk, and seeing her friend alongside her lover jarred Lacey completely out of her wistful daydreaming. Not only had John never hinted he wanted her on a long-term basis, but he'd brought Clara to live with them. Even if he had no nefarious purposes in mind for Clara, bringing her here effectively meant he wanted nothing more to do with Lacey, for they would not be able to claim one single moment of privacy.

She tugged at her neckline again.

"Come and get a fresh gown from your trunk, Lacey," said Clara, obviously misunderstanding Lacey's agitation with her garment.

"In a moment," she said, oddly reluctant to delve back into that trunk, as if doing so would mean reaching back into the past when she wanted with all her heart to stay here, in this place and time. "You should let me show you around the cabin first. John ... Mr. Bradford ... has made some remarkable innovations to this place."

She glanced his way as she spoke; it was only polite to acknowledge somebody's presence when you mentioned their name. For once, instead of looking away, his glance met hers, held it, and she felt powerless to draw away from what she read there, as if no words had ever been so precious to him as hearing her say that he had done something remarkable with his cabin.

But a heartbeat later, he turned his head and she wondered if she'd really read that in his eyes, or if she had merely wanted to see it there.

"Come," she said, tugging at Clara's hand and leading her toward the back door.

"Oh, not outside, Lacey. I've had enough of the outdoors to last me a full year."

"This doesn't lead outside." She pulled open the door to reveal the secret area John had hollowed from the hill. Only a little light penetrated that far, and so the wondrous water contraption looked little better than a collection of pieces of wood.

"What's this, a secret hiding place?" Clara clapped her hands in delight.

"A passage," John said curtly.

"Even better! Let's explore." Clara lifted her skirts, looking as if she meant to traverse the passage, and Lacey felt embarrassed that she'd not shown even a trace of the enthusiasm Clara was showing.

In fact, anybody chancing to observe them would no doubt think Clara was the woman who wanted to make this remote handbuilt cabin her home for the rest of her life.

"No exploring," said John. "It's designed for survival, not entertainment."

Clara wasn't paying him the slightest bit of attention. She'd swung open the door as wide as it would go, allowing the waning afternoon light to illuminate the cellarlike space. Lacey studied what she had not paid much attention to before: a man-sized opening near the floor, which led to the tunnel snaking back into the hill. The day before, she'd been too flustered by John's nearness, by what had happened with the water, to even look at the room, much less notice the tunnel. And earlier when she'd retreated there for safety, she'd stood in the dark.

Clara crouched down and peered into the tunnel. "My goodness, going in there would be like crawling into a grave." She tentatively touched a wall and pebbles showered down. "A grave indeed! Why, this dirt would fall and seal the hole up right behind you!"

"That's the idea."

Clara stood and brushed her hands together. She glanced at Lacey and the two of them shivered. "You're right, Mr. Bradford, it is not entertainment. I can't imagine wanting to go in there."

"You would if you were being chased," said John.

"You sound as if you speak from experience."

"I have some experience."

Lacey rolled her hands into fists to prevent herself from reaching out to stroke him. There was such a wealth of pain and sad memories in his voice. "Indians are a constant threat," she said, to spare him.

"Not Indians." John offered that tidbit of information but did not elaborate. Clara rolled her eyes toward Lacey.

"He probably based it on a skip hole he remembers from his misspent youth," Clara said with a chuckle.

Lacey was sure Clara meant the comment as a joke, but John stiffened, whitened, and seemed to stop breathing for a moment. Something about Clara's jest had struck him hard, and Lacey did not know what part of it.

She did not know anything about him, she realized. She knew nothing at all. She knew only that he bore a grudge against the Virginia Company for forcing him to come here, and that he seemed to have very fixed notions about women of high status. She laughed, a bit falsely, but she hoped brightly enough to lighten the sudden tension.

"Dear Clara, Mr. Bradford did not have a misspent youth. He's highly incensed at the Virginia Company for forcing him to come here. He must have led an exemplary life back in England."

"That's not the way it was, is it, Mr. Bradford?" Clara asked gently.

In answer, John bolted from the cellar.

Lacey heard his long, quick strides cross the wooden floor, and the sound of the door closing behind him as he left the cabin.

"Clara, what was all that about?"

"You don't know very much about him, do you?"

Lacey considered what little she did know about John. A vow never again to be dirty. The treasuring of the simple beauty found in a stone or a leaf. She shook her head. "Some things. Not much."

"They talk about him back in the settlement. He grew up an orphan on the streets of London."

"Then why—" Lacey stopped herself from speculating aloud lest she divulge the full extent of John's plans to Clara. It had been bad enough to confess the truth about herself; she didn't think she could bear telling Clara that she found herself falling in love with a man who intended to use her only for revenge, and who might at that very moment be turning his eye toward Clara for the same reason.

"Remarkable," Clara said, sweeping her hand to encompass the cabin.

"Yes," Lacey said.

She had some familiarity with homeless orphans. Although Stivington Manor had sat too far outside the city to draw the endless stream of beggars drawn to closer homes, the half-starved waifs would often accost her and Amanda when they went shopping. She remembered torn and filthy clothing hanging in tatters from starvation-racked bodies. Young faces that should have been smiling with hope and curiosity instead pinched and drawn, eyes dull with defeat. She remembered how the bravest of them would sometimes dare approach and stand before her, mumbling, hand out, face averted, as if driven by his empty belly to do things his mind was a-shamed of.

She remembered how John so often averted his face, looked away, mumbled.

"I'm surprised he holds such animosity toward the Virginia Company for bringing him here," said Clara.

"Dear God." Lacey's voice shook with emotion. "They took from him the only thing he could call his own—his freedom."

She wasn't sure Clara could understand. "Street beggars are nameless, faceless, to everyone else. They own nothing. They live and die without being remarked upon, except for when they encounter the wrath of somebody they've robbed or inconvenienced."

"I see." Clara quickly sobered. "That explains it, then."

"Explains what?"

"Why he runs whenever someone comes close to discovering his vulnerability."

Was it true? Did John Bradford run to avoid being hurt? Could that be why he had left their bed and never returned? Why he tried to shield himself from Lacey by introducing Clara as a buffer between them?

"No doubt it's made him extremely territorial, too. Protective of his den, so to speak." Clara gestured around her at the neat cabin. "Everything just the way *he* likes it."

"It is his cabin," Lacey pointed out.

"Would I be correct in guessing that you would like to make it yours as well?"

Lacey bit her lip. She debated lying. Or at least evading the truth. And then she decided she was done with that sort of thing. "I'd like to stay."

"Very well. Let's make your mark on this place, so that he can't imagine living here without you."

"How would we do that?"

"I'm not really sure. But for starts, we'll simply try to get under his skin."

"You must have a rope somewhere, Mr. Bradford."

"I do," John said. "But I'll not be stringing it between trees for foolish purposes."

Clara and Lacey exchanged glances. Clara rolled her eyes. John set his jaw.

Clara had been interfering, rearranging, poking into every corner of his place from the moment she'd arrived. The trunks he'd set along the wall had been dragged to the middle of the room, where he tripped over one or the other of them every time he crossed the area. They gaped open to reveal mounds of silks and satins and fancy fripperies. Despite looking full to the brim, items had been removed, for there seemed to be no surface, no peg, no spare inch of his place that was not covered by ladies' things.

He'd worked hard to make this cabin exactly the way he wanted it. It ought to annoy him no end to see it being overtaken by two women. Instead, he found himself feeling surprisingly . . . indulgent.

He liked seeing evidence of Lacey's presence everywhere he looked.

This unexpected gentling of his nature worried

him. She didn't seem any more eager to stay here now than she'd seemed before he brought the annoying Clara home to her. It didn't seem like a good idea to get used to seeing Lacey's belongings strewn about, if she only meant to take them all away. For the sake of his pride, for the sake of his heart, he had to put an end to the overtaking of his retreat.

"No rope for you," said John.

"It is not a foolish purpose to air out our garments. They've been stored away for weeks onboard ship."

"What do you mean to do with the garments once they're aired?"

"Return them to the trunks, of course."

"Foolish." There didn't seem any way even Clara could argue with that. "There are more pressing chores awaiting your attention, madam."

"Clara, we can lay the clothing out over bushes and branches. Maybe he doesn't have a rope."

It smarted that Lacey would think he lacked a rope. "I do indeed have a rope. But they are not easy to come by here. It would have to be watched."

Clara's eyes rolled again. "I hardly think the rope will run off, Mr. Bradford."

"Not on its own," he agreed. "It would disappear soon enough if some Indian is lurking out there and sees it."

"Clara, we should heed him."

"Don't you let him scare you, Lacey. I heard all about him and his false warnings about the Indians. He merely fears they will usurp his profits."

"No, madam, I fear they will kill us all while our backs are turned on them."

"Clara—"

"Pay him no mind, Lacey. Go ahead and smooth

out that dress over that bush over there." She shooed Lacey away, and when John started to follow her, Clara gripped him by the arm. "You stay right here, sir. I will have a word with you."

He stood there in an impotent fury while Lacey did as Clara ordered. When at last Lacey was engaged in arranging her dress over a heavily leafed bush, Clara poked him in the ribs.

"You are no gentleman, John Bradford."

"I know that." He did; he knew it to his core, but it smarted hearing her state it aloud, especially with the memory of Lacey's frightened face haunting him. "You wrong me, though, by denying the truth of what I say about the Indians."

Clara made a dismissive sound. "Botheration, Indians. If you feel it is your manly duty to warn us about danger, then you can do so in a way that makes us feel like ladies and not like little children."

"Ladies." He found he couldn't take his eyes off Lacey as she spread a frothy yellow gown over the branches of another bush. He wished suddenly that he had risked his precious rope. Her beautiful dress could disappear just as easily as his rope. And he'd already taken so much from her. . . .

"Yes, she's a lady!" Clara seemed rather agitated, and suddenly strident. "She deserves to be treated with consideration and respect, no matter . . . well, just no matter what. Any woman deserves respect. Even if . . . no matter."

She was the most exasperating woman. She was red and bothered and he wanted nothing more than to walk away from her and disappear into the woods, except he knew she was right.

He was no gentleman. He did not know the right way to talk to a lady, to act with a lady.

Clara was Lacey's friend and was also a lady. Clara understood what Lacey wanted, what Lacey needed. He did not know how to react to the things they said to him; for example, at this very moment he could not shake the feeling that Clara was both telling him a truth and hiding something important from him, and he could not fathom what it might be.

"I don't know how to be a gentleman," he said. "I would have to be taught."

This succeeded in silencing her when all else had failed. She stood staring at him dumbfounded, when he heard a loud crashing in the brush.

Indians wouldn't move so carelessly unless they wanted to be heard, and yet when he peered into the dimness beneath the trees, he could see the shadow of a man moving toward them.

"Get into the cabin!" He shoved Clara toward the cabin, deciding gentlemanly behavior could wait until later. "Lacey! Come away from the trees. Get into the cabin."

He couldn't wait for her to comply with his order, and though it was the hardest thing he'd ever had to do in his life, he had to trust that she would heed his warning. He had to leave her exposed while he ran to the cabin for his musket.

Percy stumbled his way clear of the cursed woods into the clearing, and found himself facing a nightmare: John Bradford, his feet braced wide, his eyes narrowed with deadly intent as he peered down the sights of a fully primed and cocked musket aimed straight for Percy's vitals.

His knees commenced quaking from fear on top of exhaustion; his teeth chattered with such fright that he could barely manage to issue his demand.

"I've come to take you to account for abducting those women, John Bradford."

Bradford blinked. The musket wavered.

Bradford laughed.

Percy supposed that while being laughed at was humiliating, it was also a good sign; a fellow usually squinted along the sights in a very forbidding fashion when intending to take aim and shoot.

"It's bad enough that you absconded with Mistress Cochran, but to sneak into the settlement and make away with Mistress Cutler as well . . . well, it's simply intolerable."

Bradford lowered the gun and Percy breathed a silent prayer of relief.

"She insisted upon coming here."

"She never would. She's a lady."

Bradford scowled.

"Percy? Mr. Bledsoe, I mean? Is that you?" With a flurry of skirts and flyaway red hair whipping as she ran, Clara pounded up to them, followed closely by Lacey Cochran. "Look, Lacey—it *is* him. I knew I recognized his voice!"

Percy executed a stiff bow toward them. He smiled at Clara but directed his first comment toward Lacey. Somehow he didn't trust himself to speak to Clara just yet.

"I see you are looking well, Mistress Cochran. I don't need to tell you that everyone in the settlement is worried sick about you."

"They are?"

Clara sniffed. "Then why is it that you are the only person to come to see how she fares?"

"I came to see to your welfare as well, Mistress Cutler."

"Mine?" She blushed, a wild red that Percy couldn't recollect ever seeing on a woman's skin before.

It suited her somehow. In fact, she was the sort of woman who ought on purpose to seek out unusual cuts and colors—make a show of her uniqueness rather than trying to blend in with other women.

"I told you, Lacey," Clara said, her voice sounding suspiciously on the verge of trembling. "He's the only person who's been nice to me since we got here."

"Nonsense," Percy declared stoutly. "The Hedgingses are quite taken with you."

Her eyes turned suspiciously moist, and her nose reddened even more, and for a moment he feared she would burst into tears. "Mrs. Hedgings is too exhausted to be 'taken' by anything," she said to Lacey. "It is nice of you to say so, though, Mr. Bledsoe."

For some reason, Clara looked away from him to glare at Bradford, who looked decidedly uncomfortable with all the goings-on.

"Yes, some people around here could certainly benefit from a dose of gentlemanly example—oh!" Clara clapped her hands together and yelped, adding a little jump for emphasis. "Percy, I do believe God himself has had a hand in your arrival. Could you steal time from your daily business to stay here with us for a few days and train Mr. Bradford in the art of being a gentleman?"

"Now just a minute—" Bradford began.

"I couldn't possibly—" Percy began, when he snapped his mouth shut. He doubted very much if he'd be welcome back at the settlement after the way he'd deserted the tobacco chores and charged after Clara. And Miss Cochran, of course. As for his daily business, well, he had none, save for the ceaseless tending of tobacco plants, which he despised.

And he was achingly tired, and rather unsettled from his long and harrowing trip through the wilderness. Not only was he unaccustomed to such travels, he'd been tormented the whole time by the thought of Mistress Cutler at the mercy of the savage Bradford. Mistress Cochran too, of course. He'd been conscious of every passing second, knowing each one placed Mistress Cutler in greater danger. Mistress Cochran too, of course.

Coupled with the relief of finding Mistress Cutler safe and sound—well, Mistress Cochran as well— he felt curiously drained of strength and eager to stay right where he was.

"He requires instruction, Percy," Clara said, her dear face earnest as she pointed toward John Bradford. "He knows nothing of importance."

"Actually, I would prefer it if Mr. Bradford—" *would teach me the things he knows rather than the other way around,* Percy just managed to stop himself from saying.

It was true John Bradford was a savage. And an opportunist. And disloyal to the Virginia Company and scornful of England's laws and customs. But there was something about the man that Percy envied with all his heart. A freedom, a sense of purpose, that his own life had always lacked.

"I would prefer it if Mr. Bradford invite me to stay for himself," he amended, rather than reveal how little esteem he held for his own gentlemanly background.

"I don't believe this." John glared from Clara to Percy and back again.

"You told me yourself that you required instruction," Clara said.

"I didn't mean for you to blab it—oh, never mind." With a disgusted sigh he shouldered his weapon and stared consideringly at Percy. "You don't look very useful."

"Your first lesson: gentlemen may be as indolent as they please, or can afford."

"Is that true?" Bradford asked Lacey.

"Well, I guess so. Yes."

"And ladies like men who do nothing?"

"I ... of course I can't speak for all ladies, but ... well, I often found little to admire in most gentlemen."

For some reason that seemed to cheer Bradford.

"Well?" prompted Clara. "Ask him to stay, Mr. Bradford."

Bradford scowled again. "If you stay, that makes me responsible for your wellbeing."

Percy found himself staring at the women, then back at his own self, imagining what Bradford must see: three utterly useless human beings fumbling about in the wilderness with no idea how to survive. He wouldn't blame the man one bit for sending them all packing.

"She's hopeless when it comes to household chores." Bradford angled his chin toward Lacey Cochran. "She is a bossy, interfering biddy." He nodded toward Clara. "I don't know you well enough yet to know what you are," he said to Percy.

"You might be surprised to learn exactly how little you know about anything, John Bradford," said Lacey.

Percy shrank back, wondering how the savage

would react to this show of impertinence. Lacey seemed unperturbed: She tipped her chin up and stared straight at Bradford, who couldn't manage to outstare her.

He turned away. And then just as quickly stole another look at Lacey, a look of such hunger and longing that it roused sympathy in Percy's breast.

"Please stay with us, Mr. Bledsoe. We have need of you here."

CHAPTER 14

Now there were four of them in the cabin.

Lacey stood at one end of the table between Clara and Percy, who couldn't seem to stop smiling at each other even though Clara had to look over Lacey's head and Percy had to sort of bend forward a little to look around her in order to accomplish it. She wondered if she was the only one who noticed how the three of them had gravitated toward each other at one end of the table while John stood on the other side, alone.

Did people naturally shy away from him, or did he deliberately hold himself aloof? Or could it be that years of being ostracized by society had fostered within him the ingrained belief that nobody *wanted* to be with him, and so he maintained his distance?

Clara and Percy dimpled at each other. John stood as impassive and motionless as a guard in front of Buckingham Palace. Lacey seemed the only one whose thoughts churned, balancing what she knew against what she hoped.

She had never shown John that she wanted to be with him.

Nor had she told him. But he had never told her that he wanted her to be with him for one minute longer than suited his purposes.

He was notoriously difficult to talk to.

Where talking failed, perhaps action might make do.

Saying nothing, moving as quietly as possible, Lacey went to stand beside him.

Three steps, no more. They were the hardest steps she'd ever taken in her life. With each one, her pride demanded she stay right where she was and see if he would come to her. With each one, her conscience reminded her that she had not yet been honest with this man. With each one, she expected to hear him order her to stop, or to see him back away and maintain the distance between them.

Clara and Percy were no doubt simpering at each other, but from the instant she moved, John's full attention was upon her. She sensed it, with a prickling of her flesh and a stirring of the place inside her that seemed always to respond to his presence.

She understood then that there was more than ingrained habit that had him forever ducking his head and averting his gaze. She wanted to do the same. Keeping her eyes fixed upon his face was almost as hard as taking those steps. She dreaded seeing revulsion. Or animosity.

Or worst of all, indifference.

She had one step left to take. John's head moved ever so slightly, and she felt her hopes plunge, for she was certain he meant to duck away yet again. But then, with an almost visible exercise of will, he tipped his head back and stared down at her, and she saw something hot and needy kindle in his eyes.

Something hot and needy burned inside her as well.

He shifted his feet and her hope faltered yet again, but he merely moved ever so slightly, angling his body almost infinitesimally, so that when at last she reached his side he was turned toward her, not away.

The air seemed warmer there; she fancied she could feel the invisible thump of his heartbeat across the narrow space that separated them.

She wanted to step even closer, wanted to rest her forehead against his shoulder and have his arms come up around her. Instead she forced herself to turn as gracefully as she could, given the leaden weight of her legs, and face Clara and Percy.

She fixed a bright smile upon her face to cover the tension she was certain must show, and smiled even more desperately when she heard the scrape of boot leather against wood and knew that John was on the move again.

And then a heartbeat later, his arm bumped up against her shoulder.

She had crossed three steps. He had moved three inches. Insignificant distances, but from the relief and joy shuddering through Lacey, it seemed they had negotiated the world's largest chasm.

Something drew Percy's attention, for he blinked and ceased smiling at Clara. He frowned at Lacey and John, and then at Clara. "This won't do at all," he said. "We must head back to the settlement at once."

"No!" Clara blurted.

"Not yet!" Lacey bit her lip at her outburst; thank heavens Clara seemed equally agitated and ambivalent about returning to the settlement.

"You gave me your word that you would give me lessons in the gentlemanly arts," said John.

"Yes, I did." Percy blushed furiously. "It puts me in a difficult position. I cannot honor my word without setting a bad example. This is not at all proper."

He gestured toward Lacey and John and blushed again as he encompassed himself and Clara with another broad sweep of his arm. "It's not proper at all for unmarried men and women to live together in one room."

"Oh, that." Lacey slumped with relief. "Clara and I slept in the cabin last night. John slept outdoors."

Neither she nor Clara had raised an objection about his doing so, but now Clara's brow creased with worry.

"It can be chill and damp outside at night. Perhaps we could make some arrangements in here. Hang some blankets from the ceiling to divide the room in two. Why, we'd scarcely know that other people were in the room with us."

Lacey had no doubt that Clara's suggestion was prompted by concern for Percy's health. Clara could not know that Lacey's pulse quickened at the mere thought of John sleeping in the same room with her.

It would take much more than a blanket hanging from the rafters to dim her reaction to John's being so close. More than a blanket to keep her away.

Percy shook his head. "Such an arrangement might be acceptable if there was a life-or-death reason for you to be here, Clara, but now that you've satisfied your worries about Miss Cochran's safety, there's no longer any reason for you to remain."

Percy's observation sent a chill through Lacey. There really was no good reason for Clara to stay here.

And as John had made abundantly clear, there was no good reason for her to remain, either.

"Oh, I'm far too delicate to attempt another journey through the wilderness so quickly after the first," said Clara, looking and sounding extremely robust.

Percy grinned and looked quite pleased with her response.

Clara's excuse for staying sounded so flimsy to Lacey. Percy had accepted it, though, and John seemed to be taking Clara at her word, too, even though Clara had annoyed him all day with her flitting around and disrupting his calm.

She didn't want John to remain silent and accept Clara's and her own continued presence. She yearned to *hear* him voice his desire for them— for her—to remain.

He said nothing.

"I am sure you have not yet fully recovered from your travels, Miss Cochran," said Percy.

"I stayed abed all day yesterday," Lacey said.

John moved away so that his flesh no longer bumped up against hers. She clasped her arms around her chest to ward off the chill she felt. He shot a quick look at her, and then at Percy.

"Do you want to stay?" He asked Percy the question Lacey had been aching to hear him ask her.

"I would not mind," Percy said.

"Nor would I," said Clara, although she had not been asked.

John frowned at Clara. He turned his head a little, looking at Lacey sideways, and she waited for him to ask her.

"I can't see how it's possible, though," said Percy, when John just stood there, silent.

Percy's comment hung in the air as John left the cabin.

Running away again? Or making preparations to be rid of her? Lacey was too miserable to follow him and demand an explanation. She had taken those steps to stand at his side. Her triumph had lasted maybe three minutes. She needed some sign from him that he wanted her to stay there. He'd had the perfect opportunity.

No matter how she tried to fool herself, she could find no explanation for his failure to ask her to stay other than the fact that he no longer wanted her there.

She rested her hand against the table to steady herself.

"I'm disappointed that you gave my blanket suggestion such short shrift," said Clara.

"Dear lady, you must know that such a precaution would never stand up to social scrutiny."

Their attentions were so fully focused on one another that Lacey wondered if Percy and Clara had even noticed that John had left the cabin. Apparently not, for they launched into a spirited discussion, completely oblivious to her distress, sounding for all the world like two lawyers intent upon analyzing evidence for flaws.

"Well, capable as he seems, he can't very well build another room just like that." Clara snapped her fingers. "Look at those logs, Percy. Why I imagine it would take hours to make one of those."

"Longer," said Percy. "You must first cut it down, of course, but then it must be peeled and left to season for a while—a year is ideal."

"Then a curtain it must be."

"I still feel obligated to say the right thing to do would be for you to return to the settlement."

At least John hadn't completely disappeared. Through the window Lacey could see him walking back and forth from the rear corner of the cabin toward the edge of the clearing. One time he carried a bundle of long sticks across his shoulders. Another time a mound of folded cloth.

She recalled the travois he'd used to haul her belongings here such a short time earlier and wondered if he was at that very moment reassembling the carrying conveyance with the intention of returning her and all she owned to the settlement. She wondered if he was happy that Percy had come and made it so easy for him to send her on her way.

And yet he'd gone to the settlement alone when he could have easily insisted she go along with him. He'd brought back her garments. He'd brought back her friend. None of those actions seemed as if they belonged to a man who wanted to be rid of her.

He returned to the doorway. Clara and Percy continued to argue, oblivious of his return, but Lacey could not be so unaware. The sun shone from behind him, casting his face in shadow, so she could not know whether he realized how intently she stared at him. He seemed so broad standing there, so tall. His shirt gaped open at the neck, revealing the dark thong that encircled it, and she shivered remembering the way his coin had all but branded her flesh, at how thoroughly possessed she had been by him.

It made no sense, but she ached, she tingled, she wanted him again.

"You and I will sleep outside, Bledsoe," John said.

"I'm not sure you should," Clara said anxiously to Percy. "Are you prone to catch cold easily?"

"He won't get wet or cold," John interrupted. "I've set up an Indian shelter."

"It can't possibly be snug and safe if it is something used by savages," said Clara.

"I lived in one for months while building this place. I'm not dead."

No, he wasn't dead; he was gloriously, vibrantly alive. And he wanted them to stay or he would not have erected a shelter and stood there arguing its merits with Clara.

"The women will sleep in here. Bledsoe and I will sleep outside." He lifted his chin toward Percy. "Is that proper?"

"Not really. But I suppose it will do if we adequately explain the constraints imposed by Miss Cutler's fatigue and delicacy." Percy sounded rather delighted.

Lacey wanted to cheer. And she felt oddly affected by John's competence and by the quiet, quick way he'd gone about solving their problem without asking for help. He had never been able to depend upon anyone to do anything for him, and yet when others were in need he simply went to work and got things done.

If he didn't want them to stay, he need only have remained in the cabin and let Clara and Percy argue themselves into admitting there was no proper way for unmarried men and women to live together.

He'd gone out and built a shelter.

He didn't want her to leave.

The whole time he'd been erecting the shelter, John had told himself that moving out into it with Percy was the best thing he could do. At least he'd be somewhat removed from the constant arousal that plagued him around Lacey. Once his loins settled, his brain would settle, and he would be able to think straight again.

He dropped the blanket he'd brought into the shelter and kicked it close to one of the trees he'd used as a main support. He'd done next to no labor the whole day, save for trotting to and fro to appease Clara's endless demands for rearranging, and yet he felt exhausted, dispirited, ready for nothing but sleep.

He doubted he would sleep, though, because the minute he sat idle his thoughts began swirling again.

He hated the way his thoughts had become all of a jumble, bouncing from one matter to another. Dreaming of the sounds Lacey made, the way she had felt beneath him, the touch of her hand against his cheek. He'd been so distracted by her, by his body's memory of her, that he'd scarcely spent five minutes working on his plan for revenge.

Even now he couldn't force himself to think about his revenge. He tried. He would have to be there, to watch while she walked toward the settlers, watch while they leered at her and speculated about what he might have done to her, watch while they reluctantly parted to allow her to join them. Forced by their own strange code to accept damaged goods. Forced to acknowledge that he'd had his way and they were left with his leavings.

That was what he'd wanted.

He felt almost physically ill. He cursed and wiped that image from his mind.

Maybe some of his discomfort stemmed from being in such close contact with other people for such a lengthy amount of time. He was a loner. Always would be. No wonder he felt sick. No wonder his thoughts churned. A man could only focus on so many things at one time. He required all his thinking time to hone his revenge. And now he had to worry about Indian threats, and ropes for airing silk gowns, and taking lessons at the knee of a gentleman. . . .

He cursed again.

"Ah . . . should I come back later?"

Percy Bledsoe had just that moment poked his head into the shelter. John fancied he could still hear his curse echoing through the space. He made a noncommittal sound. He really did need some time alone, and yet at the same time he felt reluctant to tell Percy to go away.

"Do you have a particular area you'd like to pursue?" asked Percy.

"What?"

"The gentlemanly arts. You requested my instruction."

"I'm reconsidering that."

But then he thought about Lacey and how she'd objected to returning to the settlement, and he reconsidered again.

"Tell me, do you think she likes this place?"

"She certainly seems interested in arranging matters to her liking."

Percy was talking about the redheaded witch. John shook his head. "Lacey."

"Oh . . . Miss Cochran." Percy's face creased with thought. "She did chime in with agreement when Clara said she didn't want to return to the settlement. I would say that means she likes it well enough to stay—at least for a while."

Maybe if he polished himself up a bit, she'd like him, too.

"How long?"

"How long will she like it?"

"How long to learn to be a gentleman?"

"It depends on the pupil, of course." Percy gnawed worriedly at his lower lip as he studied John. "It could be a rather lengthy process."

Well, that was it, then. He didn't see how he could trick her into staying here long enough. And if that were so, then there was no need to take lessons.

"Never mind, then," he said.

No, he'd be better off devoting his mind to his plan for revenge. At that moment, however, his mind felt completely blank.

"We could practice the art of conversation," Percy suggested.

"I don't talk much," said John. "In fact, I'm tired of talking already."

He closed his eyes and leaned back, pretending to take a nap, even though he never did such a thing. Never sat on a blanket in broad daylight doing nothing, either. Nothing about his life was going the way it had gone just two days ago.

He tried to summon some enthusiasm for returning to his old ways. Tried, but the awful blankness remained.

"This is rather nice," said Percy.

John opened one eye and glared at him.

"Nobody relaxes at the settlement. There's always the infernal tobacco to tend, or land to clear."

"There's plenty to do here, too."

"Oh? Could you teach me?"

Percy leaned forward, all but quivering in his excitement to learn what John knew. Ha! What an about-face; Percy was supposed to be teaching him, not the other way around.

But there didn't seem much point in taking lessons in gentlemanly behavior when he had no intention of behaving like a gentleman once Lacey was gone. He didn't see how he could turn down Percy's offer to tutor him without hurting the little man's pride, but maybe he could just avoid the lessons by filling Percy's day completely with woods lore.

"You mean like a trade?" John said. "I teach you in exchange for you teaching me?"

"Exactly! Except, it hardly seems a fair trade."

He'd been worried about hurting Percy's pride; it seemed Percy had no compunction about hurting his.

But he soon found out he'd wronged Percy.

"You can teach me how to survive in the wild, Mr. Bradford. I daresay there's not another man in this settlement who could do what you do. I have nothing to offer in return save for inessentials, frippery. I am getting the best of this bargain by far."

John felt the oddest sensation.

Percy admired him. Him, John Bradford. The outcast, the former guttersnipe.

If not for Lacey, for trying to please her, he would never have known that at least one man in the settlement held a decent opinion of him. When John indulged his dreams of revenge, he'd always thought of the settlement as a thing, a single entity. He'd never thought that there might be one or two individuals among the hundreds who did not deserve his scorn.

"We must make a plan," Percy said. "I have no experience with teaching, but it seems to me that it will be rather difficult to teach the gentlemanly arts within the rather Spartan confines of this shelter. And with only each other to practice upon." He frowned. "I have it! We will eat our meals each day with the women."

"I have excellent table manners," said John. He'd learned them in the good days, before his parents had died.

"No doubt you do. But only with women present can I gauge the extent of your ability to discourse and show courtesy. In fact, in thinking further upon it, not only shall we eat with the women, you will also walk out at least once each day with Miss Cochran in order to put into action the lessons you learn."

Walk out with Lacey. John's heart quickened. It seemed a blessing, to be given a brief while alone with her each day, and then be shielded from temptation the rest of the day by the presence of the two others.

How different a man's day might be, he reflected, if rather than spending all his effort on planning revenge, he had the delightful prospect of an hour with a beautiful woman to look forward to.

"If I am alone with Lacey . . ." John began, and

he felt his heart lurch in a strange manner. He started again, feeling obliged to point out a potential pitfall to the plan. "If I am alone with Lacey, that will leave you all by yourself with Miss Cutler."

"Why, so it will." Percy blinked, and smiled. John found himself smiling back.

CHAPTER 15

"Lesson number one: You can't walk out with a lady while garbed as a savage."

John shook his head. "That cannot be Lesson number one. Clothes cannot be the most important factor in being a gentleman."

If that were so, he'd need only acquire a set of fine garments and strut about calling himself a gentleman. Nobody knew better than he how ridiculous that would be.

"There's a country full of well-dressed idiots, drunkards, and windbags calling themselves gentlemen who would say you're wrong." Percy shrugged. "Sometimes fine clothes are all that remains, save for a title, when a gentleman has gambled away his fortune or otherwise squandered his inheritance. Or, as in my case, the title and wealth were given to the older son while the others are left to fend as best they can."

Percy did not seem disturbed, and yet his comment surprised John. In some ways Percy had been abandoned by his family, and all because of birth order. Left to fend for himself, and he'd ended up here. They had something in common.

"You're right in some respects," said Percy. "True gentlemanly qualities come from within. But for far too many it is only the veneer that matters. And unfortunately, in our situation, polishing the veneer is both our most pressing challenge and our best shot at success."

John glanced down at himself. The deerskin breeches and shirt had served him well for some time. "These are my best garments," he said. "They are clean. I cannot abide foul smells or filth."

"Well, yes, they are clean." Percy tugged at his cravat, and straightened his shoulders as if to show off the fine cut of his jacket. "Even so, you must have some more civilized clothes."

"Must I? Where would I have gotten them?"

"The clothes from your journey."

John gave a short laugh. "Even if I had been given the opportunity to pack, there would have been nothing to spare, and nothing that would fit me now." The rags he'd worn in Groat Alley had scarcely hung together long enough to last out the journey. He could still remember the acrid stench they'd given off when he'd burned them out in the woods—when he'd made his vow to never be dirty again.

Percy was blushing, as if he had been responsible for John's forced arrival in this place. "But since then you must have . . ." Percy's voice trailed away and dismay deepened his blush. "I forgot. You don't trade with Company merchants."

"Nor do private citizens have anything to spare,

even if I were inclined to deal with them," said John.

Percy slumped and appeared so dejected that John wished he had a silk waistcoat hidden away somewhere in his cabin.

"Well, then, we're reduced to the worst option," said Percy.

The worst option, in John's mind, would be to cancel his walking-out with Lacey.

"She is accustomed to seeing me dressed this way."

Percy gave him a withering glare. "You misunderstand. You must borrow my clothes for this occasion."

The suggestion was ridiculous enough to inspire laughter, but it caused instead a curious tightening of John's throat that felt nothing like amusement, to think that this man he barely knew was offering to loan him his clothes.

"I'm a head taller than you."

"A good deal of your extra height is in your legs."

"I'm quite a bit broader than you as well."

"And look how loose this shirt and jacket are upon me." Percy flapped his arms rather like a duck, setting the folds of the garments flapping. "Off with your shirt."

John sat paralyzed for a moment while Percy tugged loose the cravat and shrugged out of jacket and shirt, revealing a scrawny physique and a near-hairless chest more suited to a young Indian than an Englishman, save that his skin was so pale.

"Quit dithering, Bradford. A gentleman never keeps a lady waiting."

Scarcely crediting what he was doing, John pulled his shirt over his head and then stole a covert glance at the other man. He and Percy might have belonged to two different species, they were so unlike physically.

But Percy was the gentleman, and he the farthest thing from a gentleman. Lacey's previous lover may have been someone very much like Percy. Did she find John unattractive in comparison? He felt rough and primitive: too dark from spending many hours shirtless in the sun; too lumpy from the heavy work of digging and hauling logs; too hairy.

"That medallion must go as well," said Percy, indicating John's blood-money coin.

"I will never remove this."

Percy leaned forward slightly and squinted. "Oh, it's a coin. Sentimental value?"

"Something like that. It reminds me of what's important."

To John's intense relief, Percy seemed to lose interest. "Try on the shirt," Percy instructed.

As John suspected, it would not meet over his middle. Percy frowned in thought, and then brightened. "We will make do." He pulled the hide laces free from the front of John's discarded shirt and ordered him to string them between buttons and loops. John did so and scowled down at the gap, inches wide, crisscrossed with rawhide over whorls of springy black hair, and the dull shine of his coin peeking through.

"We'll fashion the cravat to cover all that," said Percy, and he did so, tying the length of silk into a simple knot with the ends trailing down John's front. It did hide his bare middle, providing he limited himself to shallow breaths.

"Now, for the jacket."

The jacket was even worse. The shirt had been cut and sewn generously across the back and sleeves. Not so the jacket. John all but strained his shoulder tugging it on, and then it stretched uncomfortably tight across his shoulder blades. He had to hold his arms cocked back; if he dared move them forward, an ominous ripping sound hinted at disaster. They had not a prayer of fastening it, no matter if they used an entire spindle of rope and a winch.

"It's the thought that counts," Percy said at last. "Mistress Cochran will be so pleased with the care you took with your appearance that she will not notice at all that the clothes are a bit snug."

John had been set to rip the clothes away until Percy said Lacey would appreciate the effort. He frowned down at himself. "You are certain?"

Percy nodded, but with less enthusiasm than John found reassuring.

He looked down at himself and understood Percy's lack of enthusiasm. He looked ridiculous. He shook his head, ready to abandon the plan. He found the leather lace's trailing edge and made ready to tug it loose when he was struck by yet another odd sensation.

Percy had quite literally given John the clothes off his back.

All in the interest of pleasing a woman. A gentleman had handed over his garments as if one man were the equal of the other, kindred spirits in this quest for a woman's heart, with no social barriers between them.

John could not remember the last time another person had given him anything. Trying to recall roused old memories that he'd forced himself to bury so long ago that it almost hurt to resurrect them. But the pain was tempered by pleasure, as he could swear he could hear his long-dead mother's voice reminding him of his manners.

"I should thank you."

"It's not necessary."

"It is. I remember . . . being told to thank someone when a gift is given to me."

"You remember?" Curiosity quickened Percy's expression. "I must say I am somewhat surprised by you on occasion. Your table manners, for example, are quite good. You had told me they were, but I must confess I did not expect them to be, considering what I know of your unfortunate background."

"I did not always live in the London gutters," John said quietly.

He reeled as wave upon wave of the newly released memories crashed through him. It hurt, yes, to remember those long-ago days when he'd been part of a family, when his mother tucked him into bed each night, when his father hefted him up on his shoulders and played horse through their cottage.

And yet there was an unexpected sweet joy in seeing them again in his mind's eye, in knowing that their much beloved faces and voices weren't really gone forever. He'd done his best to smother those memories. He'd denied himself the pleasure; he had to stop himself from laughing aloud with the delight of finding that they had been abiding inside him, waiting for all these years until . . . until . . .

Until he'd reached out to other people.

"I suppose I never thought about it before," Percy said thoughtfully. "How people might have lived before being forced into begging on the streets, I mean," he added.

John wondered if this, too, was a lesson in gentlemanly behavior—an invitation to speak about his past if he was so inclined, and yet without the pressure of a direct question.

To talk about it ... to voice aloud to another person for the first time the heartache, the despair, the utter sense of isolation, the terror that had been his only legacy when he'd been orphaned so young.

He'd never been able to tell anyone. He'd had to be tough and cold to stake out a place in the London gutter, and within no time at all he'd learned that the youths who scrabbled for survival with him would grant no quarter to a lad who'd thrived in the loving care of two parents until he was all but a man in their eyes.

To talk about it . . .

No.

He could not shake the feeling that it would make him appear weak in another man's eyes. No matter that Percy seemed friendly, interested, genuinely curious. A man did not bare the agony in his soul to the eyes of another—ever. A man could never trust anyone with knowledge so potent.

"I think it's time to fetch Lacey," he said, deliberately changing the subject.

He learned something then about the way a gentleman responded to an insult, for Percy merely glanced away and assumed a carefully neutral expression, as if he'd never expressed the slightest curiosity, as if he'd never invited John to take a step that might have forged the beginnings of a friendship between them.

John should have felt justified—and relieved—to have deflected the situation. Instead, he couldn't shake the sense that he'd turned away from an opportunity that could have changed his life for the better.

Clara bit her lip, and Lacey felt her confidence plunge to her toes.

"You think I should change again?"

Clara looked as if she meant to agree, and then shook her head. "The yellow silk is totally impractical for a walk in the woods. He already thinks you're incompetent. You don't want him thinking you're a fool as well, to wear your best dress on an outing where it can only get ruined."

Lacy smoothed the sturdy blue serge cloth over her hips. "Mr. Bradford is, above all, a practical man," Lacey agreed.

"A trait that is to be desired in a man," said Clara, sounding even less enthusiastic than Lacey felt.

"Practicality is a trait highly prized in a woman," Lacey whispered. "Practical women don't get themselves into trouble for the sake of love."

"Practical men don't lose their heads and make fools of themselves for the sake of love."

Lacey's appalled expression met Clara's.

"Oh, Lacey, if we hurry we can get you out of that horrible blue dress and into the yellow one. . . ."

But it was too late. Even as her fingers tugged at the infernal tiny buttons, Lacey could hear the murmur of male voices that meant John and Percy were crossing the small clearing to the cabin.

She smoothed the dress again and felt the material rough against her fingertips. A little rough, a little nubby, the sort of garment a woman might wear when she meant to sweep the kitchen floor. That was what he would feel when he touched her—if he touched her. She might not know if he touched her, for the thick, serviceable cloth might well shield her from all sensation, not like whisper-light silk that would be no barrier at all between a man's heat and a woman's soft skin. . . .

"This is the right dress," she said firmly.

And then he walked through the door.

She thought at first that he must be carrying something, for the line of him seemed wrong. Then she realized it was Percy's cravat tumbling down his chest, and that he'd somehow managed to squeeze his broad shoulders into Percy's shirt and jacket.

The tiny part of her that clung to the belief that she ought to strive for practicality told her that he must surely look ridiculous. The rest of her threatened to melt at knowing the practical John Bradford had done his best to dandify himself for their outing.

While she greeted him in serviceable blue serge suited for housework. Her fingers tightened in the folds of the skirt. She'd worn the wrong dress.

His glance flicked over her, impossible to read. He bowed forward slightly from the waist, a movement that parted the cravat from his shirt and revealed bronzed skin and curling black hair, revealed the coin he always wore, through a gap in the shirt. Lacey's cheeks tingled, remembering the feel of that skin, that hair, against her face as she'd rested against him, the hard imprint of that coin between her breasts.

Stop it! she scolded herself silently. John was here only because Percy had insisted he learn the arts of a gentleman. He'd dressed this way only at Percy's insistence, she was sure. He hadn't betrayed the slightest flicker of disappointment over what he could only believe to be her own lack of care in preparing to walk out with him. This walk with her was nothing more than a chore, an assignment.

"You look lovely, Mistress Cochran." Percy's stage whisper could be heard throughout the cabin. Beside her, Clara stifled a giggle.

John scowled at her.

And then he lurched forward, and Lacey realized Percy had shoved him from behind.

"You look lovely," Percy coached again.

"You look lovely," John said, without looking at her.

"Curtsy!" Clara hissed at Lacey from the side of her mouth.

"What?"

"Curtsy!" Clara accompanied the instruction with a jab of her elbow.

Lacey had not been prepared for the jab. Nor, apparently, had John been expecting a second nudge from Percy. The two of them, sent off balance by their well-meaning friends, collided in the center of the cabin and landed in a heap of blue serge and silk cravat upon the floor.

"Oh, dear," said Percy.

"Oh, dear," Clara giggled.

Oh God, thought Lacey as her body surged with pleasure from the feel of John pressed hard against her. His eyes met hers; in them she read dismay, embarrassment, and something else—something dark and hot and savage that stole her breath away.

It was gone as quickly as it came, and so was he. He sprang away from her, lithe as a cat. As if he couldn't get away from her fast enough.

"Offer her your hand, John," Percy said quietly.

He did. She took it and tried hard not to notice that he did not need to labor at all to pull her to her feet. Percy's continual prompting reminded her that everything John did with her was part of his lessons in gentlemanly behavior, nothing more.

She'd worn the right dress.

"Offer her your arm, John."

John crooked his elbow toward her. She slid her hand into place. Her fingers curled over the too-tight sleeve, sensing at once the bulging strength contained within. She wanted to stroke the corded muscle. She opened her hand so that only her palm, rather than her sensitive fingertips, rested against him. It helped. A little.

"Shall we?" He inclined his head toward the door.

She managed a smile and nodded. It would be better outside, she thought. As they crossed the clearing, she glanced back to see Percy and Clara standing side by side, smiling and waving and looking quite pleased with themselves. She smiled back. As soon as they were beyond the clearing, she would let go of John's arm, and he would revert to silence, and nothing untoward could possibly happen. Couldn't possibly.

So much for believing he'd made progress in learning to become a gentleman. A gentleman would never be so clumsy as to tumble to the floor with his lady. A gentleman would certainly never want to stay there on the floor with her, reveling in the feel of her body beneath his, even as two wide-eyed witnesses snickered over his lack of grace.

And a gentleman would certainly never find his private parts throbbing huge and hard just because the lady walked at his side.

A lady with sense. She had not bedecked herself in silly fripperies. He felt like a court jester garbed in Percy's too-small garments, which felt even more constrictive from his physical reaction to Lacey. How ridiculous he must look to her! She'd made no comment on his attire. Nor could he think of one single thing to say to her. All day long tutoring with Percy and he still didn't know how to do or say the right things.

Always, when faced with such evidence of his inadequacy, he'd fled rather than reveal his weaknesses. How comforting it would be to disappear into the woods, where his lack of polish would not show. But running now would mean leaving Lacey. That seemed far too high a price to pay simply to spare his pride.

The gentleman introduces an innocuous topic of conversation. He could hear Percy's lesson in his mind.

He wished he could disappear into the woods. At the same time, he knew he couldn't take a step away from her to save his life.

"These garments belong to Percy." That seemed innocuous enough.

"I thought they might."

"Your dress is your own." He winced at the ineptitude of his remark.

"Yes." She seemed to falter in her step. "I did not realize we were to . . . dress up for these outings."

" 'Tis a silly notion of Percy's."

"I suppose it is." He fancied she sounded wistful, as if she had hoped the garments had been his own idea.

All of this had been for naught. She was still as much a mystery to him as she'd been that first day, when he'd sensed she was hiding things about herself. He'd made love to her, lived with her, eaten with her, submitted himself to these ridiculous lengths for her, and still he knew nothing more about her than he'd known that very first day.

Nothing, save for the fact that she had bewitched him.

By no means does the gentleman become too personal in word or deed.

The hell with that.

"I wish . . ." he said. "I wish we could speak plain to each other."

She stopped walking. She dropped her hand from his arm. But if he had thought that voicing his hope aloud would ease things between them, he'd been dead wrong. She appeared stricken, her skin pale, her eyes wide and shimmering with unshed tears.

"Don't," he murmured, cursing himself for suggesting something that so obviously caused her distress. Never again would he voice such a thought. "Don't cry." He reached out and awkwardly touched her cheek, the way he'd seen Clara, her friend, do to express tenderness and caring.

She reached up and covered his hand with her own. She moved such a little bit that her skirts barely rippled, but it was as if she'd crossed some invisible barrier that let a magnet inside his body draw hers closer. He didn't know if he pulled her tight or if she pressed against him, only that she was there, nestled against him, his chest bearing the sweet weight of her with each breath he took.

He wanted to pull her closer and yet dared not move at all for fear that she would step away, and also because her nearness intoxicated his senses so thoroughly that no part of his body seemed inclined to obey the commands of his brain. He wanted only to feel her, to breathe in her scent . . . to taste her.

She lifted her face toward him and he indulged his appetite.

Her mouth beneath his pulsed with her life force. It molded softly against him, warm and insistent, driving his hunger for her to a fever pitch. She answered with gentle, tentative touches of her tongue, with breathy sighs that drove him wild. His whole body ached with the need to cover her, to probe into her, to possess her, and his muscles shook with the effort of holding those impulses in check lest he crush her. He let his hand roam the sweet line from her waist to her neck and accidentally dislodged some of the pins holding up her hair. It tumbled down, releasing the heady scent of lavender and vanilla, tormenting his skin with its soft silkiness.

She trembled and yielded in his arms, and he knew that there was nothing that would stop him from taking her again, here and now, outdoors on the ground. He would bare those long, beautiful legs of hers to the light of day with nothing but lush grass for their bed and nothing but blue sky for a blanket.

A gentleman wouldn't do such a thing.

A man who knew the lady meant to leave him shouldn't be so overcome by passion that he ignored the temporary nature of their arrangement. He should worry more about how a life that had been barely tolerable before might be completely intolerable now that she had lighted it so briefly and would soon leave him in the dark.

A man who loved his woman would care nothing for the restrictions imposed by gentlemanly behavior, and would worry not at all about his own bleak future while the woman he craved with every ounce of his being rested willing and ready in his arms.

Virtually every action of his adult life had been calculated to avoid future pain. He cast aside all those careful habits and lost himself in the sensation of loving Lacey.

He ripped the lace from the shirt and shrugged it off. Something hit against his chest—his coin. With a quick tug, the old leather thong broke away. He cast it down and didn't bother looking to see where it fell.

He lowered them both carefully to the ground and broke off kissing her only to run a quick hand over the grass to make sure no large rocks or branches would make things uncomfortable for her. He found the hem of her dress, slid his hand under, ran his hand up her legs. Found the edge of her cotton stocking and moaned at the pleasure of touching the impossibly soft skin of her thighs. He reached higher and gritted his teeth against the searing ecstasy of finding her damp and ready for him.

She gasped at his touch and pulled him closer. He could not stop himself from pressing hard into her, from letting her feel the evidence of his desire for her. He caught her hand and placed it against himself, then nearly screamed with frustration when she tried unbuttoning the front of his breeches and couldn't unfasten them. It was the work of a moment for him to tear himself away from her and undo the buttons himself, but the time away seemed endless and yawning, a hint he did not dare think as to what a lifetime without her would be.

"John," she whispered his name. She stroked his belly with her fingers, and then lower, and when her hand curled around him he thought he would burst. He moved to cover her and meant only to revel in the sweetness of her body rounded and curving beneath his for a time, meant to gradually ease his weight onto her, meant to spare her his weight by keeping his elbows firmly planted on the ground. He meant to do all that, but his mind fled when she moved beneath him, when she freed her legs and wrapped them around his waist.

He'd grown so large, so hard, he was half-afraid of hurting her, but her body welcomed him with sweet, warm dampness and the last fleeting shreds of sanity deserted him. He had dreamed that if he ever had the chance to love her again he would take his time and let her experience a woman's full joy before losing himself in pleasure. He'd imagined that maybe if he could show her what she meant to him with his touches, if he could give her ecstasy she'd never known, then she might be able to overlook his rough way with words, his lack of social graces. All those half-formed doubts and plans dissipated into thin air as he drove into her, as he claimed her body and marked her forever-more as belonging to him.

He could feel her moving beneath his thrusts, moving *with* him, *with* him, as if there were no place on this earth she would rather be, and that inflamed him even more. He had to have her, all of her, now and again, or he would die of the need.

She made a sound of excitement. Of wonder. It pierced his numbed mind and he was able to draw back, just a little, and watch her as sheer delight lit her features and curved her sweet lips. Her whole body quivered, outside and in. Her legs tightened around him, her arms wrapped around his shoul-ders. He buried his face in her hair. She clung to him so tightly it seemed that they were for a heart-beat one person as ripples and spasms coursed through her body, shaking him to his core until he, too, lost himself in shuddering ecstasy.

They lay clasped together for a very long time, until their breathing slowed, until his flesh cooled and he began to worry that she might catch a chill lying there on the ground.

A dilemma. He wanted nothing more than to keep her there, pinned beneath him, half-naked, rosy with satisfaction, and content to be with him.

"John." He quivered at hearing his name come from her lips. "What you said before about speaking plain to each other . . ."

He pressed a finger to her lips, remembering how his suggestion had caused tears to spring in her eyes. "It's not important."

"It is. There are things about me you must know. I don't know where to begin."

"We started this before, Lacey. I know you did not come here untouched."

"The man who was my lover was above me in station."

A jolt of jealousy so sharp that it was painful shocked John. If her former lover had been so far above her, he must have been important indeed.

"And now your lover is below you in station. Perhaps it evens out."

She blinked up at him, wide-eyed, her mouth trembling as if she wasn't sure he'd jested. John didn't want to hear about her former lover. He claimed her lips for himself, branded them with his touch, his taste, and long minutes later when he finished he thought he'd distracted her enough.

But no.

"I must tell you how it all came about," she said.

"There are so many things about me you don't know."

"I don't want to know."

He wanted no part of knowledge that made her pale with agitation. Didn't want to hear her admit to ever having been attracted to another man. Didn't want to know details that would forever leave him imagining Lacey on the arm of someone wealthy, someone influential, someone who could have given her a life of luxury while he, John Bradford, hoped to convince her to embrace a life of hardship and uncertainty.

"We know enough about each other," he said.

"You only *think* you know about me."

Her agitation was infecting him. He felt restless and had to quell the urge to rise from the ground and lose himself in the shelter of the woods. All that stopped him was the utter certainty that he had to find words to reassure her, to tell her that whatever had happened in the past was over and done, that he loved the woman she was today. That he knew her to be sweet and loving and willing to see through a man's hard shell of protection and dare to love him. "I don't want to know those things. What I believe to be true about you is all that matters to me."

"I see."

Her appearance was at odds with her comment. Her lips had gone pale and bloodless, her eyes stark with sorrow. Somehow he'd failed to make her understand.

He would show her instead of tell her.

He kissed her again. Touched her. Stroked her until high color warmed her face and that terrible sorrow was concealed behind eyes that squeezed shut with pleasure.

"Yes, you see," he said. "I don't want to hear about it. None of it."

He loved her, and he let his body say everything for him.

JUST THE WAY YOU ARE

CHAPTER 16

"This cornbread puts to shame any I've eaten back at the hundred," said Percy, holding aloft a chunk of the bread Lacey had baked the day before. "I'm quite astonished that a woman of your background has such a gift for baking, Clara."

"Oh, I—" Clara began.

Lacey kicked Clara's shin under the table, and sent her friend a quick shake of her head to remind her not to reveal their secret. Clara frowned and bent to rub her leg. Lacey shot a quick look at John, who appeared to have noticed nothing, since he was concentrating on scraping the last morsel of porridge from his breakfast bowl.

"About this bread," Percy said.

Lacey wished he would just shut up about it.

Percy continued. "I am puzzled about another thing. I did not think you traded with the settlers, John. How do you happen to have flour on hand?"

"Trade with the Indians."

"But I thought you didn't trust them."

"I don't."

"Yet you trade with them."

"Cheaper that way."

"Corn is absurdly expensive."

"Not when you don't much care whether you get it or not." John glanced up away from his plate. "Indians know I don't need it, so they don't ask for much in trade from me."

"Why, that's downright dishonest! If the settlers knew, they would not stand for it."

John's lip quirked in a half smile. "Wouldn't they? I've warned them time and again about more serious threats from the Indians, and they continue to trust them."

"You live out here virtually in their midst."

"And I have an escape tunnel that took me many months to build. I hardly believe that one of the settlers from the hundred will come out here to murder me while I sleep. Nobody came even to challenge me when——" He flushed and bit off his comment.

Silence fell. Lacey waited in a fever of anticipation, praying that now that he'd mentioned the subject, he might take it one step further and say he was glad nobody had come. Or glad that she'd decided to stay.

"I have an escape tunnel," he repeated. "That should tell you whether or not I believe there is danger."

"Perhaps we should not go hunting today," Percy said with a nervous look toward Clara. "Perhaps we should stay near the cabin and keep watch."

"We won't go far." John stood. "And we shall check the immediate area before venturing into the woods. I'll be teaching you to recognize Indian sign as well as animal sign. One day your life may depend on it."

The men left.

"I'm beginning to believe he may be serious about the Indian threat," Clara said. She gave a shiver.

"Let's stay busy," Lacey said. John's refusal to say anything about her continued presence confirmed that he was equally serious about not wanting her to stay. She prayed Clara wouldn't remark upon it. She collected the plates from the table. "There's so much to do. We need more bread. We can cook—"

"Why wouldn't you let me tell Percy that you baked the bread, Lacey?"

"You know why. John thinks you are doing all the household chores."

"Surely after what happened between the two of you yesterday, there's no longer any need for that deception."

Lacey's face flamed with heat. She'd confessed nothing to Clara about the wild lovemaking she'd done with John in the woods. She'd feigned sleep the night before rather than share whispered confidences. Somehow, though, Clara had known.

Her joy, her despair, must have been branded on her for all to see.

"I tried to tell him everything. He wouldn't listen. He doesn't *want* to know the truth about me."

"That's a curious thing to say, Lacey."

"Not so curious, Clara. There are still some things you do not know." Lacey bit her lip. "Not about me—I've told you everything there is to tell. But I never told you why John brought me here in the first place."

"I just assumed it was because you're a beautiful woman."

How nice if it could have been so simple. How wonderful if he had thought her beautiful. He'd never said. Lacey shook her head. "You are well aware of John's animosity toward the settlers. Claiming me so that a loyal Company supporter could not was the crowning achievement in his plan to gain revenge against the Virginia Company for bringing him here. He chose me because he wrongly assumed I was highborn, wealthy, and of good family. It would devastate him to know the truth."

"I think you're wrong about him, Lacey. I've seen the way he looks at you. I suspect the man loves you."

Curse the hope that always lived within her! It surged to life at Clara's remark, and Lacey sternly tamped down the joy that bloomed through her. "If he loved me, he'd want to know everything about me."

"Perhaps he does. Perhaps he thinks it's a sign of his love that he doesn't want you to feel obliged to reveal matters that might be of some embarrassment to you."

Lacey remembered her agitated state when she'd tried so hard to confess to him. She had been nervous, shaking, terrified of seeing the warmth in his eyes chill into the frost of disgust.

"Think of how he lived before he came here, Lacey. I've done some charity work in my day, and I know that the orphans who live in the gutters prize their privacy above everything else."

"It's the same for servants," Lacey said. In a life where the clothes you wore, the food you ate, and the bed you slept in belonged to someone else, your secrets were the only thing you could truly call your own.

"It's always a woman's lot to understand a man's shortcomings, to make allowances for his mistakes. Give him the benefit of the doubt, Lacey. Vow here and now that you will *force* him to listen to the truth about yourself."

"What if . . . what if he turns away from me after I tell him?"

Clara picked up a stray chunk of cornbread. "You made this with your own hands. I'd wager that every thought you had while preparing it revolved around him in some way. You watched him eat it. You watched him take pleasure in doing so, and no doubt felt some satisfaction in knowing that your work nurtured him. But he doesn't think you had any part in making this bread. He will never know unless you make him hear the truth."

"I don't want to spend the rest of my life living a lie," Lacey whispered. "But I don't want to lose him, either. I have to confess that part of me was somewhat relieved when he refused to listen."

"That's the part of you that's just like him."

"What?"

"That part of you wants to run away rather than reveal its vulnerabilities."

"You're right. I've thought many times that it would be so much easier to simply return to the settlement and never let him know the truth about me." She paused. "He told me that I should always fight for what I want."

"Fight for him, Lacey."

"I will."

"When they return, I will lure Percy away on

some pretext to give the two of you some time alone.''

Lacey nodded.

John stared down at the slight indentation in the earth. If the Indian who'd left this evidence of his presence was watching them, as John suspected, he must be cursing his carelessness at that very moment. "You've learned well, Percy," he said. "I might have walked right past it myself without noticing."

There was no *might* about it; he would have missed the sign. Only a small part of his mind was engaged on this all-important scouting expedition. Too much of his attention wandered where it shouldn't—toward Lacey and her inexplicable withdrawal from him after their shattering closeness the day before.

Percy nodded but did not appear pleased by John's compliment. "I imagined that learning tracking skills would fill me with a sense of accomplishment. I did not realize that the knowledge would give me more reasons to be afraid." He swallowed. "How have you endured this, John? Knowing they are around all the time, watching, waiting . . .''

"I've tried to warn the settlers. None will heed me."

"Because your actions run contrary to your warnings. How can anyone believe you when you consort with them on a regular basis?"

"How else was I to learn their methods?" John was surprised at the anger that surged through him. "Why do you continually point out my attempts to gain familiarity with them as something wrong?"

"I see!" Percy leaned forward, excitement clear upon him. "So *that* is why you have never allowed anyone in the settlement to get close to you: You worried that they would get to know your churlish demeanor hides a generous heart."

Percy's observation left John speechless for a moment. How dare he say such a thing. "We're talking about Indians."

"If you say so."

John snorted with disgust. "And here I had credited you with having more sense than the other settlers. The more you fear an enemy, the closer you ought to get to them. How else do you learn their ways?"

Percy considered for a moment, and John knew Percy must be observing the rigid stance, the frightfully blank expression he'd deliberately mustered. He did not know if it was part of the gentleman's code, or a simple lack of interest, that caused Percy to drop his probing and allow John to change the subject. He only knew that he felt a little empty and sad when Percy appeared to return wholeheartedly to the topic of Indians. He reached toward his neck in a gesture he'd made times beyond counting, to stroke the pierced coin and remind himself of what had happened to him. His hand found only his own flesh. He remembered then that he'd ripped the thong from his neck and thrown it down. He'd never looked for it.

"I must admit your logic about getting to know them makes a kind of sense," said Percy, oblivious to the turmoil circling through John. "Why haven't you ever presented that argument to the settlers?"

Because he'd always been so consumed by the need for revenge against the settlers that he'd never tried to make them understand. He'd used their refusal to accept everything he told them without question as yet another reason to let his anger simmer within.

How thoroughly that drive for revenge had numbed him. Now that he'd lost his taste for revenge, he was continually plagued with other emotions that had lain dormant for years: loneliness, regret, anger, remorse.

Joy.

He'd found joy within Lacey's arms, only to have it snatched away when she'd gone silent and tearful after their lovemaking. His natural inclination was to return to the blessed numbness that would mean an end to the pain. But something within him rebelled at giving up that joy, so newly found, so briefly held. Something within urged him to move away from his old ways and try something new.

He didn't know how to do it. Percy would have to teach him. Fast. An ever-present sense of dread clung to John, a dread he knew had nothing to do with the danger from Indians, but from the more devastating possibility of losing Lacey.

Percy squared his shoulders. "Well, since it appears we two are the only ones who recognize the danger from the Indians, you had best speed up the woods lore lessons."

"No."

"No?"

"Lessons in the gentlemanly arts."

Percy scowled. "John, there are Indians afoot. We must be on guard."

"I've been on guard against them for years. It's time someone else takes up the responsibility."

Odd how, as soon as he said it, he recognized the truth in that outlandish statement. Alone, unacknowledged, he'd been keeping watch over the struggling settlement, doing his best to keep them informed of the danger, urging them to be prepared. Just as he'd done in the gutter, he realized with a start. Despite all his pretense of holding himself aloof, he'd spent years casting his scanty protection over those who were weaker than he was.

Even his burning need for revenge had not been so much for himself as to convince *them* that he was worthy, that he was strong and brave.

Perhaps it was time to step away from all that and truly seek out something for himself.

Such as Lacey's heart.

"I must say that gentlemanly arts don't seem all that important out here," Percy said unhappily.

"They are important to some people."

"Not to me. Not anymore."

John couldn't help smiling at Percy's misinterpretation, and Percy reddened.

"Oh my—you mean Mistress Cochran."

"Aye."

"She doesn't say much," said Percy. "I've never heard her make the slightest sound of disparagement over your lack of gentlemanly arts."

There were many sounds Lacey made that Percy had not heard: sounds only John had heard, sounds he wanted her to make only for him in the future. "We got off to a bad start, she and I," he said carefully. "I led her to expect certain things. . . . I need to convince her I am capable of changing."

"Truth to tell, John, the lady fairly glows in your presence. Perhaps she likes you just as you are."

If only it were true. "I have reason to believe she would not entertain the notion of remaining with me unless I can prove certain things to her. I need your help to do so, Percy."

"Oh, well, if you need my help." Percy looked

down and scuffed the Indian sign into oblivion with the toe of his boot. His face was flushed with pride and pleasure. John did not know what it was about admitting a weakness of his own that had pleased Percy so much. Or why doing so made him feel so good himself.

Lacey prepared herself for their outing. She wondered what toll her sleepless night had taken on her appearance. Her eyes felt gritty and puffy. John's small shaving mirror was out in the shelter with the men, and there was no glass in the cabin, no shiny surface where she might inspect her face to see if nervousness had turned her pale as a ghost.

This time, she had no problem choosing her dress. The blue serge was the right dress to wear when telling John the truth about herself. Fancy silks had gotten her into this mess in the first place. She was happy to set them aside forever.

"The men are coming," said Clara.

Lacey moved to the doorway. She leaned against the jamb, overwhelmed suddenly by a trembling in her legs as she watched John stride purposefully toward the cabin. He was so tall, so fine. Her skin tingled from the memory of his flesh pressed against hers. Her entire inner self was in a turmoil, her secret places quivering with need for him, her soul churning with guilt and trepidation over how he would react to knowing the truth about her at last.

She would force him to listen to her during this outing. She would not let this deception continue for another day. But oh, God, how she dreaded doing so.

He glanced up. Saw her. Her heart lifted when

she saw the undisguised delight light his eyes, but all too quickly he masked that reaction. She did not even have time to regret its passing, for he turned stern and forbidding. "Lacey, get back into the cabin."

She could not tell him the truth about herself in front of Percy and Clara; John's command was a reprieve! But even as part of her welcomed the chance to postpone her confession, she steeled herself to proceed as she had vowed to do. She stepped forward, away from the supporting door. "We are going out."

"No."

Percy nodded vigorously. "We saw sign in the woods. There may be Indians in the area."

Clara stepped next to her as the men drew up to the cabin. "Do you think they mean us harm?"

"When they're not up to mischief they stop here to let me know they're in the area," said John. "I do the same when I venture into their territory. By not following this usual courtesy, it leads me to suspect trouble."

"Are they watching us now?"

"That's what's so troubling; I think one of them has been here and gone."

"I spotted the track," Percy puffed with pride.

" 'Twas almost as though someone merely stopped to check we were in residence, and then left." John sounded puzzled.

"Maybe it was just one lone savage who dared not approach since we are four in number," said Lacey.

"No, courtesy would reign. He would know we would not harm him if he came in peace."

"John." Percy spoke his name very quietly.

John shot him a troubled glance.

"I hear something."

Once again John had allowed his inner turmoil to distract him from the job at hand. How could he not have noticed that the wild sounds had gone quiet? He closed his eyes, concentrating on hearing. "There is the sound of men on the move. Armed men."

Clara gripped Lacey's arm while Lacey strained to hear. She heard nothing. Nothing. No bird song, just the light flutter of wind through the leaves.

"Someone approaches," said John. "A party of men. They are making no effort to conceal their presence. Something is afoot."

He and Percy took position in front of Lacey and Clara.

They waited.

He was wrong; surely he was wrong, Lacey told herself as long minutes passed with nothing happening. But with each passing minute he grew more tense, more alert, and it was almost as though his more highly attuned senses lent strength to hers, for eventually she could hear it, too. The far-off sound of something big moving through the trees. And occasionally the clink of metal.

"Indians move silently," she said, and was rewarded with a curt nod from John.

And yet it was an Indian who ventured from the woods to the clearing.

"You!" cried Clara.

"That's Opechancanough," said Percy. "He often brings turkeys and rabbits to the settlement."

"I know him," said John. He called out a word in a language Lacey could not understand. The Indian paused in midstride at the greeting, and then glanced down and away, almost as if he was embarrassed.

"He's betrayed us," said John.

Lacey soon understood what he meant. Two men holding muskets against their shoulders moved into the clearing. They looked to be settlers from the hundred. Behind them, a half-dozen soldiers with sabers clanking at their sides marched out of the trees.

"We've come for the women," said one of the soldiers.

Emotions surged through Lacey. Despite her determination to tell John the truth, she couldn't help feeling the tiniest bit of relief that she could put it off just a little longer. Immediately that relief was squelched by despair, that she'd put it off so long and now wouldn't be able to tell him in front of all these witnesses.

Topping it all was anger, that men she didn't know would think they had the right to tell her where she could live. *We've come for the women,* as if she and Clara were no more than two cows who'd strayed from their pasture and had to be herded back to the proper stable.

"Now that we have no interest in being rescued, you come," Clara sniffed disparagingly. "Well, as you can see we are in excellent health. You may return to the settlement straightaway."

The man who'd spoken stepped forward. Lacey thought he must be of some importance within the British army, considering all the fancy embellishments upon his uniform. "Captain William Throckmorton at your service, madam. I'm afraid that returning to the settlement without the two of you is quite impossible, mistress. We're under orders to save you and bring you back immediately."

"Who issued these orders?" questioned Percy.

"And where did you come from? There haven't been any British soldiers in the settlement throughout my entire stay there."

"We arrived just yesterday on the frigate *Chalcedony*," said Throckmorton.

Lacey couldn't believe they were engaged in such banal conversation. She met John's gaze and saw that he was as paralyzed by the situation as she was. Percy and Clara carried on, badgering the soldiers for information while she and John just stood there. Lacey could not divine John's motives; for herself, the paralysis stemmed from despair. It was over. Their brief interlude, their temporary withdrawal from reality, was at an end.

But it didn't have to be. All she had to do was tell these soldiers that she was no fine lady in need of saving, and declare once and for all that she loved John Bradford and wanted to spend the rest of her days with him.

"Percy, leave off interrogating the captain," said one of the non-uniformed men who'd accompanied the soldiers.

"I'm not interrogating him, Winston," said Percy.

Winston. Percy and he knew each other, which meant Winston and the other similarly garbed man must be settlers.

Her swirling emotions rocked her again. If Lacey revealed the truth about herself in front of these men, then John's revenge would be spoiled.

She wished she could curse God for the unfortunate timing of her rescue, but she knew she had only herself to blame. She'd had days and days to tell John the truth about herself, and she'd let every opportunity slip by. It was too late now. It would always be too late.

And it worked both ways, she realized. John had

had plenty of opportunities to let her know that he'd set aside his plan for revenge. To tell her that he, too, had found something rare and wondrous in her arms. But he hadn't.

Maybe because he didn't love her the way she loved him.

Maybe because his revenge was still the driving force in his life.

She could still confess the truth. She could admit her love for him here and now, tell the truth about herself, and see whether he returned her feelings.

But if he didn't . . . if he didn't . . .

Oh, God, then she would have humiliated herself for nothing. And destroyed his revenge.

She could endure the humiliation. But she could not endure hurting the man she loved, even if he didn't love her in return.

All of a sudden she felt tired. So tired she could barely stand upright. Tired of her deceptions. Tired of praying that John might love her as she loved him. Tired of waiting for him to say something to give her hope.

Amanda Stivington would have looked upon these soldiers as salvation from an intolerable situation.

All the while that her thoughts had been racing through her head, Percy had been arguing with Winston and Captain Throckmorton. As her head cleared, snippets of the argument penetrated Lacey's confusion, and what she heard only threatened to kill her on the spot.

"We came as escort to an important personage," said Captain Throckmorton. "When he heard that one of the Company's brides had been abducted, he demanded a rescue party be formed immediately."

"Well, at least one Englishman has manners," grumbled Clara resentfully. "Not that I'm happy to see you, but I was soundly ignored by all and sundry when I demanded a rescue party. Who is this mysterious important personage?"

"Sir Pumphrey Fallsworth," said Captain Throckmorton, and it seemed to Lacey that the earth shook beneath her feet.

"Pumphrey *Fallsworth?*" Clara squeaked out the surname, and she and Lacey exchanged dismayed glances. "*The* Sir Pumphrey Fallsworth?"

"So far as I know there is only one Sir Pumphrey," said Throckmorton.

"It cannot be him," Lacey said, almost to herself. Terror streaked through her. Surely Pumphrey had been boasting when he'd claimed there was no place on this earth where she could hide from him.

"You know this Sir Pumphrey?" John asked.

"We are . . . acquainted," Lacey said. She could feel the embarrassment heating her face. She saw understanding flare in John's eyes. His mouth thinned and tightened.

"He came for you, didn't he?"

She couldn't answer him. Throckmorton was rescuing her in a way that he surely did not realize he was doing.

"Sir Pumphrey is a stockholder in the Virginia Company. He has come to inspect his holdings." Throckmorton threw her a resentful glance. "But as a true gentleman, he demanded action when he heard one of the ladies had been abducted. He worried for your gentle person, mistress."

"He did not worry enough to come himself," Percy muttered.

Throckmorton grunted in agreement before catching himself and pretending to change it to a cough. "Gentlemen don't trouble themselves with rescue parties. We soldiers are better suited for rough treks through the wilderness."

Despite his self-professed suitability, Throckmorton and his fellow soldiers appeared disgruntled at the assignment. Lacey thought she understood: He'd expected an easy assignment and now had ended up marching through the woods to save a woman who had no desire to be saved.

Especially now.

If she admitted the truth to all of them, the resentful Throckmorton might well take out his anger against her in ways she did not care to contemplate.

She was well and truly caught.

And John had still not said one word or made one gesture to indicate he wanted her to stay.

She lifted her chin. She assumed her haughtiest expression. "It's about time you got here," she said. "It won't take more than a moment to pack my belongings."

"Lacey!" Clara cried.

"Our ordeal is at an end," Lacey said, avoiding Clara's appalled expression. "We did what we had to do to survive, and now we can return to where we belong."

She had no idea if she managed to pack all of her belongings. No care for the way she stuffed her things into her trunk. Her eyes were blurred with tears the whole time she prepared, and in some way she welcomed the tears, for they dimmed the sight of the small cabin she had grown to love.

Clara worked near her, silent and angry. Percy lurked unhappily near the door, watching them.

John had disappeared into the woods.

"How are we supposed to carry those trunks?" grumbled one of the soldiers, but Throckmorton silenced him with a command, and soon they were moving across the clearing, into the trees, heading toward the hundred.

He hadn't even said good-bye to her.

He hadn't cared enough to stand by and wave as she walked away from him.

But soon a prickling at the back of her neck told her she was being watched. And not by the soldiers, not by Clara, not by Percy. Everybody else seemed oblivious to the sensation. But she felt it in her heart, and when a few hours later she whirled about she caught a glimpse of a shadow flitting from behind one tree to another. John. He'd followed them the whole way, separately, apart, watching over them to grant them safe passage through the wilderness.

She did not know how long it took them to make the journey, for she passed it in a kind of numbness that she welcomed. Better this lack of feeling than the pain of knowing John had not loved her. Better this absence of sensation than the fear and dread she ought to be feeling over confronting Pumphrey once more. She would like to stay this way forever, moving about, surviving, numb to everything.

They reached the settlement and the soldiers herded them toward the largest, finest house, where Pumphrey Fallsworth had taken residence.

Lacey managed to hang back so that she was the last one to pass through the door. She turned about and took the final few steps by walking backward. The door swung closed very slowly, narrowing her vision, and she saw him again, standing alone at the edge of the forest, alone, an outcast.

The door closed, locking her inside with everybody else, locking him away.

And she realized that her heart had not gone numb at all, for it had never ached the way it did now.

CHAPTER 17

"Hello, Lacey."

Pumphrey reached toward her, but she flinched away.

She adopted a ramrod-stiff posture, but she was not able to still the shivering that radiated from her core. She stared straight ahead at the wall. Not at him.

He walked slowly around her. Each thunk of his boot heel against the wooden floor made her want to flinch again. She felt his eyes all over her. Her skin crawled with revulsion. Oh, God, how had she ever endured his actual touch?

"I wish I could say you're looking well, but I've not seen a more bedraggled woman. I must insist you abandon this fashion once you are back in England with me."

His pronouncement shocked her out of her silence. "I'm not going back to England."

"Now, now, is that any way to express your gratitude that I've come all this way to fetch you?"

He stopped prowling around her and stood directly in front of her, so that she had no choice but to lower her gaze or stare at him straight on. She would not lower her gaze.

"You should not have bothered." Her lips had gone icy, so that she could barely tell if they moved.

Pumphrey's eyes flashed with anger, and when she trembled again it was from fear.

"I should not have had to bother," he ground out. "You caused me no end of inconvenience by running away."

"Pumphrey, matters were ended between us."

"No."

"I agree I should have said good-bye, but—"

"But it's difficult to say good-bye when you're trying to avoid being discovered as a liar."

Oh, God. Lacey's heart thumped with dread. Pumphrey could not have known that much unless Amanda had broken her word, had divulged their secrets.

"Oh, Amanda," she whispered.

"Yes, your *dear cousin* grew quite garrulous when I, um, encouraged her to tell me where you might be found."

"You didn't hurt her?"

"Hurt her? I'm not a monster, Lacey."

Lacey bit her lip to keep from shouting that she found him to be one.

"Miss Stivington was a veritible font of information. Such as telling me who and what you truly are. Such as admitting to me that you had wearied of your little game and decided to stop playing before I was ready. If you were truly the lady you claimed to be, you would know that it's not nice to play so unfairly. You would know that cheaters never win."

Terror surged through her. "I regret misleading you—"

"Misleading me? Pretending to be Amanda Stivington's cousin, flirting with me, engaging my heart—you call that merely misleading?" His eyes bulged with anger. "You played me for a fool, Lacey Cochran. Well, the joke's on you. I quite enjoyed having you as my little bit of fluff, and I have decided I want you back."

"I don't want you."

He laughed. "What a serving girl wants or does not want hardly matters, does it?"

Her cheeks burned. She still shook, but rage replaced some of the terror. "I don't love you, and I never will."

"You can't possibly believe that matters to me."

"It should. Things are . . . different . . . between a man and a woman when love is involved."

He grew very still. "The only way you could know that is if you experienced it for yourself."

She couldn't answer.

"Well, well, this adds an interesting turn to the proceedings. Dare I guess that you fancy yourself in love with the savage?"

Again she could not answer, and her silence spoke the truth. Pumphrey laughed. "Oh, how delicious. I'll break your heart the way you did mine."

"I didn't break your heart. You are merely angry—"

"Enough! We can continue this discussion on the ship. We sail back to England in two days."

"I won't go."

"Won't you?" He laughed cruelly. "Right now,

the settlement believes I am an investor come to examine the Company's holdings. I need only reveal the truth about you and you won't be able to hold your head up here. You'll be happy to slink away with your tail between your legs."

Oh, God, her deception was hemming her in at every turn. She didn't care for herself, but if the truth came out this way it would devastate John. Why, oh why hadn't she made him listen to the truth about herself? Her mind raced, seeking a way out.

"You can't tell the truth about me without admitting to the world that you were taken in by a serving girl who fooled you into believing she was Quality. They'll know a nobleman came chasing across the sea for a woman beneath his station. You'll be a laughingstock."

Pumphrey whitened with anger. She had hit home, but she felt no triumph.

"Then we must keep the truth to ourselves. Fortunately for me, I foresaw the need for another bargaining chip with you." He smirked. Her heart turned with dread. He strode to the door and summoned one of the British soldiers into the room.

"Throckmorton, kindly tell Miss Cochran what you have just finished doing."

Throckmorton assumed a military stance. "Captured the notorious kidnapper John Bradford as you requested, sir, and incarcerated him to the extent possible by binding him with ropes in the community stable."

"No!" Lacey cried.

"Well done, Throckmorton," said Pumphrey.

Throckmorton saluted and turned on his heel. Pumphrey closed the door once again.

She trembled, all but overcome at the thought

of John bound, his strong arms lashed behind him, his ankles hobbled, his freedom once again taken away from him. Because of her.

"You can't do this," she said.

"I did."

"You have no reason."

"I have every reason in the world. He abducted you. He must be made to pay. Kidnapping is an offense punishable by death, you know—if someone in authority is inclined to pursue that end."

"He was kidnapped from the streets of London and brought here against his will. Nobody was executed for the crime against *him.*"

"Isn't that a shame." Pumphrey crossed to her and stroked her cheek. She forced herself to remain still and not cringe away.

"You can't put him to death over something that has given me great joy."

She thought for a moment that he meant to hit her. She closed her eyes and tensed in anticipation of a blow.

The blow he dealt was not physical, but it struck with fierce power regardless.

"The ordeal must have been terribly difficult for you, Lacey. I see you still have not regained your wits. I can be gentle and understanding under the circumstances. I can be merciful as well."

"Please." She would not beg for herself, but she would beg for John. "Show mercy."

"I might be so inclined. . . . If I were persuaded by the victim that she has quite overcome her trauma, and if I found myself escorting that same victim back home to England where she longs to be, then there would be no accuser to hold the man up for justice."

Her freedom for his. That was what Pumphrey's extortion amounted to.

No matter how she twisted and turned it in her mind, it boiled down to one thing: All of this was her fault. Her fault for agreeing to Amanda's schemes. Her fault for dallying with Pumphrey. Her fault for running off to Virginia to escape a situation she found intolerable. Not her fault that John chose her, perhaps, but her fault that he was paying this terrible price for all her other mistakes.

"You win," she said. "I'll go with you."

"A kiss to seal the bargain," he said, moving toward her.

She averted her face. "Release him."

He tried once again to kiss her and once more she evaded him. His mouth thinned. His complexion whitened. "Do you plan to deny your favors until I meet your terms, Lacey?"

She could hear John's voice in her mind. *There is an advantage to be found in every situation.* Pumphrey had just offered one to her.

"Yes."

"I see. So, if I order Bradford's immediate release, you will leap into my arms with enthusiasm and we may shock the entire settlement with our passion."

Revulsion coursed through her. "If you release him now, then yes, that could happen."

"As appealing as you make it sound, I believe I'll wait to order his release. Not that I doubt you, my dear, but I'll feel a bit more . . . comfortable . . . if we are safe at sea before the savage is set loose."

"I insist you give the order now."

"You are not in a position to insist on anything."

She wasn't. She was thoroughly put in her place.

A serving girl at the beck and call of one of her betters.

But these days of freedom, these days of loving John, had strengthened something inside her. She refused to cower away from Pumphrey's power. "I insist that you place an order for his release to take effect when the ship sails. In front of witnesses."

He smiled, appearing amused. "Very well. Then I'll insist on a condition of my own. You confront the lout and tell him you are going with me of your own free will."

"That would not be the truth."

"Based on my experience with you, Lacey, you have the habit of being less than truthful with the men who adore you. Was it any different with your savage?" She could feel the heat rise in her face, and knew she'd betrayed herself when he laughed again. "It shouldn't be at all difficult to convince Bradford that you want to leave him."

"I don't want to lie to him again."

"Then you are signing the man's death warrant. I don't see how I can order his release if I have to spend the next few years worrying that John Bradford might take it into his head to chase after you and rescue you from me."

He would do it, too, Lacey knew. John would come after her and free her from Pumphrey if he knew she was being forced into the situation against her will. She had played right into Pumphrey's hand. She had not gained any advantage at all.

Too late now to wish with all her heart that she had been honest with John about her experience with Pumphrey. She had lied to herself and convinced herself that she'd kept the truth about her past from him in order to enrich his revenge. She saw all too clearly now how that excuse very conveniently fitted into her own need to avoid the embarrassment about revealing what a liar she'd been. In doing so, she'd only made it easier for John to believe that she would want to run off with somebody else.

She would have to lie to him yet again—this time not from choice, but to save him. And no matter how desperately she yearned to tell him the truth— all of it or even just the final part of it—she would not be able to tell him.

Withholding the truth this time would kill her soul. It seemed somehow to be a fitting punishment for all she had done.

A commotion at the stable door roused him from a light doze. An arm dangled a lantern inside, illuminating the area enough for John to see Lacey as she walked into the barn, followed closely by the bearer of the lantern. A soldier.

The soldier took up position near the door.

She walked toward the stall where John stood tied like a recalcitrant gelding, and the only thing worse than the blow to his pride from having her see him like this was noticing the fatigue darkening the skin below her eyes, the puckers creasing her forehead, the general droopiness of her posture. It had taken no time at all for the hardships of this rough land to take their toll upon her.

She gripped the top rail of the stall. Tears shimmered in her eyes. "I'm so sorry," she said.

He couldn't stand to see her so dejected. He shrugged, so emphatically that his joints ached from the pressure of making the motion while tied. "They've been threatening this for years. It was bound to happen sooner or later."

"Your incarceration is only temporary. You will be released as soon as . . . within two days."

He cocked a brow. "All of this is to teach me some sort of lesson, then?"

"No," she said. "To teach me."

She looked so thoroughly miserable that his arms ached with the need to hold her, to smooth her hair back from her face, to comfort her if he could. "Lacey—"

"I have to tell you as much of the truth as I can. I want you to hear it from me. It's my fault completely that you are here, like this."

"I kidnapped you, Lacey. The charges were quite clear."

She shook her head, refusing to be absolved. "That's only the surface excuse. The real reason you are here is because the sins of my past have risen to haunt me. You were right about what you said back at the cabin. Pumphrey Fallsworth came here for me."

"Fallsworth . . . and *you.*" He'd suspected as much, but hearing it validated by her own lips stunned him into numbness. She had said her lover was above her in status. He had not dreamed how high. Lacey and a man who could order British soldiers to do as he commanded. Lacey and a man who had the wealth and power to arrange virtually instant passage on a ship in order to come after her.

His efforts at learning the gentlemanly arts must have seemed so pathetic as to be amusing to her.

But she had not laughed. And the woman who had made love to him had not thrown comparisons in his face.

She peered over her shoulder toward the observant guard. Her head lowered with embarrassment. "Pumphrey wants me to go back with him."

"And you want to go with him?"

The soldier stirred. He leaned forward, clearly eavesdropping, and obviously did not care that John noticed.

She bit her lip, and gave one quick nod.

He sagged against his bonds. She'd never made so much as that gesture in all the time she'd been with him, when she'd hinted she might like to stay. She was leaving. There would be no chance to let her get to know him, to convince her that he loved her, to watch over her and protect her and live out his days with her.

She was going away. With another man.

He tried to take some comfort in knowing she would soon find herself in England's gentle breezes, with her food and shelter provided, with no threat of Indian attack hanging over her head. When he'd been arrested by the British and dragged through the hundred, he'd noticed that none of the preparations he'd suggested, none of the changes requested by the Indians, had been undertaken. The Indians wouldn't wait long to strike against the settlers. Lacey, at least, would be safe.

The notion did not make him want to leap with joy, but it left him with a very small measure of peace.

And gratitude. Perhaps the lessons he'd learned in Groat Alley had served him well after all. Perhaps holding back his feelings for her, staying aloof and not letting her know how deeply his heart had been touched, had been the best thing to do. He would look the total fool if he did as his heart urged and begged her to stay, to wait until he got free of this place, to maybe consider putting her heart and her trust in him.

"It is for the best that you go," he said, keeping his voice netural. "What awaits you here . . . would not be pleasant."

She shivered.

"When do you leave?"

"Within two days."

So soon. She couldn't wait to be rid of this place. Of him.

"Perhaps I'll be freed by then and be able to wave goodbye from the shore."

She stole another look toward the guard. "I don't think you'll be released until I am gone."

"Ah. Does Mr. Fallsworth fear I might try to spirit you away again?"

"Would you?"

She gazed at him, and it must have been a sign of his own need that caused him to fancy she begged him with her eyes to kidnap her once again.

"He need not worry," John said more harshly than he'd intended.

With each comment he told her she meant nothing to him. He wondered if she knew how it hurt to drag each word from his lips when he wanted nothing more than to beg her to stay and give him another chance.

She gave him a bright smile. "Well, then, I see you are in good spirits and I need not have worried about you. I will take my leave of you now, as I am sure I will be too busy to see you again before I leave."

He nodded, not trusting himself to say anything.

She left.

* * *

Lacey and Clara lay side by side on the small mat in the Hedgingses' storage room. The couple had reluctantly welcomed back Clara and had agreed to allow Lacey to stay with her on the condition they would both seek new lodgings as soon as possible.

Lacey could not stop trembling.

"Are you cold?" Clara asked. She rested the back of her hand against Lacey's forehead, as if testing for signs of fever. Lacey shook her hand away.

"Not cold."

"Perhaps not. Your teeth aren't chattering."

They weren't chattering because she was holding them clenched tight. Against the pain of seeing and hearing John dismiss her as if she meant nothing to him. Through the pain, though, she recognized something more: anger.

"They get everything their way," she grated out.

"Who gets what?"

"Men. They always turn matters to their own advantage."

"Well, yes they do—but what on earth brought that on?"

Lacey told her. How John had gotten what he'd wanted from her and was now content to see her leave the country and trouble him no more. How Pumphrey would soon be triumphant.

"Maybe you could run away," Clara suggested.

"I couldn't. John would be at Pumphrey's mercy then. I'm trapped, Clara."

Trapped between one man who wanted her for all the wrong reasons and a man who didn't want her at all.

"Are you so sure about Mr. Bradford? I have good reason to believe he cares about you, Lacey."

Lacey laughed with no humor. "He seemed positively happy to be rid of me. I asked him flat out if he would kidnap me again if he had the chance, and he said no."

"Humphf. That's why men get their way—they simply reach out and take whatever it is they want without explaining themselves and without regard to the consequences."

The truth of Clara's statement deepened Lacey's anger. "Well, maybe women ought to turn the tables. Maybe we should reach out and take what *we* want for a change."

"Why, that's an excellent idea, Lacey!"

"What is an excellent idea?"

"Kidnapping Mr. Bradford."

"What?"

"Turn the tables! Do unto him what he has done unto you, or something like that."

Clara grew excited. "Just think of the possibilities, Lacey! Kidnap Mr. Bradford and disappear with him into the wilderness, and in one fell swoop you will have solved all your problems."

It was ridiculous. Audacious.

Appealing.

And exactly the sort of thing John had promised to teach her to do—seek out and seize an advantage in any situation.

"What if he doesn't want me?"

"By the time you find that out, Mr. Fallsworth will have sailed back to England and you will still have accomplished the goal of freeing Mr. Bradford from incarceration."

"I couldn't do it alone."

"I will help you."

"Do you think we could? He's terribly strong. He might struggle."

Clara frowned. "Perhaps Percy would help us."

"He wouldn't think it at all proper, I'm afraid."

"No, he wouldn't. But that could be the very best thing for him, to engage him in a daring rescue mission. He's entirely too stuffy. If I can talk him into helping us and get him away from this infernal place with his infernal need to maintain appearances, why, he might turn out to be fun after all."

"So in a way you would be kidnapping Percy at the same time I am kidnapping John."

They reached for each other's hands in the dark and burst into giggles.

Nervous giggles.

"He's bound very tightly with stout ropes," Lacey said.

"I'm sure there's a large knife that will slice through that rope as if it's not there. Percy will know where to find it."

"I somehow can't see him just following meekly when we announce he's being kidnapped."

They fell into thoughtful silence.

"I have it!" Clara exclaimed. "We shall tie him with our own bonds while he is still roped up."

"He might yell out."

"We'll gag him."

"He's too heavy to carry."

"We'll fashion one of those hauling contraptions he rigged up to move our trunks through the woods. The travois. Percy learned how to make one."

"We *could* do this," Lacey whispered in awe.

"Yes, we could. The question is, will we?"

They gripped their hands tightly.

"If I don't do this, I'll be sailing to England with Pumphrey in two days' time. I will never be able to tell John that I love him."

It wasn't as hard to say it out loud as Lacey had imagined it would be. She loved him. She knew it. Clara knew it. The only one who didn't know it was John, and by God she would do all she could to make him listen to her while she told him.

"If I don't help you," said Clara, "I will spend the rest of my days as a spinster while the man I love continues to believe himself unattractive and ultimately returns to England."

"We have nothing to lose and everything to gain," Lacey said.

"Everything."

"Then we shall do it." Lacey straightened her shoulders. "We shall make our preparations during the day tomorrow and kidnap our men tomorrow night."

"Tomorrow night," Clara echoed faintly. She cleared her throat. She stiffened her shoulders and stuck out her hand. Lacey gave her a quick handshake.

They giggled.

CHAPTER 18

The stable door creaked.

In itself, the creaking was nothing new. The poorly fitted and shoddily hinged door groaned with every gust of wind. But this was different. The whining creak hinted that someone might be pushing the door tight against its hinges in order to minimize the sound. They weren't succeeding very well.

Shafts of moonlight penetrated the gloom as the door edged open. He was able to spot the moon—past midnight. His instincts alerted him to danger. Nobody had any reason to approach him so stealthily at this time of night . . . nobody with good intentions.

"Who goes there?" he called.

" 'T-t-t-t-tis me, John. P-p-p-p-ercy."

Relief swept through John, but he wondered at the shakiness in Percy's voice. Percy slunk from the door to a shadow and then crept to yet another darkened space, giving the man the look of a foot-pad sneaking in toward his next victim.

"As far as I know, visitors have not been forbidden to me," John said.

"Have you had visitors?" Percy rasped from the dark.

"Just one." Lacey. Nobody in the settlement thought of him as a friend, and he'd expected no others.

He didn't expect her to be back, either.

But Percy had come. John felt an unexpected fullness in his chest.

"I can't see you," John said.

Scurrying sounds marked Percy's progress. John heard the fumbling of flints, and soon a small candle flickered in Percy's hand. John couldn't tell whether it was the flame's movement that cast strange shadows, or if Percy's eyes really were darting from side to side. Percy lodged the candle in a crack that split the topmost stall rail.

"I brought you some water. Here, let me help you."

He bent to one knee next to John and drew a water skin from his belt. Galling as it was to have a man hold a jar to his lips so he could drink, John welcomed the cool water.

"That's it, drink it all," Percy urged. "Tilt your head back. It'll go easier."

His captors had not denied him food or water, but they had not provided enough to meet his full needs. John gladly obliged Percy's request, closing his eyes in the sheer pleasure of slaking his thirst as he tipped his head back.

"Sorry," Percy whispered.

The bag fell away from John's lips, and the remaining water spilled over his shirtfront. Percy, acting with a quickness John had never noted in him, whipped a rolled rag from his pocket and shoved it into John's mouth, which was still gaping open like that of a baby bird awaiting another droplet from its mother's beak. Percy yanked the rag tight and knotted it behind John's head, effectively gagging him.

John might not have been able to talk even had he not been gagged, so stunned was he by Percy's action.

He shook his head, trying to loosen the gag. He lunged toward Percy, but his bonds held him in place. Furious but impotent, he had to settle for glaring at the man whom, mere moments before, he had thought his only friend, when a movement near the door caught his attention.

Clara Cutler tiptoed into the barn.

Lacey followed right on her heels.

Lacey. The small candle barely illuminated the stable, but it provided light enough for him to see her beloved face, her enchanting form. She looked beautiful in candlelight. His hands were tied at the wrists, but that couldn't stop him from making the gesture that had been so much a part of him for all of his life. He committed the sight of Lacey walking toward him in candlelight to memory, then closed his fist around the memory to seal it forever.

He'd saved so much in that way, the way Rob Marton had taught him. Now it seemed a futile action. Trapping a memory of Lacey was futile— reliving a memory could never equal the glory of actually touching her with the hand now fisted.

Just thinking about having her, warm and soft and pulsing against him, made his flesh tingle anew, with the itch to stroke her, to cup her, to caress her from head to toe.

All those years, he'd used that motion to capture feelings such as anger, vengeance, hatred. He'd wasted so much time.

He couldn't even tell her.

The women drew closer and he saw they both carried ropes.

"Hurry!" Percy said hoarsely.

Lacey knelt beside him. She placed her hand against his breast. She leaned toward him. Dear God, she couldn't mean to kiss him now, with his mouth occupied by a gag! The minute he escaped this ridiculous situation, he would draw and quarter Percy Bledsoe, and then he would kiss Lacey the way he'd dreamed of kissing her. . . .

"Sorry," she whispered, just as Percy had done.

"Yes, sorry," said Clara grudgingly as she, too, dropped to her knees on the stable floor, on his opposite side.

With a precision that made John believe they had practiced the maneuver, each woman fastened one of his arms with a rope. He tried asking what they were doing. They ignored him thoroughly. They swapped the ends of their ropes and pulled, managing to painfully draw his wrists close together behind his back. The pain broke him out of his stunned torpor. He yelled, but the sound was absorbed into the gag. He struggled, but his bindings gave him no room.

"Shhh," Lacey whispered into his ear. "We're setting you free."

Setting him free? By gagging and breaking his arms? He struggled and protested even more.

They immobilized his legs next.

When John couldn't move at all, Percy severed the ropes that had originally bound John to the stable wall with several loud thwacks, until only those new ropes put in place by his lover and his friends held him helpless as a swaddled babe.

The three of them toppled him to lie face-down on the littered straw floor, and then Lacey and Clara sat on him while Percy dashed out of the stable and returned with a travois. With much groaning and—humiliatingly—muffled giggling, they then rolled him onto the travois and secured him to it with yet another rope.

Whispering, cautioning each other to be quiet and careful, the trio smuggled him out of his prison.

"You are moving rather smartly despite your load, Percy," said Clara.

Percy shrugged modestly and then realized Clara probably didn't notice the movement because of the poles pressing down on his shoulders.

"It is remarkably easy to move heavy weights with this travois," he said, noting with pride that his breathing showed not the slightest sign of exertion. Overall, he felt stronger and fitter than ever before since adopting John Bradford's way of life. "I dare-say Mr. Bradford weighs as much as Miss Cochran and I put together, and yet it's no work at all to pull him along in this thing."

"I watched Mr. Hedgings struggle a great deal with his small wheeled cart," Clara said. "It would be a great boon to the settlers if they, too, had copied this contraption from the Indians the way John has done."

"They won't pay attention to anything John tells them," said Lacey.

They were conversing so lightly, so happily, that an observer could not be blamed for thinking they were on a pleasant stroll through a park rather than their true mission: smuggling a prisoner of the Crown through a dark wilderness.

Percy knew they should be walking silently. Knew they should move faster and more warily. But the three of them were all giddy with the success of their venture, and none of them seemed able to remain solemn for more than a second.

Percy glanced back over his shoulder at the prisoner in question. A little of his lightheartedness deserted him at seeing John Bradford tied so securely that he could not move. Thank God John wasn't facing him, for Percy knew he'd see rage and disgust in his expression over the part he was playing in this strange abduction.

John might not be able to see him, but he apparently sensed Percy's regard, for he commenced struggling against his bonds, and muffled sounds came from behind his gag. Percy couldn't tell whether John was uttering threats or warning them of some danger.

And danger there might be. He'd spent so many hours of the past couple of days learning woods lore from John—so many hours to barely scratch the surface of what John knew—he'd learned just enough to know that he was pitifully incapable of fending off the dangers that could be lurking all around them.

Percy Bledsoe, former indolent gentleman, of late reluctant tobacco farmer, now found himself responsible for the safety of two helpless women and one man so thoroughly incapacitated that he would no doubt starve or thirst to death if they simply abandoned him and left him tied to the contrivance.

He wondered for the first time how his older

brother Ambrose felt about the responsibilities that had descended upon him as the family heir. The tenants. The buildings. The crops and the animals. His role as arbiter of disputes.

For most of his youth Percy had resented the impoverishment that his birth order had decreed for him. He'd been so resentful of Ambrose's good fortune that he'd secretly rejoiced when his brother's time became totally devoted to estate duties while Percy had the run of society. By the time Percy's father had died, Ambrose had assumed all control, and they barely exchanged two words through the course of a day.

He had assumed his brother was joking, was attempting to make him feel better about his lot in life, when Ambrose had unexpectedly shirked his duties to mark Percy's last day in England. He'd accompanied Percy to the dock on the day he sailed for Virginia, and at the last moment had sworn he wished he could trade places with him.

Ambrose would have liked John Bradford. He would have understood, too, how Percy felt being in charge of this little group.

Percy wished Ambrose were here now. He might have liked the man Percy felt he was on the verge of becoming.

The back of his neck prickled, whether from realizing how unprepared he was for shouldering responsibility, or because someone was watching them, he could not say.

"Perhaps we could free Mr. Bradford now," he suggested. "We're far enough away from the settlement."

"Not yet," said Lacey.

"I'm rather enjoying having him trussed up like that, to tell you the truth," said Clara.

Percy's senses signaled a warning again.

"Perhaps we should try to move more quietly, then. We are crashing about with such abandon that we won't be able to hear what's around us."

"It's so late, even Indians must be asleep," said Clara. "Besides, we can't be that far away from the cabin. Why stop now?"

"When we get there," said Lacey, "I want you and Percy to lock John and me into the cellar. He will have no choice but to listen to me—or crawl through the escape hole to avoid what I have to say."

"I'm sure John would be happy to listen to you at any time," Percy said. "He'd listen to you right now, in fact. He wouldn't have much choice about it, would he?"

Clara clapped her hands together. "Percy's right. John could always crawl through that escape hole, but he can't get away from you now."

Lacey halted in mid-stride. "I *should* do it now," she declared. "Insisting on going all the way back to the cabin—why that was just another way of putting it off."

Percy gladly stopped. "Do it," he urged, not knowing what "it" was, but only that once it was finished they could free John from the travois and Percy for one would feel much safer.

He certainly didn't feel safe now. The prickling sensation crawling along his skin had grown almost physically uncomfortable. Now that they'd come to a stop, he could see what poor woodsmen they'd been, for the forest was ominously silent around them. They'd frightened off every wild thing.

A branch snapped.

But not off in the forest, where it would cause him to panic—no, this snapping noise came from right behind him. No doubt John's travois rested on a fallen twig and it had cracked beneath the weight.

Or perhaps Lacey had broken it when she knelt down on the ground next to the travois. "If you and Clara would give us a few moments of privacy—"

She screamed.

At her outburst, Percy twisted his head to look over his shoulder, and only sheer terror numbed his throat enough to stop him from shrieking out loud like a girl.

Standing in a semicircle behind the travois stood six Indians.

Terror froze Lacey in place.

Six pairs of eyes glittered in the moonlight. Six dark shapes loomed huge and menacing. She ought to faint, she supposed, or scream, or run.

Instead, anger—hot and thick—bubbled its way through the fear.

She would *not* be thwarted again in her attempt to tell John the truth about her!

With a wordless cry of rage, she flung herself at the closest Indian and pushed him in the chest.

"Oooof!"

From him she went to the next and then to the next. So much frustration roared through her head that she scarcely noted Clara's frantic "Lacey!" or Percy's urgent "Miss Cochran!"

She pushed back yet another Indian. "You will *not* interfere now! There is nothing that will stop me from telling this man what he needs to know."

She moved to shove the final Indian, and his hand snaked out and caught her wrists in a crushing grip. The pain of her bones being crushed together brought her to her knees. He held her there, making no move to scalp her or slit her throat, while her anger ebbed and the terror began to crawl back into place.

She hung there, hurting, panting, and gradually her senses returned.

Oh, God, what had she done?

She'd accosted six Indians in the middle of a dark forest.

The Indian murmured something to his companions, no doubt listing the ways he meant to torture and kill them. She had brought this on; she had condemned her friends and the man she loved to certain death because she'd been thwarted yet again in her need to tell John the truth about herself.

The Indian's companions answered, and then they all seemed to grimace frighteningly at the same time, for the moonlight flashed from six sets of broad white teeth. . . .

And the Indians burst into laughter.

CHAPTER 19

It did no good, John reflected as the travois imprisoning him bumped along the trail; it accomplished nothing whatsoever for a man to vow he would never again let himself be forced to do things against his will.

He'd sworn to remain his own master all those years ago, the first time in his life that he'd been bound and gagged and hauled against his will.

And yet here he was again: bound and gagged and hauled, conscripted by a crew consisting of two women and a fop, and now pirated by a far more sinister bunch.

He'd been caught because he'd forgotten the standards he'd set. He'd let himself fall in love. He'd let himself worry about others. He'd let his own safety take second place to concern for others. If he hadn't fallen in love with Lacey, hadn't followed behind to make sure she and Percy—and yes, even Clara—were escorted with honor and dignity, well, the British soldiers wouldn't have taken him by surprise, wouldn't have caught him.

If he hadn't fallen in love with Lacey, he would still be free.

If he hadn't fallen in love with Lacey, he would still be completely and utterly alone.

She walked alongside the travois. From time to time she would look down at him, and he could see the sweet curve of her cheek, the soft arch of her lips. He could find but one advantage to this situation: He would die with her beloved face filling his vision as he left this earth.

He wished he'd been able to tell her.

It appeared unlikely he'd ever have the chance now.

He recognized two of the Indians who now shepherded their little group through the forest. Only two. That meant there were four new faces—twice as many unknowns—and that did not bode well, not well at all.

He'd struggled and strained against his ropes for so long that he had no strength left, but just to be sure, he tried once more to escape. Curse Percy for learning knot-tying lore so well! He broke out into such a sweat that anyone chancing to see the moisture beading his forehead and darkening his shirt would think he was chopping firewood rather than lying almost perfectly still.

The warnings he'd heard from Opechancanough just days earlier echoed through his brain along with his regrets about Lacey. He'd made only the slightest effort to convince the settlers, and he'd given Lacey no chance at all. He hadn't tried hard enough with either of them. The ache in his soul told him how wrong he'd been in thinking he would protect himself by staying aloof.

He'd made only token efforts to convince the settlers of the seriousness of the Indian threats. He'd backed off all too quickly when they derided him and scorned his opinion. He'd permitted himself to feel self-righteous, had lied to himself that he'd done all he could.

He'd outright feared baring his feelings to Lacey. Keeping them to himself hadn't stopped them from blossoming, though. He loved her. He loved that little minx, loved her spirit, loved everything about her. He'd never have the chance to tell her now.

He would lose them all now.

And he hadn't even saved himself. All of his careful aloofness had done nothing but diminish the glory of the years he had been blessed to have lived. Now he would spend eternity regretting his mistakes.

John didn't know how much time had passed when finally they reached a small clearing deep in the wilderness.

Dawn was a mere hint in the sky, so the light was poor, but John thought he might have been here before. It was difficult to tell, because the last time he'd been here, there had been no cluster of Indian shelters, no burning campfires, no dozens of Indian warriors standing grim-faced and silent watching them approach.

Their captors stopped. The warriors circled around.

It was a war camp. The Indians had gathered to attack the settlers, just as Opechancanough had said they would.

Lacey and Clara clung together. Clara's face was streaked with tears, but Lacey stood with her chin tipped slightly upward, her stance rigid and defiant.

He felt an overwhelming surge of pride in her. What a remarkable woman. She had to be terrified, but she let nothing show. Her staunch show of bravery earlier with the Indians had touched him as nothing ever had in his life.

At the same time, her courage shamed him. Lacey had only wanted to talk to him and he'd refused time and again to listen. He had wanted to talk to her and had been unable to summon the words. It looked as if they would go to their deaths with the most important things forever left unsaid, because he'd been too cowardly to reveal the secrets in his heart.

The sky brightened a little more, revealing masses of Indian warriors standing behind those who directly surrounded them.

"The advantage, John," Lacey whispered to him. "There is one."

The pupil's skill exceeded that of the teacher. He couldn't see it.

"You are the only one of us four who could cause trouble for them. While there were only six, they feared letting you loose. Surely they won't be afraid to set you free now."

She was right. The advantage seemed so slight as to be infinitesimal. . . .

"When you are free, anything can happen," she said.

She had an exaggerated sense of his fighting abilities if she thought he could fight their way out of this. But . . . if he were freed, he could speak the words he'd wanted to say.

She dropped to her knees alongside the travois, prompting a guttural objection from one of their captors. She paid him no mind.

"John, this really is not the best time for this,

but I fear there may be no other. I spent hours and hours going over this in my head, trying to find the right words, and now realize I don't have the luxury of a long explanation. What I've been trying to tell you all this time is, I am not a lady of noble birth. I'm a common serving girl. This is all my fault, and I wish I could change things, but I can't. Oh, and I love you."

For once, the gag didn't matter, for there was nothing John could think to say.

She smiled down at him, a bittersweet curving of her lips, and stroked his cheek. "I really do love you."

The caress didn't last half as long as John wished, for one of the Indians caught her by the arm and pulled her back to her feet.

The crowd around them parted, and to John's intense dread he recognized the imposing figure and noble, hawklike face of the man who passed through the path thus made.

Ipitaquod. The *werowance*. The man the settlers referred to as the Indian chief.

Ipitaquod's presence meant the Virginia settlers had run out of time.

Ipitaquod spoke too quietly for John to hear, and a brave approached. He crouched next to John's travois and pulled a knife from the scabbard at his waist. Lacey cried out and bent toward him, but another Indian caught her by the shoulders and drew her back in place.

The knife hovered near his neck. John would not close his eyes. If he was to meet his death lying helpless against it, he would not do it blind as well.

But the blade merely hovered near his ear, and then with a quick slashing motion the brave cut through the gag.

Ipitaquod approached. He made a sign of respect, and John answered in the only way he could, with a nod of his head. His mouth was dry as sand and his throat seized up from the long hours of gagging. He swallowed frantically.

"Opechancanough tells me he has asked you to warn your people," said Ipitaquod.

"I did."

"They have not changed their ways."

"They do not believe me."

"Then what Opechancanough promised shall be done." Ipitaquod's eyes darkened with sorrow.

"Wait—please." John knew that the gag-instilled dryness of his throat did not account for his difficulty as he begged. "Their failure to understand is my fault. I did not try hard enough to convince them."

"Why?"

"Because I have spent most of my life behaving like a fool," said John. "They should not be made to pay for my mistakes."

Ipitaquod looked up at the sky for a long moment. At last he said, "Are you asking me to give your people another chance?"

"I'm asking you to give *me* another chance."

"If I grant this chance, tell me what you will do."

"I will tell this woman standing next to me that I love her," said John.

Lacey gave a wordless cry and pressed her fist to her mouth. She stared down at him with joy illuminating her from within.

Ipitaquod chuckled. He made a motion with his hands, and the Indian brave sliced through the ropes binding John to the travois. Ipitaquod extended his hand and helped John stand. John opened his arms and Lacey hurled herself into his embrace. He pulled her close, scarcely daring to believe that he held her, that he breathed her scent, that she'd heard what he said and didn't run away.

"Opechancanough says your woman fought like a she-bear for you."

"She is brave."

"Women such as she might help your race strengthen its weak blood."

"Yes."

"You will sire children upon this woman?"

"If we are given the chance." John took a huge breath, and grew daring. "If we are given the chance to live, I would ask her to be my wife."

"And you would stay in this land?"

"Yes."

Ipitaquod nodded. "We admire strong women. We admire a man who has tried to learn our ways and live with this land instead of forcing the land to live with tobacco. Are these others who are with you of the same mind?"

"Yes."

"Then you four are welcome to live."

John felt boneless with relief, but soon his conscience stirred.

"The others, Ipitaquod?"

"Go to your people. Try—one more time. Convince them that we must see a sign within three days that shows their willingness to live at peace with us. Three days, John Bradford. If we do not see the sign, then you know what will happen."

It seemed the most precious gift of all, this chance not only to save lives, but to redeem his soul from the bitter need for revenge that had consumed him for too long.

And Lacey had brought it all about. Made him

care enough to try. Fought for him and impressed the Indians with her strength.

"Ipitaquod," said John. "Would you do the supreme honor of joining me with my woman?"

"You want to *marry* me?" Lacey whispered.

She clung to him. Gloried in the strong thump of his pulse beneath her palms. Reveled in the weight of his arms, the strength of his embrace.

She'd told him the truth about herself, and he wanted to marry her.

"Ipitaquod would join us as man and wife in the Indian way. 'Twould not be a legal marriage in the eyes of the English. It would be a sacred bond to me."

"And to me." She lifted her face for his kiss, and felt that any words said over them after that were mere formalities; in her heart, she belonged to him now.

Forever.

Even if their time on earth proved to be shortened, the vows of their hearts would bind them together for eternity.

"Oh, Lacey!" Clara sobbed.

Clara. Oh, God, she'd made a pact with Clara.

It seemed a lifetime ago, when she'd happily seized on any excuse to avoid her wedding night. She'd recognized the selfishness of her pact at the time she made it, and had promised herself to change away from doing that sort of thing. She could not now back away from the bargain just because it suited her to do so.

Reluctantly, she disengaged herself from their embrace.

"I promised Clara I would not marry for two weeks, or until both of us found husbands," Lacey said.

"Nonsense, I won't hold you to that," Clara said.

Percy slipped his hand over Clara's mouth.

"Miss Clara Cutler, would you do me the supreme honor of joining with me?"

The Indian joining ceremony was simple, and perfect for two people the likes of Lacey Cochran and John Bradford.

And Percy Bledsoe, gentleman, and Miss Clara Cutler found it very much to their liking, too.

"I think I was fourteen when I began to believe I would never marry," Clara said to Lacey.

"I'm not sure I ever thought I would marry," Lacey mused.

Marriage had not seemed something worth dreaming about. The wild yearning that had been a part of her for as long as she could remember had made it impossible for her ever to consider marrying any of the men she'd known back in England. Marriage in her class promised nothing but endless drudgery with no hope of ever escaping it.

She'd had that brief affair with Pumphrey, but never had fooled herself into thinking anything permanent would come of it—and at the end had deliberately run away from it. She knew she'd be expected to marry a man here in the Virginia Colony, but in her heart she hadn't believed a marriage would last once her deceptions were revealed.

But John knew everything about her now. John had asked the Indian leader to join them, and spoken sacred vows that would bind them together for a lifetime.

"Look at us now. Traveling through the wilderness while our husbands—our husbands!—walk on ahead." Clara shook her head in wonder.

"Are you tired?" asked Lacey.

"I certainly should be. We trekked half the night before the Indians captured us, and now we're heading straight back to where we started from."

"We have to warn the settlers."

"Yes, we do."

We. Such a small word, so easily formed with a kissing motion of the lips. *We.* Linking Clara with her in lifelong friendship. Linking the four of them in pursuit of a common purpose. Linking her forevermore with John.

She slowed for a moment to watch him. The effortless way he moved. The shape of him, so perfect to her eyes, so exciting, making her so aware of her own shape and how it was fashioned to fit with his.

"I must say this is not the way I envisioned spending my wedding night. Back when I used to imagine I might marry, I mean," said Clara.

"Nor I," said Lacey, and at just that moment John looked back over his shoulder. He caught her staring at him.

He smiled.

"Go walk with him," Clara said, giving Lacey a little push.

Lacey quickened her step. John slowed; Percy almost stopped. In no time they'd all rearranged themselves without a word being exchanged.

John's arm curved around her waist. She knew they wouldn't be able to walk side by side for long; the trail was too narrow. But it felt nice for that moment to be tucked up against him, to feel his body moving next to hers. She smiled up at him.

He winked at her.

"John Bradford!" Delighted, she smiled again, and then cried out with surprise when he quickly spun her off the ground and lunged off the trail and into a quiet little pocket of space with a perimeter thick with leaves and tangled branches.

He pressed her up against a tree. She could hear his heart thudding against her, and behind her she could hear Clara and Percy stifling giggles as they moved past the little rendezvous.

"I am in desperate need of a kiss," said John. He proved his desperation with a thorough claiming of her mouth that left her breathless and shaking.

"I wish you would let me take you to the cabin," he said when he finished.

"I wish we didn't have to go to the hundred."

"I must go."

"I know. And I must go with you."

His arms tightened around her. She felt his lips move against her hair.

"This journey might be our only time together as man and wife," he said.

"I know." Her throat tightened, and she swallowed against the pain.

"If anything should happen at the hundred—"

"Nothing will happen."

She tried to sound assured. But inside she knew his warning ought to be heeded. Pumphrey was still there. The British soldiers were still there. John was an escaped prisoner, and she the object of Pumphrey's obsession, as well as a culprit in helping John to escape. Clara and Percy, too, had broken such law as existed in Virginia Colony.

There was no logical reason to expect they could walk into Malvern's Hundred, speak their piece, and leave without something terrible happening.

She would urge him to abandon this mission, but

she was certain that turning him away from doing what his honor demanded would be even more terrible.

"Did you ever consider not going?" she asked. "Consider disappearing into the forest and letting them pay the price for their stubbornness?"

"I've been equally stubborn, Lacey. But I am not a complete fool. We shall head for the wilderness ourselves if they won't listen to reason."

"You want them to have a chance."

"Aye."

Her heart surged with love for him. "This is who you are," she said. "You care about others so much that you'll risk your life for them."

"My mother tried to teach me to watch out for those who are weaker. I conveniently forgot her lessons for far too long."

"John." Lacey reached up and stroked his cheek. "Your mother would be proud of you."

To her consternation, her observation brought tears to her husband's eyes. Tears, followed by a blindingly brilliant smile unlike any she had ever seen on him before.

They returned to the trail and hurried to catch up with Percy and Clara. When next she shared confidences with Clara, she would be sure to tell her that her wedding night had exceeded even her wildest dreams.

CHAPTER 20

John chose the least direct route to the center of Malvern's Hundred. Not because he wanted to prolong their arrival, but because he knew the settlers at the farthest-flung homesteads would already be out working their tobacco and would need time to come into the heart of the settlement.

The added distance meant more effort from all of them. John knew that Lacey and Clara—probably Percy as well—were dead tired from their long night of adventure. None of them complained, but John couldn't help wishing anew that the women had agreed to return to his cabin and wait for . . . for whatever would happen. Both women had refused.

He and Percy had chosen well.

They forged on. He knew their presence would rouse curiosity, but he wasn't sure curiosity alone would be enough to draw the settlers in to hear what he had to say. He taxed their flagging energy even more as they crossed the seemingly limitless acres, sending one off toward a lone figure engaged in the never-ending hoeing, sending another into a shack where smoke hinted that someone might be cooking, sending another into a copse where crab apples were known to be found, in the hope that some people had had the sense to go and gather some of them.

He didn't want to approach the settlers himself. There'd been too much animosity between them for too many years. He feared that they'd welcome the chance to refuse a direct request from him, just to spite him to his face.

By the time they neared the center of the hundred, a long line of settlers straggled behind them. Somehow, others from the opposite end of the hundred had heard word of something going on— no doubt some of those Lacey and Clara and Percy had rounded up had sent children or bondsmen running ahead to warn the others. John didn't care how it came about. He was only happy to see the crowd.

Well, happy to see most of the crowd. He wasn't quite thrilled with the way the small British Army contingent stepped forward in lockstep as John's little group approached the tobacco shed. And he had to forcibly restrain himself from throwing his fist in the face of Pumphrey Fallsworth when he realized that the so-called gentleman was using the soldiers as a personal shield.

"Arrest this man!" Fallsworth called. Throckmorton put his hand on his sword hilt.

"On what charges?" Percy had moved to stand next to John.

"Kidnapping."

"I went with him of my own free will!" Lacey's voice rang with sincerity.

The townspeople stirred. Some pointed fingers, some talked behind their hands. John's anger at Fallsworth roiled outward to include all those who dared whisper insults about the woman he loved.

She sensed it in him. She placed her hand on his arm. "Let it pass, John. That isn't important now."

He put his hand over hers. Felt her pulse, strong and true, beating in time to his own. His anger ebbed. "It *is* important. But it must wait."

Fallsworth stormed to the front of the line of soldiers. "Arrest him, I said!"

"But sir, if the lady says she wasn't kidnapped—"

"I don't care what that strumpet says!"

A gasp swept through the crowd. John's fury leaped to greater heights.

"She run off with him twice!" called a man.

"That redhead, she run off with him, too!"

Percy, trembling with rage, had to be restrained by John. "Mr. Hedgings, you have a nerve to condemn Clara for something that was honest and pure and—"

"Calm down, everyone!"

Malmford, the tobacco factor, pushed his way through the crowd. "Mr. Fallsworth, I understand you represent the Virginia Company's interests, but you are not the law here. And as for you, John Bradford, I'm damned curious to know what you're up to, marching in here like you're leading a parade."

"I've come to warn you all," John said.

"Oh, lord, not this again." Malmford shook his head. "John, if you staged this little scene just to give us the same old song about the Indians . . ."

The old fury seemed to swirl like red mists through John's mind.

Run.

He grabbed Lacey's hand, and some of the drive to flee disappeared.

His breath came hard. He'd tried. They had no use for him or for what he knew. God curse them all. What idiocy had made him believe he should forget all the years when nothing but his thoughts of vengeance had sustained him?

Run. Lacey's hand gripped his, harder, holding him there.

If he ran, he could escape from the humiliation, from the pain. . . .

The pain?

It hurt to have Malmford doubt his word.

Hurt.

He took a shuddering breath. The vengeance had masked the hurt, and now that his thirst for revenge was gone, he felt the real emotion he'd masked with his vengeance.

He didn't hate these people. They were his own kind. Battered down by life in one way or another, but striving to rise above what fate had handed them—just as he had done. He loved them. Against all odds, he loved them. And only by allowing his heart to open for Lacey had he learned the truth at last.

He prayed they would heed what he said.

"Listen to him, Mr. Malmford," Percy spoke out earnestly. "Please."

They quieted then, listening to Percy where they'd been reluctant to listen to John, and yes, it hurt, but not so much as condemning them to their deaths would hurt. He repeated the warnings. He retold the story of his meeting in the woods with Opechancanough. He watched their eyes widen with fright and disbelief when he recounted their experience with the war party in the woods.

He doubted he'd ever spoken so many words all strung together at one time in his entire life.

Lacey stood tall and proud beside him through every word.

"If you do not heed the warnings, you will die," he finished.

Silence gripped the crowd.

The snuffling of wild hogs rooting beneath the oak trees for forage broke the quiet. And then soon after, a huge flock of birds flew overhead, darkening the sky, their wings creating a din that seemed to echo through the air. The signs of plenty made mock of his words that the game supplies were dwindling because the settlers did not grow enough food for their needs.

He watched while some of their eyes flickered toward the sounds made by the hogs. Some looked up at the sky. Some stared at their toes.

A lone handclap sounded. And then another. Pumphrey Fallsworth walked forward, clapping exaggeratedly.

"I see the British stage lost a fine actor when you came here," Fallsworth said once he had everyone's attention. "Pay no mind to his dramatics, my fellow Englishmen. The Virginia Company won't stand idly by while savages massacre our brave colonists."

"What's the Virginia Company going to do about it?" called a settler.

Fallsworth gestured toward the soldiers.

"But I hear you and the soldiers are shipping out tomorrow with the *Chalcedony*."

"There will be other ships. Other soldiers."

"But will they be here when we need them?"

Another silence settled, so profound that John thought they might all hear the racketing of his heart. They sounded as if they were coming around to believing him.

"Just suppose we were to indulge Mr. Bradford and his Indian cohorts. What would you suggest the settlers do to appease the savages?" Fallsworth taunted.

Dread curled through John. He knew of only one sure way to convince the Indians that the white man would respect their wishes. One way.

. "Pull up the tobacco."

Fallsworth snorted.

That quickly, he lost them. John could feel them withdraw from believing him as denials were shouted, and disbelief overtook their confusion.

Within him a profound sadness bloomed.

"You can't expect folks to do that, John," said Malmford, shaking his head. "They've spent every minute tending that tobacco."

"That's the problem. Pull it up. Plant corn and beans, peas and pumpkins instead."

Malmford shook his head again and said nothing more.

"Be off with you now," said Fallsworth. "And as for *you* . . ." he lunged for Lacey.

John's hand shot out and caught Fallsworth's. "Don't." He fixed every ounce of rage he'd ever felt into one commanding glare. "Don't . . . you . . . ever . . . touch her."

Fallsworth backed away.

"We're finished here," said John. "It's time to go."

Lacey cast one final, sorrowful glance over the assembled settlers.

She knew none of these people, save for the women who'd arrived on the *Talisman* with her. Already it was difficult to sort them out from the others, so closely had they aligned themselves. It shouldn't matter to her whether they lived or died. They certainly hadn't cared about her fate.

Something twisted in her heart, though, to see the lank hair, the dejected postures, the pasty complexions. She wondered if they failed to heed John through stubbornness as he'd claimed, or through being so thoroughly defeated that they simply couldn't summon the energy to do as he asked.

When one felt helpless against the odds, it was by far the easier route to stay the course.

She prayed John would not be haunted all his life by his inability to whip enthusiasm into people who were too dispirited to care whether they lived or died.

"Would it be a sacrilege," she mused aloud, "if I said that I doubt Moses himself could urge these people to cross the Red Sea?"

Clara looked at her in astonishment, and then burst into giggles.

Giggling. Laughter. It sounded so good and yet alien in this place of gloom. Lacey vowed then and there that she would laugh often in her new home. She noticed that the four of them drew together and turned as one as they began to walk away from the settlement. She slid her hand into John's, and he gave her a squeeze. She wondered if he was remembering, as she was, that just a mere day or two earlier she had stood with Clara and Percy at one side of the table while he'd stood alone. Now, they were united. Now, none of them were alone.

They had almost gained the woods when a young

man sidled up to them. "Johnny, you remember me? Benny Carter?"

John stopped. Lacey felt a slight tremor run through him. "Aye, I remember you, Benny."

"Back in Groat Alley, you never steered me wrong. I don't know how I'd forgotten."

"Groat Alley was a long time ago," said John, but Lacey knew from the tension in his grip that Groat Alley would never be far away from the man she loved.

This Benny must be one of the men Clara had told her about—orphans who'd been taken off the streets of London and forced here against their will, just as John had been, who had been toiling ever since as indentured laborers. They'd turned their backs on John because he'd had the courage to refuse the bonds that the Virginia Company had tried to impose on him.

"Johnny ... I—I believe you. About the Indians." Benny's dirt-streaked face fell into bleak lines. "Can I go with you?"

"I'd like to go with you, too." A voice came from the trees, where its speaker must have hidden.

"Me and my family, too," said yet another person from behind them. Lacey turned to see a haggard man and woman balancing children on each hip. "What you say has always made sense to me, John Bradford. I just never had the guts to up and agree with you in front of everyone else, till I saw these little ladies here—and you, too, Percy."

"There are more of them coming after us," Clara whispered.

They came toward them like wraiths, bone-thin men and women, children with fear-etched faces.

Maybe two dozen in all, just a handful of the Malvern's Hundred settlers.

"This isn't what John had in mind." Percy raised his voice to address them all. "You can stay if you pull up the tobacco and—"

"We won't pull it up if we stay, Percy. And even if some of us did, would the Indians spare us while they massacre the others?"

Percy slumped. "I know you didn't intend for this to happen, John."

"No."

"They'll be helpless in the woods. Just as I was."

"You sorted out rather quickly."

Percy beamed.

John studied his ragged would-be followers. "They have the look of survivors. They can come."

Lacey's heart surged with love and pride.

"In two days."

"Two days! But what if—"

John silenced the objector with a wave of his hand. "Two days. Go home. Gather what's most important to you for survival. Nothing frivolous. Then come out to my place. You all know how to find it."

Some shook their heads. Benny spoke up. "I know where it is. I sometimes would go there, in hopes of seeing you, but I never had the courage to approach."

John's eyes darkened and looked suspiciously moist.

"To tell you the truth, Bradford, I don't have anything back at my place that's worth going back for."

John drew Lacey close. "Two days," he repeated.

"I need a little time to become better acquainted with my wife."

The two days passed in a haze of laughter and lovemaking. Percy and Clara happily confined themselves to the Indian shelter outside, while John and Lacey became very closely acquainted indeed with the bedroom portion of his cabin.

It would never be their cabin.

They would be leaving as soon as the settlers arrived from Malvern's Hundred.

"Will you build a skip hole in our new cabin?" she asked.

"I don't think I'll have as much spare time as I did before." He gave her a cocky grin.

"Do we really have to leave, John?" She patted the water contraption forlornly. How she would miss its convenience. "Ipitaquod said we were welcome to live."

"Welcome to live. Not necessarily welcome to live *here*. Besides . . ."

"Besides?"

"Screams can be heard for miles."

At first she smiled, thinking he was teasing her about the sounds he drew from her when they made love. But then something in his tense stillness penetrated her besotted daze, and she realized what he really meant.

"I hope the others get here soon," she said.

John figured he would know the right place when he found it. Nobody questioned his lack of a plan. They followed quietly, intent upon conserving their strength while he led them through forest, over hills, through creeks and ravines.

Five days later, when they hacked through a particularly vicious section of vine and stumbled into the clear, he knew he'd found it.

Lacey came to stand beside him. Her breath left her in a whoosh that managed to convey awe and delight.

Spread out before them lay acres and acres of glorious green meadow dotted with wildflowers. Softly rounded hills rose in the distance. Though he could not see the water, he could hear the rush of a strong creek.

"Could it be ours?" Lacey wondered aloud. "It's like paradise."

"Aye, paradise." John's arm curved around her waist and he drew her close. "We'll settle here."

"What about title, John?" Percy asked.

"There may be nobody . . . available . . . to grant it to us just now," he said, his heart heavy with sorrow. "We'll settle here. We'll live in peace with the Indians. And some day, we'll get everything set right."

"But if everybody has been killed—"

"They'll keep coming." John knew this to be true, knew that his countrymen would never lose the thirst for land of their own, for the chance to make their fortunes away from England's long-established strictures. "The Indians will kill some, but others will arrive to take their place. Some day the Indians will be the ones to leave."

Nobody challenged his prediction.

"We'll say a prayer for the ones who are gone," he said.

"You have forgiven them?" Lacey looked up at him, hope and concern written all over her.

"Aye."

"No more need for revenge?"

He laughed. Softly at first, and then louder, until the sound boomed across the verdant meadows and seemed to echo from the far-off hills. Rich with life, full of promise. "Pursuing revenge was wrong," he said. "But look what it got me."

Lacey looked, toward the grasses, the flowers, the trees, until he caught her chin with his fingers and tipped her face up for a kiss.

"You need a mirror to see the treasure I found," he said softly. "I got the best the Virginia Company had to offer. Stole it right from under their noses."

Discover the Magic of
Romance With

Kat Martin

__The Secret
0-8217-6798-4 $6.99US/$8.99CAN

Kat Rollins moved to Montana looking to change her life, not
find another man like Chance McLain, with a sexy smile and
empty heart. Chance can't ignore the desire he feels for her—or
the suspicion that somebody wants her to leave Lost Peak . . .

__Dream
0-8217-6568-X $6.99US/$8.50CAN

Genny Austin is convinced that her nightmares are visions of another
life she lived long ago. Jack Brennan is having nightmares, too, but
his are real. In the shadows of dreams lurks a terrible truth, and only
by unlocking the past will Genny be free to love at last . . .

__Silent Rose
0-8217-6281-8 $6.99US/$8.50CAN

When best-selling author Devon James checks into a bed-and-
breakfast in Connecticut, she only hopes to put the spark back
into her relationship with her fiancé. But what she experiences at
the Stafford Inn changes her life forever . . .

Call toll free **1-888-345-BOOK** to order by phone or use this
coupon to order by mail.

Name_____

Address_____

City _____ State_____ Zip_____

Please send me the books I have checked above.

I am enclosing	$_____
Plus postage and handling*	$_____
Sales tax (in New York and Tennessee only)	$_____
Total amount enclosed	$_____

*Add $2.50 for the first book and $.50 for each additional book.

Send check or money order (no cash or CODs) to: **Kensington Publishing
Corp., Dept. C.O., 850 Third Avenue, New York, NY 10022**

Prices and numbers subject to change without notice. All orders subject to
availability. Visit our website at **www.kensingtonbooks.com.**

Romantic Suspense from
Lisa Jackson